# BLACKWARDEN

# BLACK WARDEN

## CIARA HARTFORD

First edition: 2025

Paperback ISBN: 978-1-963524-06-2
Hardcover ISBN: 978-1-963524-07-9
Hardcover (Event Special Edition) ISBN: 978-1-963524-08-6
eBook ISBN: 978-1-963524-05-5

Edited by Bibliobean
Proofread by Sara Michelle Rebekah
Cover art and design by Ciara Hartford
Interior art and formatting by Ciara Hartford

For more information, please visit ciarahartford.com and stay connected on Instagram, TikTok, and Threads: @ciarahartford.author
Zephi Press, LLC is a publishing imprint created and owned by Ciara Hartford

*To all those who risk their heart
with a second chance at love:
may you find your midnight apple.*

CONTENT WARNINGS
# My Dearest Reader,

**This book was written for an adult audience.** I've covered some graphic themes that may not be suitable to readers under the age of 18. Here's a list of content that some readers may find triggering. This is not exhaustive, so please, take care!

- Brief mention of infant death*
- Description of blood
- Gaslighting
- Grief/loss of a loved one
- Magical violence
- Psychological abuse
- Sexual assault and rape**
- Sexual content

* non-violent recount of sudden infant death sydrome

** **PLEASE NOTE THIS IS DESCRIBED ON PAGE,** but it is not between the main characters and has not been done to illict titillation

Run your fingers gently
Through the field of wildflowers
Blooming from the cracks in my armor

And I'll scratch my nails slow
Down the watercolor mural
We painted on your crumbling walls

*by Essie Rowley*

## CHAPTER 1

# The Name Called

### ROSALIN

I couldn't let them take my sister to the Dark Fae monsters, not when I was a childless widow burning with hatred. The moment I heard Renee's name from the Magistrate's lips, I knew what I had to do. She had so much of her life left to live. And the life I'd always wanted had been taken from me, all because my husband was in the wrong place at the wrong time.

I stood and took confident steps to the dais before Renee even had the chance to acknowledge her name had been called. She was likely too shocked for the words to sink in. I would have been, if I'd just found out I was being sent to the Dark Fae—the terrifying creatures we'd read about in children's stories. The same ones that had spent the better part of a hundred years systematically slaying humans during the Fae Wars. Dark Fae, like the one who'd killed my husband.

"The name I called was Renee Stormbeck, *not* Rosalin Greene," Magistrate Thompson said, voice stained with impatience. I pretended not to hear him. "It was your sister I called." He reached a hand forward to stop me.

I couldn't ignore him anymore. Mostly because my resolve was crumbling, the terror of what I was choosing to do sinking into my flesh like dark claws. By the time I'd taken the final step I was trembling, my confidence blowing away in the bitter, winter breeze.

"Pretend I'm her. Let me go in her place," I hissed, hoping not everyone in the crowd heard. Not that most of these people didn't know who my sister and I were already. Fennigsville was a small village.

"The person whose name is selected, is who must—"

"Please. My sister has her entire adulthood ahead of her. I'm a widow. No one wants me." I hated the pleading in my voice, the way my heart raced faster with every word that tumbled out of me. "I fit the age criteria. I have no children. Let me go in her place. I beg of you."

Thick silence had fallen over the crowd. I tried to ignore how their eyes burned the surface of my skin. I stood a little straighter, wiping sweaty palms on my dress. I hadn't exactly prepared for the choosing of our town's sacrifice. Instead, I'd worn my old brown work dress and a simple woolen cloak, my hair pulled into a loose braid. Most of the girls wore their finest gowns, with elaborate plaits and gaudy makeup, as though they were attending a formal ball. They all knew there was a chance they'd be taken away and without knowing what would become of them, they wanted to be prepared.

My name hadn't even been included in the choosing. I'd escaped the archaic requirement when I'd married Bastion. I had only come to support Renee, because I knew, if her name was called, I couldn't let her go.

"Rosalin!" Renee yanked at my arm. "This is my burden. You're—"

"My life is spent. Yours is just beginning." I pushed her back as two men in dark leathers stepped forward on either side of the Magistrate. "Besides, one of these Fae monsters killed my husband. Maybe this will give me a chance to find some closure...or you know, put a knife in someone's gut."

A sad smile tugged at her lips at my attempt at humor. It was fleeting. She stared at me, her eyes growing glassy as she clung to my arm.

"Say your farewells, Ms. Greene. These men shall escort you to the Gatehouse."

I willed a shiver of terror back down into the pit of my stomach. "Can I grab a few things from my—"

"Anything you should need shall be provided to you."

"But I—"

"Say your farewells," Magistrate Thompson spat, turning away as the other two men stepped forward, all frowns and folded arms.

I'd made my choice. I had to go with them, or my sister would be dragged away—and I refused to let that happen. I turned to Renee and immediately wished I hadn't. Tears streamed down her cheeks, and I struggled to hold back my own sorrow. I needed to be strong, for her. *For me.* I pulled her into my arms and held her as tightly as I dared, her shoulders shaking as she cried. I choked on a sob as I gripped the back of my baby sister's head. This would be the last time I'd get to hug her, and I'd make it count.

"It's going to be okay," I whispered, even though I knew it was lie.

"It's *not* going to be okay," she said, between snivels. "I'll never see you again!"

"We'd never see each other again anyway, whether it was you or me going."

She refused to remove her face from my shoulder, holding me tighter than she ever had, and I refused to let go. I wasn't ready to say goodbye.

Not yet.

"It should be me. He called me," she whimpered.

"You still have so much to live for. I've had nothing since Bastion was killed." I pulled her back, holding her at arm's length before cradling her face between my hands.

I couldn't help my lower lip from quivering. She was my little sister. As far as I knew, she'd never even held a boy's hand. Never been kissed. Never made love. She hadn't lived, not really. And now I wouldn't get to see her fall in love, or braid her hair on her wedding day, or hold my nieces and nephews in my arms. But at least I knew she'd have a chance to have these things.

"Let me do this," I said, with as much authority as I could muster.

Her blood shot eyes glared back at me before she finally nodded swiping at her tears with the organza sleeves of her gown.

This is how it had been, me, protecting my precious little sister, and no matter the cost, I would *always* pay it. Renee was ten years younger than me. She had been my entire world before I met Bastion and she'd been my light through the darkness of losing him.

We had a brother between us. His name was slashed into the fabric of my sorrow. I was four, and I'd been so excited to be a big sister the day Romie was born. When my mother found him cold in his cradle, I thought she'd died too. She didn't speak or eat for days. My father and I did our best to continue on, as if the cruel world hadn't just dealt us our greatest misery. Then one day, she picked herself up, smiled at me, and became my mother again. To this day I don't know how she'd overcome such grief.

Six years later, Renee blessed us with her squeaky cries. They'd been the best days of my life—holding her as she squirmed in my arms. I cherished every moment, every adventure we embarked on through our village. Every time I'd braided her golden hair. Every time we'd sneak away and steal an apple from the neighbor's orchard to pass between us, taking monstrous bites and giggling until we were both in tears.

And now, I had to tuck those memories away before my world collapsed again, like it had the day I lost Bastion. I had to be strong a little longer, even though everything I knew was being ripped from my fingers.

I didn't know what would happen to me. No one knew exactly what happened to the human girls taken to the Gatehouse every five years. We only knew that it had been a century since our village had been required to provide a maiden, and that the names were drawn from a collection of unwed women ages eighteen to thirty, with no children. Girls married as soon as they could to escape the choosing—myself included.

The two guards stepped forward before grasping me by my upper arms, my spine stiffening at the callousness as I was quite literally torn from Renee's grasp.

"Hey, I'm not going to run," I said, but their grip only tightened. "For the Mother's sake, I'm *choosing* to go."

Renee crumpled into a pile of chiffon and organza, wailing like a toddler, as the two men yanked me toward a carriage waiting at the base of the dais.

"Renee! Pick yourself up!" I swallowed back the first of my tears, desperate to keep them at bay a tiny bit longer. I needed to be strong and apparently, she needed her big sister to yell at her one more time. "I love you, Renee. You have to live your life. Live it for me!" I tried to pull myself free from the guards long enough to turn back to her. "Tell Mother and Father, I love them. Now, get up!"

Before I could say another word, I was crammed into the carriage, the door slammed in my face. For a long moment I could do nothing but stare in disbelief at the wood grain that surrounded me, my sister's tear-streaked face burning into my memory. I promised myself I'd never forget it. I had sacrificed myself for my miracle sister. The one who pulled my little family from the depths of our darkest despair and made everything whole again. I'd done it so she could have the life that had been stolen from me. I'd done it for Renee, but in all honesty, I'd also done it for myself.

I couldn't lose another member of my family. Not after all I'd endured in the last year, losing Bastion. He'd been the center of my life, carved from my soul before our own family could grow.

I collapsed into a heap of tears on the floor of the carriage. The latch clicked loudly as it was locked from the outside before lurching into motion. Every thread of my being unraveled as I let the wall I'd built around my heart since my husband's death crumble into a pile of broken dreams. If I hadn't thought my life destroyed before,

I did now, because I was on my way to the mysterious Gatehouse, to be prepared for whatever the Dark Fae would do with me.

It was said the maidens were used for cruel experiments, hunting rituals, or turned into servants for the households of the Unseelie Court. All their free will stripped, leaving them nothing but human puppets, emotionless and empty. But I suspected there was a far darker purpose. Why would the Fae require slaves? They controlled powerful magic—the Dark Fae especially. They were mysterious and evil and relentlessly uncaring of what their edict did to the families stripped of a cherished daughter.

My vision grew dark around the edges as I tried to take long, slow breaths and failed. The Dark Fae were the monsters that crept into homes in the middle of the night to spirit away loved ones. They were the evil that destroyed households, the crafters of curses designed to inflict anguish for generations. I squeezed my eyes closed as I curled into a ball, pressing my legs tight against my chest. I was going to the Dark Fae. The source of every nightmare I'd ever had.

Behind my eyelids terrifying creatures with taloned fingers reached for my throat. I couldn't do this. Why had I thought I could? Bile burned in my throat, and I swallowed it back down, gulping in shallow breaths.

I dragged myself up, hoping to draw more air into my lungs and distract myself from the death I was being dragged to. With trembling hands, I pulled myself to the carriage window and peeked out. A cold landscape slipped past. The day had been new when the Magistrate gathered us at the base of his dais. Now the sun hung at its highest point, washing away the shadows and turning everything the same drab gray of winter. I pulled my cloak tighter around my shoulders. Exactly how long would the journey to the Gatehouse take? Hours? Days? I wasn't sure I wanted to know how much longer I had to live.

*Three days.* We rode for three days. Other than to relieve myself, I was not permitted to leave the carriage. I was given bread, cheese, and water to sustain me. It was miserable. My abs hurt from crying. Every time I blinked it felt like sandpaper scraping over my burning eyes. The motion of the carriage made me so sick; I struggled to keep any food down. I was used to riding on the backs of horses, not in wooden prisons on wheels. At some point, I stopped caring that I was likely going to my death and began praying for it to hurry up and take me.

The first day, I tortured myself with memories of every happy moment I'd spent growing up with Renee—the trips to Fennigsville, rising with the sun to do chores around our tiny family farm. When I moved home after Bastion's death, we went back to sharing our little attic bedroom, almost as if I hadn't spent six years being a wife.

The second day, I devolved into a weird delirious state, reliving every moment before I was shoved into the rickety carriage. The memory of learning Bastion was dead seemed superimposed over it, like a curtain of black, sheer fabric. I thought I'd cried myself dry, but apparently, I'd been wrong. Renee's anguished face wouldn't leave me alone. My skin burned with every fresh tear that carved a path down my cheeks.

As the third day waned, I grew antsy. I was ready to face whatever would greet me after this wretched journey. Perhaps, it was because I'd already been torn apart by the year I'd endured at the loss of Bastion, but I felt hollow and hopeless. Who needed hope anyway? It was such a fickle thing. Something that could be stripped away in seconds and replaced with the darkest shadows of despair.

The carriage driver must have felt the same growing dread that simmered in my gut, because our pace slowed, even though the road conditions hadn't changed. The landscape outside my prison hadn't changed much either. We'd passed fields and villages, then desolate stretches of land, nothing but untamed grass swaying in the bitter wind. The walls of the carriage weren't thick enough to keep the winter wind out, and I was chilled to the core, my threadbare cloak barely kept me warm. The cold settled so deep in my bones, it would take a blazing fire—and possibly a blistering hot bath—to thaw me out.

As the sun painted the sky pink, we passed through an unassuming stone gate, which marked the border of a forest. I was relieved by the change in scenery, until I noticed the trees seemed trapped in endless summer, leaves clung tenaciously to the branches even though we were deep into winter. They crowded the road with their full leafy canopies, until there was no light at all. And those leaves— they slowly changed color, from the brilliant green of summer to the black of death itself. Eventually, it grew so dark I wasn't sure if the sun had set or if the trees had smothered it entirely. The only light came from the lanterns mounted to the sides of the carriage, casting sinister apparitions against the tree trunks as we passed.

After what felt like another hour, the carriage came to an abrupt stop. It was at that moment my bravery decided to betray me entirely. I straightened the skirt of my brown work dress with trembling fingers, waiting in the stillness for what would happen next. The moment stretched thin and brittle, and I nearly fell off the bench when the lock finally clicked open. One of the guards who had ripped me from my sister's arms greeted me with a pale face and wide eyes.

"Hurry now," he said, holding out a shaking hand.

To see a grown man—a guard of the Magistrate—terrified, did little to calm my own fear. I took his hand and let him help me down. I wouldn't have managed on my own otherwise. The stiffness from sitting for days was so complete, I stumbled on the steps, thankful for the guard's iron grip on my upper arm. When I turned and faced the dark structure known as the Gatehouse, I shrank back in terror. I knew then, I'd been insane to think I could exact some sort of revenge on the Dark Fae who killed my husband. I was hardly brave enough to take a single step forward.

Onyx spires rose several stories into the air from either side of massive double doors which stood taller than most of the buildings in my village. The entire structure was made of some kind of black stone that seemed to soak up every drop of the remaining light. Dark windows gaped like empty eye sockets, glaring down at me as the guard pulled me forward. Stone steps led up to the door, framed by black metallic sculptures of grotesque serpent-like creatures. They twisted together until they were nothing but indiscernible limbs and long bodies. They reminded me of the illustrations from my favorite picture book—nightmares I'd always known as the Dark Fae—evil creatures with evil intentions.

I'd been both mystified and scared of the stories as a child, addicted to the monstrous depictions in a way that had bordered obsession. Bastion's death only renewed my nightmares. And now? I was in a living nightmare, staring up at what I had always told myself was nothing more than a fairy tale, because how could something so wicked, so foreboding, be real.

Vines with the same black leaves from the forest clung to the dark facade like spindly fingers, climbing over twisted ornate trim and up the eaves and gables. Two braziers mounted on either side of the door, burned with mocking warmth, but I knew the truth. My death awaited on the other side of those doors.

"Hurry," the guard said, as he pulled me along. "I must see you into the Gatehouse before nightfall."

I swallowed the fear that crept up my throat. This was just another step, another thing to conquer. If I was brave enough to take my sister's place, then I needed to be brave enough to pass through these doors—even if I knew I would likely never step back out. The guard knocked three times, and with the third knock the doors creaked open, swinging inward with a torturous slowness to reveal a pitch-black hall beyond.

How had I gotten myself into this?

Why had I ever thought I was brave enough?

A cold numbness crept through my limbs as I waited for some sign of what to do next, or where I should go. Or if I'd be left in the Gatehouse alone until I was dragged to the Unseelie Court by some bloodthirsty monster made of nightmares.

From the far end of the hall, two braziers flared to life, their eerie warmth oozing through the darkness. Something stepped out of the murky depths, more braziers igniting as it approached. No matter how much light those braziers emitted, the figure remained cloaked in shadow.

I wrung my hands, trying to keep them from trembling, but it was useless. A deep fear settled in my marrow, it was all I could do not to turn and run. The guard rushed down the steps, eyes wild with fear, followed by the faintest scent of urine as he passed.

The closer the figure came the more it appeared to be a man. Tall and slender with strong shoulders. Dark hair hung messy around his head, but it was what was on his head that caught my breath in my throat. Two horns sloped back over pointed ears. Horns as black as the stone and glittering with high polish—demon horns.

*Dark Fae.*

I took a sharp breath, trying to keep my knees from collapsing. I had never thought I'd see one with my own eyes. His pale skin seemed to solidify from the shadows as he came to stand at the entrance of the Gatehouse. A long face framed by a sharp jaw drew my eyes down to the deep neckline of his finely embroidered doublet, unapologetically revealing a slice of toned chest.

The Fae kept themselves far from humans. The ties they had to the magic of the Earth Mother made them arrogant and self-centered. They isolated themselves in their courts which required magic portals to enter. I knew Fae could be beautiful, but I hadn't been prepared for *how* beautiful.

Behind me, the driver of the carriage snapped the reins and sped away. I risked a glance over my shoulder in time to see it disappear into the forest. When I looked back, I found the Dark Fae waiting, his gorgeous face showing no emotion. He had a slender nose and angular, arched eyebrows that rested over almond-shaped eyes as black as his doublet. They watched me with an intensity that bordered on creepy.

"Welcome to the Gatehouse." His voice was a song I'd never heard but had dreamt of all my life. It curled around me, pulling me forward as my gaze fell to his perfect lips.

He was gorgeous.

*And truly terrifying.*

He held out his hand, stretching elegant fingers toward me.

"Come," he commanded.

The fear that had rooted my feet firmly in place released its grip, and I took one trembling step toward him. I wasn't sure where my bravery had come from.

Was I meant to take his hand? I hesitated, while he continued to hold it out. I'd anticipated he'd be cold, like the dark shadows that seemed to cling to him, but instead his skin was warm and soft. He curled his slender fingers around mine possessively as he pulled me through the door.

For a second, I thought about yanking my hand free, to turn and run in the same direction the carriage had gone. Perhaps, I could get out of the forest, through the gate, and down the road to the last village we'd ridden through. Maybe I could get away. I could hide for a time, before making my way back to my village and to Renee.

No, I'd given myself in place of her. I had a purpose to fulfill. I was the sacrifice so she didn't have to be.

It hadn't completely sunk in yet that I had chosen to take Renee's place—that I would stand at the entrance of a massive black mansion with my hand captured by a beautiful Dark Fae's. I hadn't known what I was truly volunteering to do, and as he pulled me further through the doors, I realized this was likely forever. I was never going home. I was never going to see my mother, father or sister again. *This* was the choice I had made.

And my life was well and truly over.

## CHAPTER 2

# The Gatehouse

## ROSALIN

Fear and sorrow swirled around me in a horrible haze of silence as he led me down the massive main hall of the Gatehouse. Had my eyes not been affixed to my hand firmly clutched by his, I might have taken the time to look around. He didn't look back, didn't ask my name, and didn't offer his own. Instead, I was left with a simmering dread squeezing my throat as shadows clung to him, creeping up his legs and snaking along my hand and arm. I flinched when braziers lining the walls burst into flames as we walked past. He must have noticed, because he tightened his grip on my hand, steadying my rising panic just enough to keep me from bolting in terror.

*This* was my introduction to magic—my first brush with the shadows of the Dark Fae. The culmination of every frightening childhood story coming to life as I was led down the hall to my doom. Each time a brazier ignited I squeezed my eyes closed, desperately trying to keep from hyperventilating. This couldn't be real, could it? But when I opened my eyes, it was all still there. The shadows, the self-lighting braziers, *him.*

He guided me into a dimly lit dining room with a table that could easily seat a dozen people. Pulling out a chair for me, he then took the one directly across. I could see him more clearly here. His hair was...*blue*, the color of a midnight sky and lay in soft waves around his head. My fingers itched to sweep it back from his face. His eyes were black, threaded with silver that caught the light when he turned just right. There was a strange, almost violet cast to his alabaster skin, his lips a soft pink. He was truly flawless, his age impossible to discern. He could have been thirty. Or three hundred. Or three thousand, really.

"Are you hungry after your journey?" I startled at the sound of his calm voice.

I'd been staring at him this entire time and he, in turn, had been staring back. His dark eyes, two bottomless pits of mystery. I tried to find my voice but failed and shook my head instead. His lips tugged up in a small smile before smoothing back into a cold reticent expression.

"Very well then." He made a dismissive gesture at the room around us. "This is the dining room. The Gatehouse provides whatever it is you wish to eat, you have only to think of it, and it shall appear."

*More magic.* I wrapped my arms around myself, following his downcast eyes to the empty plate in front of him. Before I could grasp what was happening, the air above it shimmered, and a modest portion of roast and potatoes appeared.

I leaned away, unsure if I was more shocked by the fact that magic had just plucked his desires from his mind and created a meal before my very eyes. Or that he'd chosen something as pedestrian as meat and potatoes. Then, the smell of it hit me like cold water to the face. It was the scent of my mother's kitchen—fresh herbed gravy and onions. Instead of leaning away I began to lean forward, my stomach suddenly reminding me it was desperately empty.

He cut a piece of roast with his elegant hands, and I was transfixed—an intoxicating mix of terror and curiosity coursing through my veins. My eyes followed the bite to his mouth, his lips parting to receive the nibble of meat. I held my breath from the intimacy of the moment as he pulled a clean fork from between his lips and chewed slowly, his eyes never leaving mine. The muscles in my shoulders tightened, heat rushing into my cheeks as I tried, and failed, to look away.

Goosebumps rippled down my arms. Was this more magic? Had he put me under some strange spell to seduce me? I'd heard stories of such things—Fae wooing humans away from their homes or lovers, glamouring themselves to appeal to the baser desires of their prey. I felt hot all over as he brought a full glass of wine to his mouth, his tongue brushing the rim before he tipped it to take a drink.

He took another bite, and my body refused to cooperate. I'd gone from hot to numb, frozen in place, unable to break free.

"Tell me your name."

It wasn't a question, and he didn't offer his own.

"Rosalin Greene."

"Where are you from?"

"Fennigsville."

"And you were the chosen?"

"Yes," I lied. I wasn't ready to risk someone dragging my sister here in my place if for some reason this broke a rule I wasn't aware of.

He nodded as he took another bite, chewing slowly, sending another flush of heat through me.

"Are you sure you aren't hungry, Ms. Greene?"

With shocking clarity, I seemed to break free from whatever spell he'd cast on me. Was it my name? Or was it simply that I was, in fact, *very* hungry?

"The Gatehouse seems to think you are." A wicked smirk crept across his face.

I swallowed hard, too scared to look. What had I been thinking about that might have materialized on my plate? Because I knew I hadn't been thinking of food.

To my morbid embarrassment, slices of some foreign dark purple fruit rested in a pool of honey. I'd never seen anything like it. It looked like an apple, but the peel was the color of a twilight sky, and its flesh a deep violet.

"A midnight apple," he purred.

I shot him the fiercest glare I could muster, his eyes firmly planted on mine once again as he cut another bite of his roast.

"Seems you're hungry for...Fae fruit."

I knew the double meaning of his words. He controlled this moment entirely, and I was desperate to break free, finally ripping my focus from him to the fruit in front of me. I hesitated, taking a sharp breath as I considered my options. I'd heard somewhere never to accept food from the Fae, that they took debts, even something as simple as nourishment, very seriously. The last thing I wanted was to be bound by an obligation.

"Please, eat. Food is given freely here."

I blushed. Did he know what I was thinking? Was this a trick to ensnare me once and for all? My stomach made my decision for me, grumbling so loudly I wondered if he'd heard. Was it better to be indebted to a Dark Fae than starve? I would take the risk and add it to the list of all the other risks I'd already taken.

We ate in silence. The midnight apple was delicious, sweeter and more decadent than the apples I was used to. I avoided his eyes, but he stared mercilessly. Finally, after what felt like an eternity, the Dark Fae explained the rules of my indenture as matter-of-factly as one could. It sounded like he'd recited them so often, he'd die of boredom if he needed to again.

"The Gatehouse is only a place you'll be passing through. You'll be educated on etiquette, expectations, and given eight days to acquaint yourself with magic."

What did that mean? I shivered as I found myself, once again, unable to pull my eyes from his mouth as he spoke. I hated how he drew such dangerous attention from me, like a lovesick teenager. I'd been in love. I'd been married to Bastion, our relationship built on the fondness we'd cultivated since childhood. I was not a lovesick teenager, though I had to admit the last year without him had been agonizingly lonely.

My brain was a mess of heavy, wet thoughts, and I wondered if this was more magic, or a symptom of finally being out of that damned carriage. I was unable to register everything he said as he continued listing all the rules I was to follow. I tried desperately to commit them to memory, but I was certain I'd forget something.

"If you wish to eat, you will present yourself here, in the dining room for breakfast, lunch, and dinner." He took a sip of wine before continuing. "You are not allowed to leave the Gatehouse. In fact, I assure you, if you try, you'll find the doors quite immovable."

I gripped the skirt of my work dress as I stiffened. I knew I would be a prisoner in some form, but having it confirmed made it real. All of this, the Gatehouse ripping the thoughts from my head, the memory of Renee's anguished face, it was too much.

"You may go into any rooms you find unlocked. But if you force your way into any of the others, the Gatehouse will know." A thick pause, emphasizing his next words. "*I* will know."

He took a bite of his roast, chewing slowly before continuing.

"You are under no circumstances to wander around after the stroke of midnight." He held my gaze for a long time, his jaw set in a stern line. "It's important that you follow these rules, Ms. Greene." He paused to punctuate his final point. "The Gatehouse is happy to provide for your every need, but if you disobey, it can just as easily take it all away."

His words drew a shiver down my spine. I was still grappling with being completely surrounded by magic. The fact that a house was capable of providing for my desires seemed impossible. I squeezed my skirt harder, feeling the fibers stretch.

"Is there anything else you'd like to know before I show you to your suite?"

"My suite?" The words slipped out before I could temper them.

The Dark Fae tipped his head with a curious smirk. "Did you think you'd be treated like a prisoner?" He took another sip of wine before setting the glass down between us, his long fingers lingering on the stem in a way that made my blood heat. "Ms. Greene, I assure you, you shall be a cherished addition."

Cherished addition? But addition to what? The treaty with the Dark Fae, made centuries ago, was murky at best. Concessions the humans had made after the Fae Wars. The details had never been fully explained to the common folk, instead they had been shared between the members of the Council of Magistrates. I wanted to know more, but this did not seem like the right time. I tucked his words away to think on later.

"Who are you?" This was the question I'd been burning to ask. Who and *what*, really.

The smile that had brightened his expression slipped from his lips as they parted.

"I am the Gatekeeper."

Did he truly mean for me not to know his name? His eyes couldn't hold mine. He glanced down at his fingers intertwined in front of him. Did he hesitate to answer me?

"Do you have a name, or am I to call you Gatekeeper? Dark Stranger? Hey, you?"

He smirked at this last one.

"My name is Keres."

"No family name?"

"It's not important right now."

Oh, it was important. If he wasn't telling me, it was likely *very* important. He avoided eye contact, yet again.

"Is it true, Fae can't lie?"

I'd wondered this my entire life. It seemed such a strange concept. As a human, my day was built on half-truths, and tiny lies. "How are you?" "I'm fine." "How lovely." "Tis indeed." Clearly lies. Most people were *not* "fine" or "lovely." They were sad, or starving, or terrified.

He met my eyes, his brows curving with his frown and I straightened in my seat. Even with frustration clearly written across his face, he was gorgeous.

"Your human knowledge of the Fae is—"

"So, it's wrong? You *can* lie?"

He tipped his chin up, transforming back into the terrifying Dark Fae who had greeted me at the front door, made of shadows and midnight. How could he change the way I saw him with the tiniest tilt of his head? I grabbed my glass of water, trying to ignore his glare.

"If I could lie, I might have greeted you with a different face."

I almost spit the water out that I'd just gulped down. "A different what?"

Like a melting frost from the blades of grass, his horns seemed to shrink away, his ears rounded over. Familiar golden-brown hair lengthened around his face. Slender eyebrows thickened, his nose grew longer and more bulbous, his lips thinned, and his chin widened. The muscles in his neck and shoulders stretched, pressing against the fabric of his doublet as he filled out—muscular and bulky.

I was out of my seat in an instant. The man sitting across from me was Bastion. I tried to breathe but choked on a sob as I slammed my hands over my mouth. Bastion was dead.

"Would this face be more to your liking?"

It was Bastion's face, his hair, his build, but not his voice. I took a step back, nearly falling over my chair as I tried to move further away. This wasn't happening. This wasn't real.

"No." I scrambled to put more space between me and Bastion. Not Bastion, Keres—the Dark Fae. Every fiber of my being knew the man across from me wasn't my husband, and yet…I yearned for one more embrace, one more kiss, from the man I'd loved with all my heart. And it felt so wrong. "You're a monster."

I turned to run, but before I could get far, a warm hand slipped around my upper arm and held me firmly in place. I squeezed my eyes shut, afraid to look at him, afraid to see Bastion's face again. If this was the magic I was to be acquainted with, I'd rather die. Every day for the past year, I'd tried to tuck the memory of Bastion away, my heart breaking every time the whisper of his voice came to me in a dream. I missed him, but I hated him for dying—two terrible emotions wrestling for dominance over my heart.

"Ms. Greene." I struggled against Keres until he released me, and I flew forward into the wall of the dining room, catching myself with both hands. "Rosalin." He raised his voice, and I risked looking back at him.

Dark horns and midnight blue hair greeted me. My shoulders slumped with relief. Thank the Earth Mother, Keres had donned his own face. I wouldn't have been able to handle looking into the eyes of my dead husband again.

"Please," I whimpered as he stepped forward, taking me by the upper arm more gently this time to lead me from the dining room. "Any face but that one."

He guided me down the hall, and I went with him, lost in a numb stupor. I wasn't paying attention to my surroundings as we ventured deeper into the gloom of the Gatehouse. I should have. I would need to know how to get back to the dining room for meals. But I'd turned my thoughts to something far darker. How did Keres know what Bastion looked like? How had he managed to conjure such a perfect image of him? Had *he* been the Fae that killed him? I tried to collect myself as we walked, but the warmth of his hand was enough to strip my mind bare. I was trembling as fear and frustration warred with one another for dominance. I wanted nothing more than to curl into a ball and melt through the floor.

"How could you know that face?" I wasn't sure I'd asked loud enough for him to hear. I wasn't sure I actually wanted an answer.

"It was the only face I could see tied to your emotions."

"My emotions?" I squeaked. Could he read my thoughts? My stomach bottomed out. Were they all there for him to rummage through? I didn't need anything else tearing me down at that moment. If he could see my deepest secrets, the wanderings of my mind...

"It's complicated."

"Can you read my thoughts?"

"No."

"Can you see my memories?"

"No."

I took a sharp breath. He couldn't lie.

"How could you see him then?"

"It's complicated."

This wasn't a good enough answer. I don't know where I found the bravery, but I yanked my arm from his grasp. "Make it less complicated," I demanded as I stood my ground.

When I looked up at him, his eyes were wide with shock, as though he'd never been challenged in such a way before. An ember of pleasure at catching him off guard, flared to life in my chest. It was fleeting, replaced by an anger so viscous it chased away the fear and sadness that had filled me moments before. My eyes filled with tears again, but these were born of fury.

"Why his face? Why Bastion?" My voice cracked, my hands balling into fists at my sides.

"You have heavy emotion tied to him," he said with an even tone, as if that was enough explanation.

I glared at him for a long moment, unsure what to say, before storming down the hall in the direction he'd been leading me. I had no idea where I was going, but I didn't particularly care. As though we were old friends, he matched my pace, walking beside me.

"Here," Keres said, as he turned toward a door, cutting me off.

I flinched as the brazier mounted on the wall beside us burned to life, reminding me yet again, I was surrounded by magic. *His magic.* He pushed the door open into a lavish room with wide windows dressed in black velvet. I was too stunned to move for a few seconds before I was drawn in like a moth to a flame.

I wasn't sure what I expected, but it was not...this. It was as if I'd been taken from a dark nightmare and thrust into a decadent fairy tale. My fingers danced over the wooden trim, decorated with tiny carvings of animals and fairies that meandered along the walls and around windows and door frames. A roaring fireplace cast a pleasant glow over a sitting area. An overstuffed leather chair hugged by a side table cradled a stack of books, waiting patiently for me to read them. Positioned beside it was a small round table with a single wooden chair occupying the space closest to the windows.

Bookcases lined one wall, though they were mostly empty, aside from what looked like an inkwell and a journal. On another wall was a door that stood open, a massive bed nestled on the other side, wrapped with a canopy of matching black drapes. Opposite the bedroom was another door that led into what looked like a bathroom, with glittering black and gold tiles.

"I hope your suite is to your liking, Ms. Greene," Keres said from the hall, not stepping a single foot into the room. When I turned to face him, I was met with an arrogant smirk before he bowed. "I'll fetch you in the morning for breakfast."

Before I could say another word, to thank him for the generous accommodations, to apologize for my tear-streaked face, to give him an explanation for why I'd reacted the way I had, he was gone.

## CHAPTER 3
# Burning Questions

## ROSALIN

I stood in the middle of the sitting room, shivering with cold and fear and staring straight ahead out a window to the dark forest beyond. Keres' voice echoed through my head. *"You have heavy emotions tied to him."* What did he mean by that? How could he know?

How. Could. He. Know?

I squeezed my eyes shut, Bastion's face flashing behind my eyelids. I pushed it away. My heart was too tender right now, my emotions sliced into thin strips of sorrow soaked in anger. The tear-streaked face of my sister flashed across my mind. I'd left her in a state of absolute despair. I worried she'd struggle to pull herself together enough to make it home to our parents. Three mornings ago, I'd helped her get ready to present herself for the choosing. We'd laughed about how silly the whole thing was, while I wove ribbons into her hair. We'd both been certain she wouldn't be chosen.

My chest tightened, knowing I'd never see Renee again. We'd never walk arm in arm to the market or splash each other with soapy water while washing the dinner dishes together. We would never share our cozy room at the top of the loft ladder, in our parents' house, chatting in the darkness until we both fell asleep. I'd left my very best friend behind. But if it hadn't been me to come here, it would have been her. I didn't regret my decision. I shuddered before hugging my arms around my chest. I needed to tuck these memories away, before they broke me entirely.

Flames crackled in the fireplace nestled beside the small sitting area, but I still felt cold. I wasn't ready to sit in the comfortable looking chair yet. There were too many new things, too many swirling thoughts. And there was a Dark Fae, somewhere on the other side of the door to my suite.

I spun in place, until I was drawn back to the bedroom. The further I went into my new chambers, the safer I felt. Peeking in, I found a wardrobe against one of the walls. I expected to find it empty, to be greeted by a waft of dust. Instead, I found a collection of gowns, most of them too frilly for my taste—definitely something more to Renee's liking. Had the Gatehouse known my sister's name would be called? Had someone prepared these for her?

I ran my fingers over the satiny material of a black overdress, simple and elegant. Beside it there was a cream dressing gown for sleeping and I pulled it from its hanger, suddenly desperate to be out of my travel worn clothes. How had I managed to get through this day in one piece? I pulled off my work dress, goosebumps blooming over my arms and back from the chilled air of the bedroom. With more haste than usual, I slipped into the dressing gown as thoughts of creepy mansions and dark magic turned mushy with exhaustion.

The canopy bed was perhaps the most lavish thing I'd ever seen, with carved wooden posts, heavy canopy drapes, and sumptuous pillows and bed covers. I snuck beneath them, burying myself and my sorrows. I'd be safe here, I told myself. Everything would be okay. At least as okay as it could be. I nuzzled into the pillow, wishing I could disappear. As much as I feared I wouldn't be able to still my nerves in this strange new place, I fell asleep faster than I ever had before.

Light peeked between heavy drapes and flooded the otherwise dark room with golden warmth, waking me from my hard slumber. Reluctant to remove myself from the mound of silky bedding, that was far more luxurious than anything I'd ever slept in before, I rolled over and burrowed back under the covers. I told myself that as long as I was wrapped in these blankets, I'd be safe. I knew that soon, I would need to extract myself in order to rummage up something to wear, but what would a little more sleep hurt?

I dozed for another few moments before the eerie feeling of being watched jolted me awake. Poking my head out of the covers, I looked around. There was nothing but the wardrobe, massive canopy bed, a nightstand, and a single window. A brazier beside the bed burst to life, and I yelped as I yanked the blankets back over my head.

After several minutes spent trying to calm my frayed nerves, I finally dragged myself out of bed and pulled on the black overdress I'd found the night before. It fit shockingly well. Even the length seemed tailored to my measurements. I smoothed my hands over my stomach to my hips. It was probably more magic, and I wasn't sure I would ever get used to it. Summoning food with my mind was crazy enough.

The fire sprang to life as I entered the sitting room, and I flinched back, my heart racing with adrenaline. Frozen in place, I watched the flames for a moment. Would I ever get used to Fae magic? I pushed the rush of anxiety away as I plopped down on the chair in the sitting area and started rooting through the books left for me on the side table. They were as good of a distraction as any from my situation. They were texts on royal etiquette and a history of the Fae courts. So, this was what I'd be learning. I'd only managed a cursory glance before a soft knock interrupted me. Not entirely sure why I felt the need to hurry, I rushed to the door. I knew who would be on the other side. There was only one other person in the Gatehouse as far as I could tell.

The Dark Fae was waiting, both hands tucked behind his back in a strangely formal way. His posture was confident, the slightest tilt of his head speaking volumes of how highly he thought of himself.

"Good morning, Ms. Greene."

Today, he wore a black doublet trimmed in blood red, tailored tight to his toned frame. It seemed modest compared to what he'd worn to greet me the day before, with a high collar that hid his chest entirely. As he turned to lead me down the hall, however, I was met with sheer fabric that left his entire back exposed. Every sculpted muscle and perfect curve of his form on display with shameless elegance.

It was unnerving. At the same time, my curiosity kept me from looking away. He had delicate, almost feminine tattoos wrapped around his shoulder blades and down his spine. They looked like winged dragons or serpents, but I couldn't be sure. The shear panel of his doublet was just thick enough that I'd need to step closer to see, and that was the last thing I wanted to do. Besides, I needed to pay attention to where he was leading me so I could take myself to the dining room in the future.

For the first time since stepping into this place I focused on my surroundings. I'd not been in the proper emotional state before. It was black on black on black. Black stone tile with black painted trim. Black stained wooden rafters high above. The walls were frosted with black textured paper and sweeping murals painted in drab tones of twisting serpentine dragons similar to what was on Keres' back. The beasts snaked down the wall and wound around the self-lighting braziers that ignited as we walked past. My skin crawled as I noticed the eyes of the dragons following my every step.

There were other creatures in the mural as well, ones I didn't have names for that seemed in a never-ending quest to capture the countless naked humans. Some of the creatures appeared to be ripping the limps from their prey and some devouring them whole. It wasn't these that scared me, though. It was the ones that were doing other more intimate things that caused my stomach to clench. Based on the expressions the humans wore; they weren't always consensual things. It was grotesque, but I couldn't rip my eyes from it.

I shivered, reminding myself that while my suite was peaceful and relatively normal, this place was anything but. The tingle of magic on my skin ever present. After noticing a woman who looked entirely too much like myself, with mousy brown hair, being chased by a dark creature with wings, I tried my best to avert my eyes and let them return to Keres' tattooed back.

He swept us into the dining room, a place that was at least somewhat familiar, though, like the rest of the Gatehouse I hadn't spent much time the day before actually looking at it. The table was a heavy dark wood. Not black, surprisingly. Each chair was made from the same wood and adorned with a black velvet cushion, bordered with silver studs. The two floor-to-ceiling windows were adorned with black drapes with a cold, dark landscape painting in a gilded frame between them. Everything was lavish, pristine, and just a little strange. It did nothing to calm my nerves at the fact that in a moment I'd be telling the Gatehouse what I wished to eat...*with my mind.*

Keres didn't seem to be in a particularly chatty mood. He pulled my chair out for me as he had the previous day before choosing the seat directly across from mine. There were clean black plates placed on the table in front of our two seats, and I wondered if this was where Keres always sat. His expression was innocuous, empty. His eyes seemed almost dead as they searched my face for some answer I was apparently not providing.

"Are the accommodations to your liking, Ms. Greene?"

I could only stare at him, trying to think of something to say that wasn't scathing. It was strange how my fear turned to frustration every time he spoke. It wasn't him; it was his words, or lack thereof.

Truth be told, my accommodations appeared to be perfect—like him. The only flaw was the fact that everything that surrounded me, the bed coverings, the leather on the comfy chair in the sitting area, the walls, the floors, the towels in the bathroom, *were all black.* And it reminded me of *him.* As if the rugs and the curtains and the brocade overdress that I wore were made of the same thing he was made of—Dark Fae magic.

"Are you...part of this mansion?"

I don't know where the question came from exactly, but I was happy I'd asked it, because a flash of confusion crossed his face before he smothered it with a smirk. I found it hard to hide my momentary enjoyment at confusing him.

"What makes you think I could possibly be part of a building?" Mirth stained his words in such a mocking way.

"I don't know. It's magic. You're magic. It's dark and scary. You're dark and scary. It can read my desires. You can apparently feel my emotions."

He smiled, showing elongated incisors that sent a shiver of fear down my spine. Like the creatures painted on the walls in the hall, he was a predator. A beast. I clutched the arms of my chair so tight my fingers ached. A Dark Fae, like him, had killed my husband for no more reason than saying the wrong thing at the wrong time. I reminded myself that I was a sacrifice. For what, I had yet to learn, but the girls who were brought to the Gatehouse never returned.

And I wouldn't either.

"You poor humans know so little about Fae," he sighed.

Perhaps his words were intended to scare me but they ignited a searing frustration in me instead. It was electric and alive, scurrying under my skin. Not because he was wrong. I truly only knew what I'd read in storybooks and from fairy tales passed from one generation to the next. I was mad because he didn't know me well enough to establish how much or how little I knew about anything. But what I knew for certain was that one Dark Fae had murdered my husband and another one was sitting across from me. I leaned forward, pulling his attention to my face, a momentary spark of bravery searing through me.

"Then educate me, Keres, because I'd love to know exactly what you are and why I'm here."

The muscles in his jaw tightened before he eased back in his chair, his eyes never leaving mine. His expression had melted back into that annoying stoic mask he seemed to love wearing. I hated it. I'd rather have the smile he'd just flashed a moment ago, even though it was terrifying. I'd rather have the reminder that he wasn't a placid man sent to be my guide between the human realm and the Unseelie Court. He was a Dark Fae male—a monster disguised in beautiful skin.

"I'm sorry to disappoint, Ms. Greene, but on the contrary, the Gatehouse is actually—"

He stopped abruptly, squeezing his eyes closed, his eyebrows drawing together in what looked like pain. I took in a sharp breath. He recovered quickly, but my curiosity was officially piqued. He'd nearly given something away he shouldn't have, and I needed to know what it was.

"Breakfast first, then you can ask your questions," he said, a stain of frustration in his voice that hadn't been there a moment ago.

But I wasn't hungry. At least not for food. I was hungry for more information. My curiosity was strong enough that for the first time since coming to the Gatehouse, I wasn't afraid of him. What had he stumbled over?

What was he hiding?

He glanced down at his plate, and I tried not to act surprised when two eggs resting in black glass egg cups appeared beside a thick slice of buttered toast. A tiny salt safe melted into existence beside his plate with a cup of tea. I leaned away, trying to get myself as far away from magical breakfasts and mysterious Fae as possible while still staying seated. He grinned at me as he lifted a spoon to crack the shell of one of his soft-boiled eggs.

I glared at my own plate. I had no idea what I could possibly request for breakfast. My whole life had been tasteless porridge, ladled into old, wooden bowls that were chipped from years of heavy use. My family wasn't rich and neither was Bastion's. The house my husband and I had made our marriage home had been the one he'd grown up in—modest and cozy. When Bastion died, I'd sold everything, before I moved back into my parents' home. I needed the money more than the memories. All I'd kept was my new family name.

And now, none of that mattered. I was at the Gatehouse. The newest sacrifice to the Unseelie Court. I pictured the most extravagant thing I could possibly imagine eating for breakfast and waited. With agonizing slowness the air around my plate glimmered and shifted as a bowl of fresh fruit appeared. Figs, plums, apples sliced to look like flowers, berries that couldn't possibly be ripe at this time of year. Beside this a slice of cheesecake drizzled with thick red syrup.

When I glanced up at Keres he was smiling again as he chewed a bite of toast with deliberate slowness. Even his swallowing was elegant, and I lost myself in the way the muscles of his neck moved, a work of art far more beautiful than the terrifying mural that covered the walls of this place.

"Now you understand," he said, a lustiness to his voice that hadn't been there before. "You have but to ask for whatever you desire."

His words were like fire, writhing through me and settling low in my belly. He'd said it before, but I guess I hadn't entirely believed him. It was hard not to, with a bounty of out of season fruit that looked so delicious my mouth watered. My hand hovered over the bowl, again the tickle of concern that this wasn't safe, that this wasn't real, wriggled into my consciousness. Like the evening before, my stomach made the decision to trust the food for me. I popped one of the berries between my lips. My cheeks ignited, a warmth building deep in my stomach at the way Keres watched me with dark intensity as I slipped another piece of fruit into my mouth. The heat plunged deeper into my core as his eyes followed the fruit to my lips.

How was he able to elicit such a reaction? It was terrifying. *He was terrifying.* Gorgeous, mysterious, but terrifying. I looked down at the fruit in front of me and tried to ignore how he continued to stare. We ate in silence, his eyes rarely leaving me long enough to tear another bite from his toast. When he was finished, he leaned back, propping an elbow on the arm of his chair as he cradled a cup of tea. He looked dreadfully comfortable, arrogance dripping from the way he held himself. He gazed at me with hungry eyes, like I was a honey cake fresh from the oven.

"You're burning with questions, Ms. Greene."

I wiped at the corners of my mouth with the napkin from my lap, giving myself a few more seconds to frame my first question.

"Why, exactly, am I here?"

His expression didn't change. He'd anticipated this question. I'm sure I wasn't the first girl to ask him. Which made me wonder...

"And how many girls have you dragged to the Unseelie Court?"

He sat up straight, setting his cup down and leaning both elbows on the table. There was something about the change in formality to his posture that caused goosebumps to bloom down my arms.

"You are here as terms of an agreement made between the Hag Queen of the Unseelie Court and the Council of Magistrates as concessions for a very long and very bloody war between our people. I believe you know it as the Fae Wars."

"And my second question?"

He spoke volumes with his expression, tipping his head to the side and furrowing his brows in mock confusion. I worked my jaw in frustration.

"Don't act coy. How many girls have you taken to this Hag Queen of yours?"

He leaned closer to me, cradling his face in his hands.

"Why does it matter, Ms. Greene?"

"Answering my question with another question, is not actually answering."

He smiled before leaning back again, letting those long fingers drag down his cheeks. "Isn't it?"

I sighed, folding my arms in a huff. This was impossible. "You promised to answer my questions."

"I said you may ask them. I never promised to answer."

He was right. He hadn't said anything about actually answering. My cheeks burned with embarrassment, and I pushed away from the table, done with whatever game he was playing.

"If you won't answer them, then why should I bother asking?"

"Perhaps you should ask the correct questions."

"Uuuuugh!" I stood so fast I nearly knocked the chair down behind me.

He watched me with curious humor as I bolted from the dining room, only to stop dead in the hall trying to get my bearings. I should have known what direction to go, but every time I'd been brought to or from the dining room, I'd been thinking of something other than where I was.

"It's really a rather small place. Do you need an escort?"

His voice was so close, I flinched as I turned and slammed my back against the door frame. He towered over me, midnight in his eyes. Shadows clung to his shoulders, wrapping around him as he took a step closer, causing me to tip my head up to see his face.

"I'll find my own way," I snapped.

He smirked. "Enjoy your morning, Ms. Greene." His voice ripped a shiver from me before he continued down the hall without looking back.

I stood there, staring at the space where he'd just been. My head was swimming with all manner of confused emotions. Heat seemed to creep into my cheeks from the pit of my being. This was stupid. He was Dark Fae, wielding some kind of shadow magic to make himself more alluring to a pathetic human such as myself. It didn't matter how beautiful he was, he was a monster, just like all the others, capable of murdering humans for no reason.

I retraced my steps down the hall, eventually following the mural I'd regretfully admired before. It was like the illustrations I'd loved so much as a child. I couldn't pry my eyes from the monsters of the Unseelie Court frolicking along the wall.

I stopped at the place I'd noticed before, with the girl that looked like me. The details were murky, as if whoever painted this mural had been working from old memories. The woman was medium build with mousy brown hair that fell around her shoulders in waves. Her face was nothing more than shadows. Unlike the other women, she wore a brown dress with long sleeves and a tattered hem. Lumbering behind her was a massive winged creature with all black skin and hair and demon horns that curved over its head like Keres'. The creature was significantly taller than the woman, with broad shoulders and a muscular torso tapering to a trim waist. Its hands ended in long taloned fingers that hungrily stretched toward her. The unusual thing was that the monster had been drawn with far more detail than the girl had. Almost like the girl was...unfinished.

I glared at the mural for so long that everything started to look different, like a word being spoken until it sounded foreign. I shook my head, trying to clear my thoughts and gazed around at the other monsters in the mural.

I shouldn't have. The hair on the back of my neck rose as I realized what I was looking at. Only a slight distance from the woman was another girl being held against a tree. She was naked and a green fleshed female monster with four arms clutched one of the human girl's breasts to her lips. Another hand disappeared between the maiden's legs. While the girl's face may have been one of pain, it could have just as easily been one of pleasure.

I couldn't stop staring, wishing I knew if this was a depiction of a crime or of two lovers. I was too scared to look at any of the others. Instead, I wrapped my arms around my shoulders and hurried down the smaller hall perpendicular to the main one. I needed the security of my suite and if I was correct, it was to the left. I glanced down the length of the hall to the right, morbidly curious if I'd catch some dark monster lurking at the end.

There were a number of doors. One of them was wide open with welcoming light spilling out and on to the wall across from it. The contrast of warmth against the creepy shadows of the Gatehouse was a stark warning that this place was not entirely as it seemed. But I couldn't let my curiosity get the better of me. Not while the memory of Keres so close was achingly fresh, the depictions in the mural still lingering in the forefront of my thoughts. I rubbed my upper arms trying to ward off the cold of fear then turned and rushed to the safety of my room.

CHAPTER 4

# Different

## KERES

She wasn't like the others. Her emotions were erratic, intense, and distracting. *And she could see my horns.* I'd noticed her brilliant green eyes trace over them when I'd greeted her. It only made me wonder what else she could see when she stared at me. The Gatehouse took such careful precautions to craft the glamour that made me look as human as possible to these maidens. It wasn't something I could control. It happened when I traveled through the portal.

Why was she different?

Even more perplexing were her questions, so many tedious questions. None of the other maidens bothered asking for much more than my name. Their terror a visceral thing that squeezed their throats and made it hard for them to speak to me. It was easier that way. I didn't need to get to know them, and they definitely didn't need to get to know me.

But this one...I had to keep reminding myself why she was here. There was something so charming about the way her cheeks turned bright pink when I'd answered her questions with more questions. Her frustration was a living creature that seemed to tease me as I memorized the shape of her face. Part of me struggled to look away and it didn't help that I knew my staring was driving her crazy.

I glared at my reflection in my mirror. Pale skin, black hair, dark eyes. *No horns.* I saw the same thing all the maidens could see. So, why was Rosalin different?

What else could she see?

"What are you doing?" I asked the Gatehouse aloud.

I didn't expect a response. I'd never gotten one before.

I wandered to my window and gazed out at the eternal nothingness that was the black leaves of the surrounding forest. She was older than the other maidens had been but that was likely only because most of the human girls were wed by the age of eighteen in an effort to avoid being chosen as a sacrifice.

And she'd lied about that too. I'd seen it the moment she hesitated. It was a split second, but it was there. A break in eye contact, a moment to construct a response. But why lie about this? She'd either been selected or someone else had. In all my time of taking the maidens through the portal to my queen, I'd never had a single one who'd volunteered.

I took a deep breath and reminded myself in the end it didn't matter. She was here at my Gatehouse, the Hag Queen's newest maiden. In seven days, she'd be gone, whether she was different or exactly the same as all the others.

## CHAPTER 5

# Curiosity

## ROSALIN

I worried I'd be bored, stuck in the same room until lunch after the excitement of my morning, but before I realized what time it was Keres was knocking on my door. I didn't rush this time. I set the book I'd been reading down, making sure it was perfectly straight on the side table, then walked as slowly as I could to answer the door.

"Do you plan to collect me for every meal?" I asked, as he stood blocking my path to the hall.

A slow smile pulled at the corner of his lips. "Only until you're comfortable with the arduous route." He flashed his dangerous teeth before leading me down the hall with that exceptional view of his back.

This time I studied his tattoos, allowing myself to get close enough to make out more of the details. They were definitely serpentine dragons, like the statues at the front door and the ones that danced along the walls. They wrapped around his shoulder blades, the wings seeming to flare out and disappear beneath the solid fabric on his sides. They were beautiful, and I couldn't help but wonder if there was some deeper meaning behind them.

I refused to look at the mural as we passed, but my skin burned as if the mural looked at me. I tried to focus on the way the shadows seem to follow us, making me even more dependent on the braziers as they lit the way. Another strange thing to ask him about. How exactly did his magic work? It had to be derived from darkness itself with how it always seemed to cling to him.

I summoned the most ridiculous thing I could think of for lunch, still skeptical the Gatehouse could provide whatever it was I wanted. I tried not to be surprised, yet again, when this time an entire roasted rabbit with an elaborate assortment of vegetables surrounding it appeared before me. Keres gave an amused look at my choice. I didn't regret my decision. It was perhaps the most delicious thing I'd ever tasted. At least the Gatehouse was an excellent chef even if it was creating meals with magic.

"So, how does it work?" I finally asked, no longer able to hold the questions in.

He quirked an eyebrow at me as he finished chewing a bite of potatoes. Is that all he ate? Meat and potatoes?

"How does what work?"

"Your magic."

He set his fork down and took a drink of wine, his eyes never leaving mine.

"My shadows you mean?"

"If that is your magic, yes." How was he able to draw answers out so elaborately? He was better at avoiding questions than my sister and I had been at avoiding our childhood chores.

He reclined in his chair with the wine glass still in his hand. "They're a part of me, like anything else. Like a nose or a finger. I don't always have control over exactly what they decide to do." He swirled the wine around his glass. "They simply...fulfill my desires." He took a sip. "There are limits, of course."

I let this tumble around in my mind for a moment as he took another drink, watching me with a tilt to his head that caused my heart to skip.

"Fulfill your desires? Like create things? Change things? Destroy things? What can they...*do* exactly?"

A wicked grin crept across his mouth, showing his inhuman teeth. "They can transport me places quickly. They can conjure objects. Glamour appearances. Many things."

Many things? Like turn his face into something completely different? Seduce a human? Was it the Gatehouse that created the food I ate? Or was it him? "Many things" left far too much unanswered.

"Can they..." My cheeks heated, and then I realized it didn't matter. He knew he was beautiful, and I'd be leaving in a matter of days. "Can you make someone attracted to you? Can you make someone want you?"

"Do you want me, Ms. Greene?" His voice was smooth, melting into something luscious that settled in my core. His glare was unyielding as it burned into me, my heart rate spiking.

I took a massive gulp of water to avoid answering. I had walked into the question. My eyes turned toward the door of the dining room in an attempt to escape his gaze. He laughed, an arresting sound that wrapped around me like a warm blanket. Mother save me, it was the most beautiful sound I'd ever heard, and I hated that I wanted to hear it again.

"They cannot make someone attracted to me," he finally answered, drawing my attention back to his amused expression. "Though, they can be helpful in creating the visage you see."

I blinked hard a few times. What exactly did he mean by *creating the visage*? Was this not the way he actually looked? I knew he could change his appearance. He'd already proven this but that had been for only a moment. Other than when he'd shown me Bastion's face, his appearance hadn't changed.

"So many questions," he said as he watched me. "I can see them as they grow behind every answer I give."

"I think...I think I'm good for now," I squeaked out, before I stood from the table and hurried from the dining room, walking as quickly as my legs could carry me down the hall toward the safety of my suite. I couldn't stay there for another moment. It was his voice or his face. It was something, and I didn't like how it pooled in the pit of my being, hot and delicious.

I must have stood too fast because a wave of dizziness caused me to lose my footing and stumble into the wall. I clung to the chair rail before I was able to stand up straight again. It took me a moment, but once the unsteadiness waned, I found I was standing directly in front of the depiction of the woman who scarily resembled myself in the mural. That couldn't be a coincidence. I shivered and turned, pausing when there was another wall in front of my face. I spun again, the world blurring around me before I realized I wasn't where I thought I'd just been. I wasn't in the hall at all. I was in a dark room with my back against a closed door.

"Where...?"

I tried the handle, but it was locked. Panic squeezed my chest. I wasn't supposed to be in any locked rooms. I tried again. How had I gotten in here in the first place? Keres said if I tried to force my way into any locked rooms the Gatehouse would know. But he hadn't said anything about forcing my way out. I pulled on the door, but it held firm, a cold sweat breaking out across my forehead.

I spun back to the room, my heart nearly bursting from my chest. It was pitch-black, hard shadows of what might have been windows cut crisp lines against the far wall. I let out a slow trembling breath.

"I'm not afraid of the dark," I whispered. But this was a different kind of darkness. "I'm not afraid of the dark. I'm not afraid of the dark." *But this was more.* I was in a strange place, locked in a strange room I didn't remember entering. I squeezed my eyes closed and held my breath for a moment to keep from hyperventilating. "I'm not afraid of the dark. I'm *not afraid* of the dark."

Unfortunately, repeating the mantra didn't miraculously make me any less afraid of the dark.

When I was finally brave enough to open my eyes again, they had adjusted to the low light somewhat, and I could make out a few new details. I was standing in what appeared to be a drawing room. Dark blurry lumps, likely chairs, arranged in various formations for chatting filled the space. The gentle glint of gilded frames reflected off the walls. It was impossible to see what was in those frames. More grotesque paintings perhaps? I wasn't sure I wanted to know, but I also very much wanted to know.

Swallowing my fear, I pushed away from the door and crept up to the closest frame. Even at this distance there didn't seem to be enough light to make out what was inside it. I could barely make out the shape of what might have been a face with dark hair. I leaned closer until my nose almost touched it.

Like fog melting away, I found myself face to face with a woman's portrait. I jumped back with a yelp, surprised I could see her so clearly when only a second ago she was cloaked in near complete darkness. She had spun gold hair pulled back from her freckled cheeks and piercing blue eyes—young and beautiful—maybe in her early twenties if that. I took a step back and looked around. A brazier on the far side of the room had sprung to life, illuminating a room full of frames.

There had to be nearly a hundred of them, none of them looked the same. A dark thought crept over me, sending goosebumps down my arms. Were they the other girls taken to the Unseelie Court? Had there been portraits made as trophies of each before they'd been sent to their doom? Some of the portraits were of young women but further up the wall the older the women's faces became. It wasn't these that sent a shiver down my spine. It was the ones toward the top, still cloaked in shadow. Those frames had nothing more than silhouettes with eerie backgrounds.

As though this was all I was meant to see, the brazier snuffed out, plunging me into a heavy darkness. I rushed to the door before I lost the memory of how to make it back there, but it was still locked. Shaking the handle I pulled as hard as I could. It wouldn't budge. It felt as if the shadows were wrapping around me, squeezing until my breath was frozen in my throat. I hugged myself as I slid down to the floor, my knees no longer able to bear my weight as I collapsed in fear.

"Help!" I squeaked out, knowing full well there was only one person here to help me. If I was lucky enough for him to hear, would he bother? I hadn't exactly been the most pleasant at our last interaction. Not to mention, I was somewhere I wasn't supposed to be even though I didn't know how I'd actually gotten there.

"Please, help!"

After a few moments of enduring the absolute darkness I pulled myself up from the floor, my heart still racing. Keres wasn't coming. I needed to figure out how to get out of here myself. I frantically jiggled the locked handle and pulled at the door again. Desperation grabbed hold of me as I realized I might very well be stuck in this room with these creepy portraits for the foreseeable future. I jerked on the handle with every scrap of strength until I lost my balance and fell backward, sprawling out on the cold floor when it still didn't budge.

I didn't have the strength of will to get up.

"I'm sorry! I don't know how I got here," I whimpered, hoping the Gatehouse would hear me and understand. I assumed if it could hear my thoughts, it could hear my voice. "I promise, I didn't mean to," I whispered, as I curled into a ball, tears wetting the corners of my eyes.

Maybe this was my punishment? To be stuck here in the darkness until Keres bothered to come searching for me.

The door flew open, shadows solidifying into the form of a man, but it was too dark to make out any of his features. I flinched back from him as he stooped to my level, all the fear I'd just felt at being trapped in this room shifting into absolute terror of what this monster would do to me now that he'd found me where I wasn't supposed to be. Instead, he scooped me up, cradling me against his solid chest and stepped out of the room into a pitch-black hall. The magic braziers didn't seem to be working. It didn't matter, I knew who he was.

I squeezed my eyes closed as I pressed my cheek against his neck and took a fist full of his doublet. The oakmoss and earthy scent of him wrapped around me, familiar, like a fading dream. The panic was still there, but something inside me cracked open. My fear wasn't gone; it had just made room.

"That's new," he said. "The Gatehouse has never trapped someone *in* before." His voice was low and seemed to resonate deep in his chest and into mine.

I risked glancing up at the shadowy face of Keres, my heart still racing.

"Are you okay? You're trembling." He tipped his face toward me, and it was at that moment I realized how close his lips were to mine, his soft, even breaths brushing across my nose.

"I'm…I…" I swallowed hard, trying to snuff out the warmth creeping into my cheeks. "I'm sorry. I…I didn't mean to."

He was silent as he carried me further down the hall, kicking a door open with his foot. This room was just as murky as the other, but at least there was enough light to see him more clearly. I tried to ignore how delicious the curve of his jaw looked from this angle. It was close enough I could bite it.

What madness had come over me?

How was I even having these thoughts? I had just been frozen with terror and now I was thinking of sinking my teeth into a secretive, frankly frustrating, Dark Fae? A Dark Fae like the one who'd killed my husband.

He set me down on a settee in what looked like a library before he knelt in front of me. I squeezed my eyes closed trying to figure out how I was going to explain myself as he tipped my chin up to his face. His fingers hot against my skin. Too hot. Deliciously hot.

"How exactly did you get in there?"

He didn't sound angry at least. I risked looking at him and my throat caught.

His eyes were *glowing*.

It was faint but unmistakable, a pale white light like a fading lantern. It made his face look even more terrifying, even more beautiful. His unyielding glare watched me with more scrutiny than I cared for. I wanted to melt into the cushion beneath me. I didn't want to be here. I didn't want all this magic and strangeness. Why had I thought I could handle any of this?

I took a couple of deep breaths, squeezing my hands together to stop them from shaking. If I wasn't here, Renee would be. I channeled my conviction to save my sister, taking slow deep breaths to calm my racing heart. When I looked up at Keres again, the glow in his eyes was gone, his lips parted like a question lingered between them.

"I...I don't know." I tried to hold his eye contact and failed, letting my gaze fall to the center of his chest. He was wearing a gold pendant I hadn't noticed before. It was as good a distraction as any. I needed to push away how severely he was glaring and how that glare wasn't anger but rather something far more concerning. Without thinking, I reached, and he didn't pull away. Instead, he lifted his chin to allow me to see the strange symbol etched into the surface. "What's this?"

"My family name."

"The one that's not important right now?"

He smirked. "The same." When he leaned back the pendant slipped from my fingers. "What's the last thing you remember?" he asked as he swept a stubborn lock of my hair behind my ear, his fingers pulling away quickly as if just remembering he shouldn't touch me.

My stomach bottomed out. Those dark eyes of his bore into me as he waited for an answer.

"I was...just trying to make it back to my room." I closed my eyes to try and rid myself of the distraction of his face and pull the memories forward. They were cloudy with panic and adrenaline. "But I was looking at the mural in the hall. There's a woman that looks like..." My face grew hot. "I'm sure you're well enough acquainted with the mural to know what's there."

He stood in front of me without stepping back. "You have no idea how acquainted I am." He stared at me for a long moment, his expression a strange mix of kindness and humor. Not the usual Keres expression, and I was lost in this Dark Fae, so different than the one I'd met the day before. He finally eased away, holding a hand down to help me up. "Let me take you back to your suite. You can rest a bit before dinner."

But I didn't want to rest. I had so many more questions. What was the room I'd been in? Were those portraits of the other maidens? Would a portrait of my face soon hang in that room? I took a breath to ask, but I knew he wouldn't answer. Instead, I took his hand and let him pull me to my feet before he tucked my arm under his, the warmth of his body bleeding into my skin.

"I'm still not sure why the Gatehouse would have locked you in somewhere. That's never happened before."

"How many...*befores* have there been?"

He was silent as we walked. When I glanced in his direction his eyebrows were drawn together in frustration.

"That room..." I started.

He paused for only a split second but long enough for me to notice the fault in his gait. I stopped, pulling my arm free from his. His eyes widened with surprise as he turned toward me.

"What is that room? Why is it full of portraits?"

His lips parted as if to speak but he stopped, frozen in place. He seemed to struggle for a moment before he let a breath out fast and hard, taking a step back.

"Are they the other girls? The others that have been taken to the Unseelie Court for this crazy arrangement with the Hag Queen?" I was speaking so fast I wasn't sure he'd understood me.

Again, he took a breath to speak but again he said nothing. Instead, he tucked my arm back beneath his and continued to lead me down the hall to my room.

"The fact you refuse to answer my questions makes this all a bit more ominous."

"Perhaps I'm going for ominous."

I glared at him, and I might have tried to yank my hand away again, but there was something so comforting about having it tucked against him that I needed in that moment. I was craving any kind of physical contact that would prove to me this was real and not some trick of shadow and magic.

We walked in silence until he stopped in front of my door. He stared straight ahead with concentration written across his face. I watched, wondering what he was thinking but certain he'd never answer if I asked. He was entirely lost in thought when I slipped my hand from his arm. He took a sharp breath, glancing down at me.

"Ah. Yes. Your suite." He took a generous step back and bowed stiffly. "Are you sure you're alright?"

I wasn't ready to answer, but I couldn't think of a sassy retort. Instead, I nodded and without risking looking at him again, I pushed into my suite and slammed the door behind me.

For several seconds I stood with my back against that door. The adrenaline melted away all at once and left me with a weariness deep in my bones. I sank to the floor, curling my knees up to my chest and burst into tears. What exactly had just happened? I'd been trapped by the Gatehouse, terrified beyond belief. He'd rescued me from the darkness. Keres, a Dark Fae, *a monster*, had been...kind. There had been concern in his words, in his actions, where I'd been certain he'd be furious with me for breaking his rules.

Instead, he'd saved me.

CHAPTER 6

# The Last Maiden

## KERES

I t took nearly all my self-restraint not to slam the door to my suite after I'd returned Rosalin to hers.

"What the fuck are you doing?" I asked the ceiling, my voice was loud enough it echoed off the walls.

The Gatehouse had gone too far. It had *never* locked a maiden up before, much less tried to terrify them or revealed the portraits. If the motivation had been to give her answers to questions that I couldn't provide, it was going about it the wrong way.

"And the braziers?" I took a deep breath, letting it out slowly, trying to calm the fury that simmered in my chest. "Theatrics? Really? You've stooped to scaring her?" I glared at the ceiling, my hands clenched in fists at my sides. "Don't fuck this up."

Rosalin was the last maiden I'd be taking through to the Hag Queen. She was the one hundredth to be exact. After escorting them through the shadow portal for five hundred years I could finally make a choice, and I didn't need the Gatehouse to make that choice any harder than it already would be.

I ran my fingers through my hair as I paced. It was going to be hard enough to leave this maiden in the hands of the Hag Queen and her hedonistic harem. Rosalin's curiosity was like a single candle in the dark halls of my home, growing brighter the longer it burned. I hadn't realized how despondent I'd grown until she'd stepped through my door.

I swallowed my frustration and focused on the ache that had taken up residence in my gut. I could usually separate myself from the errant attraction and shallow yearning of these maidens easily enough. The warmth of her desire at my closeness when there had been only fear and anger before was...concerning. To feel her relief when I'd pulled her into my arms...these weren't my emotions, they were hers, but they seared through me and settled in my core. They *couldn't* be mine. I needed to push them away because I wasn't allowed. I would have to try harder to ignore the indescribable longing to have her hand nestled against my side again or to tuck the stray hairs behind her ears. Little touches. My fingers brushing over her chin.

I wasn't allowed.

I took a deep breath. I needed to entertain Rosalin in the dining room one more time today. How many more questions would she have for me? Especially now that she'd seen the portraits. And which ones would I be able to answer? The more questions she asked, the more my walls crumbled away, and her emotions were too strong for that. They had a disturbing sway over my own. Every time I'd tried to cling to the anger it always came back to the face of the man she'd called Bastion. But her curiosity was worse, turning into terrible loneliness. I had enough of that to deal with, I didn't need hers as well.

"Why is this one so different?" I grumbled as I eased into the shadows, determined to be the terrifying Dark Fae monster Rosalin feared. And monsters didn't falter because monsters didn't feel.

I needed to keep it together a little longer. I couldn't mess this up. Not when I was so close to ending all of it.

## CHAPTER 7

# New Normal

## ROSALIN

When Keres fetched me again for dinner his posture had changed. There was now an urgency to his steps as we walked through the Gatehouse toward the dining room.

"Have you started reading the books provided to you?" he asked, his tone accusatory.

"A couple of them, yes, but that doesn't teach me why—"

"You don't need to know why." He stopped abruptly and turned toward me, a scowl of frustration marring his gorgeous face. "You just need to know what and how." He folded his arms as if to reiterate his frustration.

I glared at him, unable to form the words I wanted to say. Everything that came to mind wasn't strong enough.

"This is impossible, Keres. You can't expect me to have learned everything already. I've been here two days."

He continued to walk down the hall ahead of me. "Which means you only have six more left."

"What?" I squeaked as I struggled to catch up. "That's not nearly enough time to acquaint myself with an entirely new world and culture and—"

"I told you when you came, you had eight days." He didn't slow, his long strides reminding me of how much taller he was. "I hadn't realized you wouldn't take me seriously."

He wasted no time seating himself in his usual spot, his dinner appearing almost instantly. The Keres who pulled a chair out for me was officially gone, replaced by this new grumpy male. His stoic expression had morphed into a scowl of disdain.

"I wasn't exactly in the best frame of mind that day. You know, being ripped from my sister's arms and all."

He glared at me, sending me backward in my seat. I had just begun to think I didn't need to be afraid of him. But this Keres, he seemed more like what I'd assumed a Dark Fae would be—arrogant, sharp, and uncaring.

"Do I need to run through the list with you again?" He held me with his glare, waiting for my answer.

"No," I finally said, glancing down at my empty plate. I felt like a petulant child who'd just been reprimanded by her father. I was twenty-eight, far from being a child and he was far from being my father. "I remember."

"Good." He took a bite of his delicious smelling stew. "Because I haven't the time to hold your hand, Ms. Greene."

I crossed my arms but refused to look up at him. What did he spend all his time on? I didn't ask, because I knew he wouldn't answer. He never answered. I'd have to settle for wondering if this was the real Keres or if the male who'd carried me from the creepy room with the portraits was a truer representation. And I hated not knowing which one I'd have to dine with at each meal.

After I'd summoned myself a bowl of significantly less delicious smelling stew, I ate it while staring straight ahead at my glass of wine, my thoughts a jumbled mess. *Six days.* I still wasn't used to summoning food from a magic house, how was I going to remember when to bow or how to address people, or where I should stand.

"As different as all of this seems, Ms. Greene." I glanced up to find him staring at me, a sorrowful expression softening the hard lines of his face. "I'm confident your incessantly inquisitive nature will actually be beneficial in the Unseelie Court."

There was something foreboding about his words that didn't quite match the softness of his voice. I was distinctly reminded I was still in the human world. I had yet to see the true horrors of the Dark Fae. My heart skipped a merciless rhythm at the mere mention of the Unseelie Court. This place was just a preview of what I was bound to endure. I suddenly found myself no longer hungry.

After my disastrous second day in this strange place, I found I wasn't brave enough to leave my suite again. Instead, as evening melted into night, and I still wasn't tired enough to sleep, I tested the limits of the Gatehouse. Keres had said I had but to ask for whatever I wanted. In all honesty, I hadn't believed it was possible, but after witnessing the Gatehouse conjure my meals over the last two days, I was beginning to believe it was *very much* possible.

Hands on hips, I stood staring at the window that looked out to the pitch-black forest beyond, my mind going over all the things I could possibly desire. Bastion, my old life, hearing my sister's warm laugh one more time. Tears prickled at the edges of my eyes, and I squeezed them shut. Nope, I couldn't think of everything I'd lost. I knew those were things no magical house could restore.

The first thing I asked for was a horse. I thought maybe I could break out through the window and ride it to the nearest village before Keres could find me. Who could blame me for trying? The brazier on the wall dimmed slightly before flaring back to full light as a beautiful, life-sized statue of a horse, crafted from the same black metal as the sculptures at the front doors, shimmered into existence in the corner of my sitting room.

"I see. So, this is how it works." I might have felt silly talking to a house out loud, but as I did it, I found it helped with the loneliness that was clawing at my heart.

Curious if my imperfect imagining of the horse was the reason the Gatehouse had interpreted my desire as a statue, I pivoted to something a little less...sentient. I asked for an apple tree full of ripe apples. I envision the exact apple tree from a neighbor's orchard, focusing all my attention on the memory of Renee and I sitting in its shade. I was rewarded with the strangest looking tree I'd ever seen. Shiny black glass twisted into a trunk and tangled branches. The leaves, much like the forest around the Gatehouse, were completely black. The apples that hung from the branches were the same color as the one I'd accidentally summoned for my first meal in the dining room: a midnight apple as Keres had called it.

"Very funny." I put my hands on my hips. "Is it even real?"

I tried to pluck one of the apples, but it was stuck fast to the branch—a sculpture, like the horse.

"No living things then. Noted."

I thought maybe I'd try something easier. A fluffy blanket. And just to test the limits a little, I imagined it cream colored with a pattern of green vines along the edges. The Gatehouse gave me a blanket, but it was black, like everything else. Upon closer inspection, there were vines in a dark shade of gray. I sank my fingers into it and pulled it to my face, snuggling its softness. At least the fluffy part was right.

"Closer," I said, as I pulled the blanket around my shoulders like a cloak.

I wanted to try one more thing. I imagined the book of fairy tales I'd checked out from the library in Fennigsville so many times the librarian had eventually just given it to me. I wasn't expecting much. The Gatehouse could give me a blanket but apparently not the color I'd imagined. So, it probably wouldn't be able to bring me my exact book. After a moment of thinking it had ignored my request, I turned to sit back down only to find the book sitting on the chair.

My hands trembled as I picked it up. Had the Gatehouse brought me my actual book? I flipped open the cover to the end paper in the front, where I had once written my name, and there it was in my horrible childhood handwriting. I thumbed through the rest of the pages, finding my handwritten notes along the margins, or where I had labeled the things I'd found particularly interesting. It was the same book, full of fanciful stories and elaborate illustrations of the Fair Folk.

I plopped down in the chair, pulling the blanket around me, suddenly very interested in reading something I had long ago memorized.

"Thank you," I whispered, hugging the book to my chest. "I'll forgive you for the horse and apple tree."

I could be wrong, but it felt like a breeze wafted through my sitting room, brushing against the loose hair that had fallen around my face. I couldn't help but smile. It was a mansion, not a person, but hopefully after this I could try to be less terrified of it.

I waited until Keres came and collected me for breakfast. How he knew I needed escorting was concerning. He told me he could feel my emotions but could he feel them from across the Gatehouse? I was too terrified to ask because the same grumpy Dark Fae who'd been at dinner the evening before now sat across from me eating his eggs and toast in silence. When he finished, he stared at me while I ate the last of my own breakfast of pastries and clotted cream. Every second that passed urged my heart to beat faster.

"Today, I shall help you with etiquette."

I jerked my attention to his stern face, as I choked down my last bite. "Excuse me?"

"You expressed wanting to know the why but let's instead start with the what and the how."

I blinked a few times, trying to make sure I was awake, and this wasn't some strange dream.

"You said you didn't have time to hold my hand."

He huffed a short breath through his nose with a bitter smirk. "Then you should be thankful I'm making time."

"I...don't think—"

"This isn't hard, Ms. Greene."

Heat burned in my cheeks. What was he insinuating? I stood from the table, but he remained seated, his cold eyes locked on my face.

"Do you seriously—"

"There should be plenty of room here." He cut me off and with the grace of a dancer rose and faced me. "We can start with a simple curtsey."

"I know how to curtsey." I glowered at him, setting my jaw. How could he think me so unrefined? Sure, I was from a poor family, in a poor village, but this was common knowledge.

"Then this should be easy for you." His voice seemed to wrap around me and pull me toward him, the tension I felt only a moment ago melting into smooth seduction. And I hated that butterflies fluttered against my rib cage. "The Hag Queen will expect you to hold on bended knee until she addresses you." He flipped his hand, indicating I should step closer.

A flash of rage rippled through me. Did he expect me to demonstrate? "I don't think I need to—"

"I don't particularly care what you think you *need*, Ms. Greene. I want to know that you can curtsey and hold low." He took a few torturously slow steps closer, his eyes blazing with frustration. "I've made time. Don't waste it, for both our sakes."

Too shocked to move, I stared at him, a pool of hot resentment soaking into the threads of fear that had woven through my insides. Then, as if compelled by my own stubbornness to prove him wrong, I dipped into the lowest curtsey I could and held it.

He smirked, cold and humorless, tipping his chin up to look down his nose at me. And this is how we stayed for the longest moment of my life. I hadn't anticipated how long he'd expected me to remain in such a position. When my legs started to shake from the strain, I wondered if he'd wait until I broke and rose before being addressed. Sweat beaded across my forehead from my determination to prove I could do what he clearly thought I couldn't. I would prove him wrong. I had to. He finally turned and I straightened, nearly falling over from exhaustion.

"Adequate, at least," he said, with a stain of humor to his voice.

"Adequate?" I took a step toward him on wobbly legs. "*Adequate?*"

He turned back to me faster than I'd anticipated, leaving his face inches from mine. The hint of white light in his eyes sent a shiver of warning down my spine.

"Adequate," he repeated, over enunciating the T. "She's a queen, not a Magistrate. You don't want to break out into a sweat on your first encounter." His eyes traveled from my face to my toes and back, as if appraising me for the first time. He didn't bother hiding his derision. "It was...*adequate.*"

Red-hot fury seared through me. I took a slow step back, balling my hands into fists. It was the way he said it, the arrogance that colored every word. Like the kind Keres I'd seen the previous day had been a lie. I hated that I cared enough to be hurt, that part of me missed him. Yet this Keres—the cold, arrogant one—was easier to be angry with.

I fled, not looking back, not caring how much of his precious time he'd spared to toy with me. I'd had enough of him and this place.

By lunch I'd had time to cool down, but the last thing I wanted was to sit across from Keres again. He was waiting in the dining room when I arrived, his frosty demeanor melted into a gentle smile. He was like a different person entirely, it was jarring. Perhaps he realized he'd pushed too hard. That I wouldn't be bullied, even by the likes of a Dark Fae.

Unlike the rest of our time together, he seemed curious about me and my life. But after breakfast's instruction, I wasn't sure I was interested in sharing anything with him. Besides, I was definitely not in the mood to talk about the past I was leaving behind forever.

"You've come in your sister's place?"

It was hard not to fall for the tender curiosity in his voice, the friendly, open expression that lit his face. As much as I wished to ignore him, I abandoned my obstinance. I could be angry at myself for falling for his tricks later.

"I did, yes. She's younger than I am and..." I hadn't wanted to share with him that I was a widow, that my husband had been murdered by one of his brethren. I was still nervous I'd broken some rule by not being the woman actually chosen. I didn't want to add the possible violation of having been married as well. "Her name is Renee."

"Renee." The way my sister's name rolled off his tongue was languid and beautiful.

"I'm sorry I lied when I first came. I worried she'd be dragged here instead. But I guess you'd probably like her better—she wouldn't ask you so many questions." His eyebrows rose at this, and I continued babbling, unable to stop myself. "She's beautiful, compared to me, with golden hair. Delicate and feminine, and—"

"Perhaps I like your questions, Ms. Greene."

I couldn't hold the intensity of his gaze, instead I glanced down at the half-eaten contents of my plate. Another roasted rabbit, so juicy and decadent I didn't think I could ever get tired of it. In an effort to change the subject, I tried to come up with a question I could ask him that wasn't about his magic, the creepy mural, or anything related to the other maidens that had been here before me. I'd be lying if I said I wasn't dreadfully curious about him—someone who could go from being cold and arrogant to someone who seemed actually caring.

"Do you always live here?"

"The Gatehouse is my home, but I spend a significant amount of time in the Hag Queen's court."

I'd mistakenly thought he'd only need to be in the human realm long enough to acquire a sacrifice for the Queen. Now I wondered if there was a far greater responsibility to being the Gatekeeper.

"Are you the *only* Gatekeeper?"

"From the human world to the Unseelie Court, I am," he said, his voice full of soft amusement. "And I've been the Gatekeeper for a considerable time."

"And how long is considerable to you?"

He might have intended to answer but just stared at me instead before he glanced down at his plate. The muscles in his jaw flexed as he wrestled with whatever inner demon held his tongue. Silence stretched until I couldn't look at him any longer, unsure if he'd ever answer. He cleared his throat.

"Tell me, Ms. Greene, how did you spend your days before coming here?"

"Before being dragged here, you mean?"

He smirked. "Semantics."

I folded my arms, certain my frustration was plain on my face, but it didn't seem to deter his intense gaze while he waited for an answer.

"I helped my parents with their farm."

"That sounds like work. What did you do in your leisure time?"

"You act as though humans have all the leisure time in the world," I snapped.

"And you seem to think Fae do nothing but participate in acts of cruelty."

I took a sharp breath at how quickly he'd snapped back. My cheeks heated, and I dropped my hands into my lap below the table.

"What do you do in your leisure time then?" I asked, genuinely curious what a Dark Fae who was the Gatekeeper to the portal between the human world and the Unseelie Court could honestly find entertaining.

He smiled, resting his chin in his hand. "I believe I asked first, Ms. Greene."

"Fine," I said, glaring down at my wine glass. "I read, and sometimes I like to take my father's horse for long rides, but seeing as how I'm not allowed to leave the Gatehouse, I don't think that's possible anymore."

"I have a library," he said, before taking a sip of wine. "If you'd like, I can show you. You'd be welcome to spend time there, if you aren't too terrified to leave your suite."

I was instantly reminded of the room he'd taken me to after carrying me from wherever the Gatehouse had trapped me. I hadn't had a chance to look around before he'd escorted me back to my rooms.

"I'd like that very much."

For the first time since coming to this dark place, I was genuinely excited. And I'd be lying if I said I didn't like the way his face brightened with a pleasant smile. There was something so endearing in the way he dropped his eyes to his now-empty plate, which moments ago had been laden with what looked like the most delicious shepherd's pie I'd ever seen.

He stood and with a smooth stride led the way, a kind calm settling over his face. He was a different Keres than I'd seen before. There was something genuine about this one that I wasn't sure I liked. Mostly, because I could get used to him—dare I say, I could like him.

"I think you'll love it," he said, with an undeniable warmth to his voice. No seduction, no attempt to be something he wasn't, just his true voice. It was like the first time he'd spoken as I stood cowering at the front doors of the Gatehouse and his voice had curled around me like a melody.

I tried to smother the shiver of longing that stirred in my blood and instead focused on the giddiness that washed over me as I followed him from the dining room. A library was something I understood. Not magical food, grotesque murals, or unnaturally attractive Fae. It was shelves of books and hopefully a comfortable place to sit that wasn't my suite.

From the main hall we turned right instead of left and stopped in front of a door that hung open. Daylight splashed onto the floor and mingled with the gentle glow of the braziers. There was a freshness to the room that was immediately welcoming, and I hurried in, spinning in place like a little girl twirling in her best dress. My cheeks immediately grew hot as I realized Keres was still by the door, leaning against the wall with his arms folded across his chest. He watched me with those dark eyes and a timid smirk.

I nearly ran to the window where I stood looking out at the strange black-leaved trees as they crowded against the sides of the Gatehouse. It was impossible to see much else, but at least there was daylight streaming in. I spun in place, walking back toward the center of the library and looked over the floor to ceiling shelves with wonder.

"This was where you brought me yesterday, wasn't it."

"The very same."

"I wasn't in the right frame of mind to appreciate it then."

"The Gatehouse didn't know I'd be bringing you then or it might have been a tad more welcoming."

I paused, letting his words sink in. After testing the Gatehouse, I was coming to believe him when he spoke of his home as a sentient being. A tickle of unease at being completely surrounded by magic bloomed goosebumps down my arms. I rubbed them away, which didn't go unnoticed.

"Are you cold?" Keres moved like a wave over the shadows that oozed from the corners of the room. He swept an arm over his horns, wispy strands of darkness wove together until he held a black velvet cloak out to me. "Here."

He didn't wait for me to respond before he draped the cloak over my shoulders, stooping to fasten it in the front with a silver brooch shaped like a serpent. His face was mere inches away from me. As he straightened his eyes slid to mine, a heavy intensity as he watched me. I was too stunned by his closeness to tell him I wasn't cold.

I was going to thank him but paused. Some tiny memory that I should never thank a Fae—should never owe them any favors—trapped my words behind my teeth. He stepped away, as if noticing how close he was, and back toward the door.

"I hope this satiates some of your curiosity for now," he said, as he bowed and left without another word.

I was frozen in place, staring at the open door where he'd just passed through. He'd been so gentle, and then he was gone, like the shadows. It left me with nothing but more questions.

## CHAPTER 8

# Consequences

### ROSALIN

So. Many. Books.

My small village library was tiny compared to this. I didn't know where to start. I wandered to the nearest shelf, letting my fingers drag along the spines at eye level. After being trapped in a strange cycle of fear and sorrow, this seemed unreal. I traced the letters on one of the spines with my index finger to prove to myself the books were truly there. That this wasn't some elaborate trick of dark magic. Slipping one from the shelf, I lay the book open across my hand, lifting the pages to my nose and taking a deep breath. It was musty earth and leather and the hint of vanilla. My eyes slipped closed, shoulders sagging, as I relaxed for the first time since I'd been shoved into the carriage.

After what seemed like several minutes, I opened my eyes again and was thrust back into the moment. As much as I would have loved to remain lost in the worlds these books had to offer, there was a strange hum of magic reminding me I couldn't. I was only passing through. I was in the library of the mysterious Gate-house, the home of Keres, a Dark Fae. And I needed to get to work.

I took an inordinate amount of time reviewing the shelves of books before I began rummaging through the desk drawers, then the cupboards along the far wall, hoping I'd find something that might help me understand what exactly was going on in this place. Every moment seemed strange, every detail just a little off. And then there was Keres and his refusal to answer most of my questions. It was almost as if he *couldn't* answer them.

There was something bigger going on here and I needed to know if it was Dark Fae magic or something stronger. The more I thought about it, the more I was certain there was a curse at work. Whatever it was, there were too many questions Keres was unwilling to answer, and I needed to figure out why. Even if what I found just confirmed my suspicions.

"What are you looking for?"

I jumped, smacking my head as I yanked it from one of the cupboards. I wasn't sure what I expected to find when I met Keres' dark eyes. Anger or confusion, but certainly not amusement. Heat rose into my cheeks. I couldn't figure him out. One moment he was as cold as the black stone, the next he was endearing, soft, approachable.

"I'm uh..."

"I assure you, there's nothing but dusty books and stationery down there," he said, as he leaned against the arm of a nearby chair, dark eyes glittering with amusement.

But I already knew this. That's exactly what I was looking for. A dusty book that would give me the answers he refused to share.

I stood up straight, mustering my bravery, which was more difficult than usual. I hated to disturb the amicable friendliness growing between us, and I knew as soon as I said what I needed to I'd be staring at the cold Keres. The one that scared me—the one who was not amused by my questions and didn't have the patience to deal with a human. I swallowed hard, hoping my bravery wouldn't fail me.

"I'm trying to figure out this curse."

A flash of something crossed his face. Fear? I wasn't sure, but he smothered it with a smirk.

"What makes you think there's a curse?"

I swallowed the anger that sparked to life in my chest. We'd circled so many topics already with his evasiveness. Why wouldn't he just answer my questions? My hands fell to my hips. I might have practiced more restraint if I'd taken the tightness in his jaw and the arch to his eyebrows more seriously. But I was feeling particularly confident. If I was going to be dragged to the Unseelie Court, I wanted to know everything.

"The magic of this place for one. Or maybe the way you dodge every question I've asked with another question. Or the way you leave without answering at all." I glanced at the brazier before returning my gaze back to him. "It's as if you aren't *allowed* to answer."

My suspicions were growing and only being confirmed by the way his eyes grew wide as he dropped his arms to his sides. He looked...*terrified*. Truly worried by the words tumbling from me.

And I loved it.

"Like someone has ordered you to keep me ignorant," I said, as I took confident steps toward him, a smile on the edges of my lips. "Or they've made it so you can't say certain things. Maybe it's not a curse, but it's something."

I pushed past him, leaving him staring straight ahead at the cupboard, muscles tense in his shoulders. I dared to glance back. His slender fingers pushed the cupboard door closed slowly, as though his limbs were encased in syrup. I couldn't stand to stay in that room another second. I'd crack if he failed to answer any more of my questions, and a strange, simmering vengeful giddiness threatened to erupt from my skin if I didn't remove myself from his presence that instant.

I rushed from the library, the only sound was my hurried steps on the stone tile as I forced my legs to walk and not run. I needed to get back to the safety of my room before I said more. The hall felt twice as long as usual, my heart pounding in my ears.

My salvation was the pesky brazier that always burned outside my door. But as if I'd blinked and missed the moment it happened, he stepped from the shadows and leaned casually against my door. He gazed down at his shoes, radiating with the swagger of a male who knew exactly how attractive he was.

"How...?"

He met my wide eyes with that sultry smirk of his. The one he wore when he was hiding behind his beautiful face. The light from the brazier gilded his obsidian horns and accentuated the sharp angle of his jaw.

"Come now, Ms. Greene," he said, voice low and rough. "I don't think we're finished talking."

My breath hitched. Where once I'd found him terrifying, now I choked on something far more dangerous. My fingers itched to weave through his midnight hair and push the soft waves back from his eyes. To follow the pointed tips of his ears. Desire, hot and wholly unwelcome, unfurled within me and pulsed through my veins.

My mouth went dry as my eyes followed the column of his throat down. I wanted to trace his collar bones slowly with my lips, lingering at the base of his neck. I ached to close the distance between us, to map the line that ran down the center of his chest with my tongue. To feel his firm muscles beneath my fingers.

I shouldn't want him.

And I hated myself for it.

I took in a sharp breath and tried to look away, but I couldn't. I needed to, but the way his hands rested on his hips—elegant and effortless. *Those hands.* How would they feel gliding over my skin? Holding my arms over my head?

His pupils dilated, the smirk slipping from his lips as his body stiffened.

He could feel my emotions.

The heat that had been building in my core soared into my cheeks. The flicker of realization in his eyes terrified me more than anything else. He felt it all. Every. Terrifying. Desire. My hunger. My need.

*My shame.*

I rushed past him, ducking into the safety of my room and slamming the door before he could say another word.

That night I didn't go to dinner. I couldn't sit at that table and feel his dark eyes slip along the lines of my face. Not after the incident in the hall. My stomach bottomed out every time I thought of his voice, the golden light on his skin. I needed to get my emotions under control or risk mortifying embarrassment every time I noticed his reaction to one of my wildly inappropriate emotions.

At the time, it seemed like a good idea, but it was nearly midnight, and my stomach wouldn't stop grumbling. I was genuinely curious if I could scrounge up a snack. I had seen a door that looked like it led from the dining room into a kitchen of sorts. Why else would a house have a kitchen if not to store and prepare food?

I snuck out of my suite, closing the door as quietly as I could. I glanced up at the brazier, burning as though it required no fuel other than the frustration seething in my chest. An ominous slowness to the flames froze me in place as I watched, uneasiness settling around me like heavy shadows.

I cleared my throat. "I'm hungry, okay?" I had never felt so judged in all my life and by a house no less.

I slipped down the hall and around the corner to the main corridor. Keres had warned me that I needed to stay in my room after midnight. But it wasn't quite midnight, and I'd be quick. Plus, he hadn't exactly explained *why* I needed to stay in my room after midnight. Perhaps there was some monster that stalked these halls at night. Perhaps *he* stalked the halls at night. I shivered but didn't turn back.

I hadn't been aware of the stillness that smothered everything once the sun set. If I thought the Gatehouse was creepy during the day, the all-encompassing silence that cloaked the entire mansion after midnight, was downright foreboding. Most houses offered some hint of the outside world—the wind, the chirp of insects, the familiar trappings of night. The Gatehouse, however, was the purest form of suffocating quiet. It made every breath I took sound four times louder.

I exhaled a sigh of relief as I slipped into the dining room. The last thing I wanted was to run into Keres after everything that had transpired earlier in the day. It would have been hard to explain. How did you tell a broody Fae that you couldn't handle another moment gazing at his gorgeous face? Especially when he seemed to know exactly how gorgeous he was and was more than happy to stare right back.

I eased the mystery door open and was rewarded with a well-appointed kitchen. A row of cupboards lined one wall, broken into two sections by a massive workbench. A bread oven took up a large portion of another wall, with a workbench and a wash basin. Tiptoeing to the main workbench, I plucked a ripe green apple from a bowl heaped with fruit and pressed it to my lips while savoring the scent of it. The sound of my teeth ripping through the peel seemed louder than it should have, but I didn't care. It was perhaps the most delicious apple I'd ever eaten and for a moment I was lost in memories of my sister. How many times had we shared an apple at the market, or sitting in the sun-warmed grass along the road to our little house.

I missed Renee dreadfully, but I was satisfied with my choice to come in her place. She wouldn't have handled all the dark strangeness as well. She likely would have hidden in her suite, only coming out for food if she could muster the bravery.

As I took more bites, Renee's sweet smile wafted through my memories. I ran my fingers over the workbench until they met another bowl. This one was covered with a tea towel and my curiosity got the better of me. I peeked under, finding a mound of rolls nestled beneath. Taking two, I finished the apple, discarding the core in a waste bin before I ducked back into the dining room.

I ate one of the rolls while loitering at the window. I could see nothing through the darkness of night. I knew there were trees with creepy black leaves, and part of me was happy I couldn't see them. The buttery flavor of the scrumptious dinner roll filled my stomach with unexpected warmth, and I closed my eyes. I could see my mother's bread, perfectly flaky on the outside encapsulating a pillow of delicious heaven.

Sneaking back down the main corridor, I paused before turning down the hall toward my room. The library was to the right. Keres was likely asleep and couldn't disturb me at this hour. I could rummage through the cupboards without interruptions. I took a bite of the second roll and turned to the right, determined to finish where I'd left off before he'd so rudely surprised me earlier.

I opened the door just enough to slip through, praying to the Mother the hinges wouldn't give me away. There were two braziers glowing on the far side of the library that flared brighter with my presence. Part of me wished I could have avoided the attention of the Gatehouse entirely, but it was likely unavoidable. I was, after all, inside it, and whether it slept at all was a question for another time.

I scoured the shelves, fingers itching with curiosity as they flowed over the spines. If I remembered correctly, there was a book on the far wall that had interested me. A symbol on the bottom of the spine was the only identifier. Once I found it, I slipped it from the shelf and dropped into one of the chairs beside a brazier, opening the book across my lap. I stuffed the remains of the second roll between my lips and thumbed through the pages.

If I'd been more attentive as a child, I might have learned what some of the Old Fae script meant, but as it was the characters were strange, looping in and out of one another as they twined together into clusters of what I could only assume were sentences. I couldn't read it, and my frustration grew as I realized my entire midnight endeavor might have been for nothing. It threatened to burst from my chest in a loud growl. I slammed the book closed, glaring at the symbol on the cover as though it was the cause of all my troubles. I'd likely found exactly what I needed but wasn't able to get any answers from it.

I traced my fingers over the surface of the leather tooling, following the curve of the symbol. Keres wore it on a pendant around his neck. What exactly did it mean? Other than telling me it was his family name, a non-answer, he'd refused to give me more information. It was just another question he ignored. I hated that he seemed happy enough to answer some questions but not others.

Rising from the chair, I slipped the book back into its place before I eyed the cupboard again. It hadn't contained much: a pile of stationary, a collection of pens, and several vials of different colored inks. If I wasn't mistaken there had been a stack of what looked like journals as well, something I could possibly find more information in. I pulled it open but stood back, arms falling to my sides in defeat.

It was empty. Completely and utterly empty. Not a scrap of paper. Not even a smudge of ink or a speck of dust. Keres must have cleared it out. I stood, staring into it for another moment, letting my mind tumble over all the reasons he would have done this. Perhaps he feared I'd do exactly what I was doing. I wanted to get my hands on one of those journals even more. Instead, I crept back into the hall and slipped into my room, careful to close the door silently behind me.

I leaned against the door, letting my head fall back with a thud. I'd found nothing and gotten exactly zero answers.

Again.

Morning came entirely too early. From the enchanted wardrobe, I managed to find something both comfortable and modest, though today, it offered only blood-red gowns. I couldn't help but wonder if this was something Keres had requested. Still, it was better than black, which was all it had provided to me thus far.

Keres sat stiffly in his chair. His eyes followed me as I crossed the room and sat in my usual seat across from him. Goosebumps rippled down my arms while I tried to ignore how he stared. It was an unyielding glare. One that made the hair on the nape of my neck stand up.

"Midnight ventures to the library are not permitted, Ms. Greene."

My eyes snapped to his. How had he known? Did the Gate-house *actually* tell him?

"I...um..."

"If there's something you need, you have but to ask." He glanced down at the empty plate in front of him and the same boring breakfast of soft-boiled eggs and toast materialized before him.

I nearly fell out of my chair as a green apple and two rolls appeared on my own plate.

"Interesting choice," he said.

The left side of his lips quirked up when I glanced in his direction before his attention returned to his eggs. After the initial shock wore off, I grabbed the apple and pressed it to my lips as I had the night before. Closing my eyes, I let the smell wash over me, saving me from the merciless way his eyes never left me. The scent was sweet and sour, the perfect apple. The peel pressed against my lips was so soft. A memory of Bastion—how sometimes he would run his thumb over my lower lip before he kissed me. A soft touch. Bastion had always been so caring and attentive. The calluses on his rugged hands were rough, but his touch could be so incredibly gentle.

A flash of heat plummeted into my stomach as I remembered the night before he'd been killed. His hands had held me extra tight, as if he'd known his fate. How many times had I wished for those hands on my body just one more time. His lips on mine. The cinnamon smell of his skin flooding my senses and driving me to the brink of existence.

When I opened my eyes, I was surprised to find Keres staring at the apple, a bite of egg halfway to his mouth. He cleared his throat and looked away as he stuffed the bite between his lips.

Before I allowed myself to think more on his reaction I took a massive bite of the apple, chewing it loudly, hoping to elicit some other reaction from him. Instead, he continued to eat his eggs as though he was the only person in the room. He ripped a corner from his piece of toast, and I nearly lost myself watching his fingers as he slipped the bread between his lips.

He stared at me. Again. And in my attempts to avoid his eye contact my gaze fell back to his hands as they ripped another bite of toast.

Those hands. My blood seemed to boil through me at the thought of *Keres'* hands on my body. When had my traitorous thoughts changed from fear and anger to...*this?*

Another bite of apple, an attempt to distract myself from the way his throat moved as he swallowed his tea in smooth gulps, his eyes returning to me as I finished the apple and selected one of the two rolls. It was the same as the one I'd swiped the night before, buttery and perfect.

This was agony, the way my thoughts shifted back and forth between Bastion's crooked smile to Keres' broody stares.

"What is it you needed from the library so badly that it would force you from your suite in the middle of the night, Ms. Greene?"

I stiffened. I couldn't answer. My mind was swallowed up in the memory of a man I had loved, and a Dark Fae I shouldn't want. I pretended not to hear him. How many times had he ignored my questions? I should be allowed to ignore this one.

I took another bite of the buttery roll, letting it melt on my tongue. I closed my eyes and savored the comfortable taste of home. It didn't last. The thought of Keres' hands crept back in, the warmth of him, the steady thrum of his heart against my face when he'd carried me.

I ripped another bite away from the roll with my teeth, desperate to banish the ache for his touch, the scent of him.

"Very well then." He stood, leaving half a slice of toast and most of his second egg behind. "Enjoy your wanderings, but please..." he trailed off, drawing my eyes to his. He wore the face he'd first greeted me with—cold and uncaring. "No wandering after midnight."

My eyes tracked him as he crossed the dining room, a burning pit of anger simmering in my gut. Lesson learned. The Gatehouse, it seemed, had no intention of letting me roam freely without reporting back to him. If I wanted to eat, I needed to attend meals. Never wander after midnight. Always request what my heart desired, though I'd tested this and the Gatehouse did not in fact provide me with whatever my heart desired.

"I want to know more about the curse," I blurted out, my frustration bubbling over.

He stopped halfway through the dining room door and with deliberate slowness turned, his eyes making a slow journey across the floor to my face.

"What makes you so certain there's a curse?"

I was out of my seat in an instant, fury igniting my insides. "Really, Keres? What else could it be?" I folded my arms and lifted my chin, meeting his gaze without flinching. "Something's at work here. I *know* it. And I'm done pretending otherwise."

He didn't move, limbs rigid at his sides, dark hair tangled around the sharp curve of his horns. His black, bottomless eyes locked on mine, boring straight through me. He'd chosen a form fitting doublet in the same midnight blue as his hair, so dark it was nearly black, open down his sternum, the delicious line between the muscles of his chest on full display. His pendant rested against those muscles, the symbol mocking me as it rose and fell with every breath he took. He opened his mouth to speak, a flash of fear crossing his face before he squeezed his eyes and lips closed.

"I know you probably think I'm just a stupid human, but I'm not a complete idiot." I took a confident step toward him. "There is a curse, isn't there?"

Again, he opened his mouth. And again, that flash of something akin to pain or fear or despair before he closed it.

My frustration was a solid thing in my chest, clawing its way up my throat and I couldn't stop it

"I know you can't lie. I know your kind are more susceptible to magical curses." I took another step closer. "And I know—"

"Stop."

With one word he froze me in place. Ice crept through my veins as his shadows wrapped around me. It felt like shards of glass cutting through my joints, shredding the willpower from my muscles. He moved toward me with metered steps, his eyes holding mine, a darkness so deep within that look. I tried to wriggle free, but all I succeeded in doing was send flashes of agony down my arms and legs. I could do nothing but glare at him as I blinked back tears of pain. He took another step, lips parting as he came close enough that I could see the threads of silver that wove through his black irises.

He reached for my face. My first instinct to pull away failed. I was firmly frozen in place by whatever magic he had used on me. I balled my hands into fists, burying my nails in the flesh of my palms. Those elegant fingers of his slid across my jaw before he tucked an index finger beneath my chin and tipped my face to his. He shifted closer. Too close. A flash of fear simmered through me from the intensity of his glare before it sank into the depths of my core, turning my breath shallow with need.

"We won't speak of this again," he said, voice low and soft as he leaned his head beside mine. I shivered as his breath brushed over the shell of my ear. "Will we, Rosalin."

It wasn't a question. He backed away, his eyes dragging down my face to my lips and holding there. Then, before I could say another word he dissolved into the shadows, leaving me standing rigid and alone beside the table as the ice that held me firmly in place melted from the inside out.

The tears I'd held at bay broke free and pooled in the corners of my eyes until they overflowed down my cheeks. Nearly a full minute passed before I collapsed on the floor in a heap of spent adrenaline. I touched my chin where the echo of his fingers remained. How could I be so terrified, and yet, so attracted to him? Attracted to a Dark Fae—*to a monster.*

I buried my face in my hands and wept.

## CHAPTER 9

# Frozen Questions

## KERES

I t hadn't been my intention to use my shadows on her, but she wouldn't stop asking questions, ones I wasn't capable of answering. Each one stabbed into my soul like a poisoned barb, reminding me I was bound by this fucking curse. I was well aware of what it felt like. I'd endured the Hag Queen using my own shadows against me for centuries.

Rosalin's willpower had shredded my magic faster than I could press them into her muscles. With my weakened abilities I'd struggled to hold her in place and used more energy than I'd planned. Now, in the quiet of my personal quarters, I was replaying the moment her anger and pain had turned into wanting. I wrapped my fingers around my neck and squeezed before dragging my hand over my chest. The way her eyes could strip me bare was truly terrifying...and I wanted more.

It was rare that one of the maiden's feelings were strong enough to sway my own. Most of them were young, shallow creatures, barely old enough to understand the difference between love and lust. But this was different. The heat had drawn me closer like a pathetic moth to a flame, unable to stop from being burned.

*Too close,* when I knew I wasn't allowed.

She'd opened her emotions to me without realizing what she was doing, and I hadn't found fear. I'd found a searing desire that soaked into my own and set me on fire.

She left me hot, even with the ice of my magic ripping through my veins. Her name on my tongue tasted like the most delicious forbidden fruit. It snuffed out all the frustration I'd had seconds before when she'd spat my greatest vulnerabilities in my face.

I *was* far more susceptible to curses. I *couldn't* lie, like all Fae.

And I was unable to get her out of my fucking head.

I needed some distance, or I'd never manage to finish her portrait before this curse would force me to take her through the gate to the Unseelie Court. I'd be too busy finding ways to make her breath catch and her heart race. Or worse, I'd try to figure out how I could spare her from the Hag Queen's harem where she'd be forced to do degrading and hedonistic things whether she wanted to or not. I couldn't afford the distraction. Now that I'd learned about the loophole in my punishment, everything had to go exactly right, like every other time. I'd rather not spend the next five hundred years in chains beside the Hag Queen's throne again. Not when I could be free from this life.

Exhausted, I flopped down on my bed, hoping I could sleep before I'd need to endure her questions and her wanting that never failed to snatch away my breath. Wanting that was becoming so much harder to push away.

How was I going to get through five more days? Five more days of her fear mixed with tantalizing desire. Five more days of her fucking questions. And why did I crave those questions as much as I despised them?

## CHAPTER 10

# Shadows

## ROSALIN

I would have avoided him the rest of the day, but when lunch rolled around, I was starving. An apple and part of a roll wasn't enough to sustain me, no matter how delicious they were. I'd snuck into the dining room a little early thinking I could eat and leave before he arrived, but he never came.

When he hadn't shown up for dinner, worry settled like a stone in my stomach. Had I truly angered him? Was I doomed to endure the rest of my stay completely alone in this cold black mansion?

When I returned to my suite, I found another stack of books had been left for me. Keres had never stepped foot in my room before. Part of me wondered, maybe even hoped, he'd left a piece of his magic behind. Some scrap of his essence to assure me he didn't completely hate me.

Most of the books were detailed histories surrounding the war between the Dark Fae and humans. Five hundred years seemed so long ago, and yet, the conclusion of that war still shaped so much of the current world, not the least of which was the sacrifice I was here to fulfill. The other books were a collection of etiquette manuals that Keres must have felt I needed after my apparently abysmal curtsey performance—whatever would prepare me for my inevitable journey to the Unseelie Court. He was, after all, the Gatekeeper and nothing more. He would deliver me to my new home, and then I'd likely never see him again.

I shuttered. If all Dark Fae were as prickly as him, the thought of being left alone with another Unseelie was bone chilling. At least with him I had some idea of what to expect--stoic silence, unfiltered broody stares, the occasional smirk and genuine kindness that left me breathless and disoriented.

The hours slipped by faster than I'd anticipated as I thumbed through the books. I rubbed my eyes, glancing at the gilded clock on the wall beside the door. 11:44 pm. I had sixteen minutes, and I'd use every second.

I slipped into the hall and rushed to the library. As long as I was diligent, I could be back in my room before the strike of midnight, not breaking any more of Keres' precious rules. As I snuck down the hall however, I noticed something new. The brazier at the far end was lit. It had never been before. A strange tingling down my spine drew me to it. I passed the library and crept toward it, my curiosity a living thing clawing its way out of my skin.

A warm light bled from beneath the last door, leaving me standing in a puddle of gold. I stood frozen in place for a long moment, my mind tumbling over all the possible scenarios of what waited behind that door. Was it Keres? Was the Gatehouse trying to draw me closer to something? Or was this some kind of trick to lure me to yet another room I wasn't supposed to be in?

The Gatehouse had already locked me in one room. How was I to know it wasn't trying to do the same again? As quietly as I could, I stepped up to the door and pressed, flinching back a bit when it moved. A second later I found myself peeking through a crack into a mostly empty room.

Against the far wall, centered between two windows sat a massive easel. The problem was it faced away from me. I couldn't see the painting—only the painter's black loafers. But I know who it was. There was only one other person in the Gatehouse. Was Keres an artist? My mind immediately went to the mural, but I pushed the thoughts away, not ready to think about that. When he leaned over to load his brush with paint from a side table, the tips of his black horns and messy midnight hair peeked from around the canvas.

Holding my breath, I eased back from the door and crept as silently as possible down the hall to the library, my heart racing at the prospect of him finding me. And, apparently, at the Gatehouse divulging my spying. It hadn't been my intention to spy on him. My curiosity had gotten the better of me.

I pulled the library door closed behind me but to my absolute disappointment when I glanced at the clock over the fireplace mantel it was 11:57 pm. Three minutes left? How long had I stood watching the backside of an easel? I grabbed the nearest book and slipped quietly back to my room.

Just when I thought I'd made it, Keres emerged from the shadows in front of my door, freezing me in place. His dark eyes lost in the shadows until that one pesky brazier crackled to life, illuminating his perfect face.

"Cutting your time a little tight, Ms. Greene," he said, over enunciating the "T"s.

His hands were tucked behind his back, his steps graceful as ever. It wasn't until he was mere feet from me that I realized he wasn't wearing a doublet for the first time since I'd come to the Gatehouse. He wore a flowing black shirt, sleeves rolled to his elbows, leaving lean forearms exposed as he placed his hands on his hips. The laces of the shirt lay loose, the open neckline exposing a pale slice of firm muscle.

To see him entirely at ease was...startling. It was as if the pretense of being a terrifying Dark Fae had been stripped away, leaving a beautiful stranger behind. My heart fluttered at the memory of his fingers against my chin. Almost immediately I was drenched with cold uncertainty, washing away any sort of heat that burned through me. Was he angry? The raw hunger in his gaze said otherwise. I tipped my chin up.

"You're making a habit of showing up at my door," I said.

He smirked, glancing toward my suite before returning his treacherous eyes to me.

"Your interest in my library is dangerous."

"If I'm not mistaken, you gave me permission to visit your library if I wasn't…I believe the words you used were, 'too terrified to leave my suite.'"

He nodded slowly, knowing I'd caught him in a technicality of his own rules. It was still before midnight, and I hadn't forced my way into any rooms.

"Goodnight, Rosalin." He tipped his head in a tiny bow before he passed me, the shadows of the hall following on his heels.

I pressed my hand over my heart in the hope of stopping it from pounding out of my chest. After a long moment I slipped inside my room, pulling the door closed behind me and not worrying how loud it was as the lock clicked over.

Another day gone, and all I had was a frustrating lack of answers and a stack of books that didn't seem to have anything additional to offer. I plopped into the chair at my little table, dropping the latest book down on top. I glared at it, finally registering which book I'd grabbed. It was the one from the night before; the Old Fae manuscript with the same symbol on the cover that Keres wore around his neck. I traced the symbol with my fingertip before flipping the book open, hoping maybe I'd been wrong, and it wasn't written entirely in Old Fae. But the words were the same confusing patterns that flowed in and out of lines on the page. I couldn't make sense of it.

I turned to another page, finding it was the same. I kept flipping until I came to an illustration that had been added along the outside margin. It looked a lot like the strange beasts that snaked along the walls of the hall and down Keres' back. Goosebumps prickled over my arms. I flipped past quickly, as if fearful the monster might leap off the page if I stared too long.

I let my fingers drag over the characters I couldn't read before flipping through several more pages until I came to another illustration. This one was of a massive mansion that looked a lot like the Gatehouse, except it was missing the distinct dragon sculptures that had been so intimidating when I'd first arrived. I thumbed through more pages, hoping for more illustrations and finding nothing more than the strange flowing writing that didn't make a single scrap of sense to me. I slammed the book shut with more vigor than I'd intended. A slip of paper that had been tucked into the back cover peeked from between the end pages. It was yellowed from age and torn on one side, as if ripped from a journal.

*I was wrong, and I shall be doomed to give my soul in pieces until I fulfill her punishment. I refuse to submit a maiden to the same fate as my beloved. May the record stand; I have protected forty-three from their suffering. Their faces eternally recorded, that I might be reminded of my mistakes until this curse consumes my shadows entirely.*

The hair rose on the back of my neck. *This was confirmation of a curse.*

I read it twice more, each word searing into my memory before I slipped the page back into the book. I felt as if I'd peeked into something far more private than I should have, even though I had been searching for some clue of what was going on. A piece of me needed Keres to be the cruel Dark Fae monster he was supposed to be. But this?

Now I needed to decide if I was willing to expose my snooping and confront him or continue to pepper him with questions he likely wouldn't, or couldn't, answer.

## CHAPTER 11

# The Details

## ROSALIN

I stood in the hall, heart racing. The mural was...*different*. At first, I thought I was going crazy, but the more I studied it on my way to the dining room, the more I was certain I wasn't. It was definitely different. The creatures had moved, and now different humans were being chased and restrained. The demon who had been approaching me now loomed over me, reaching with hungry, taloned claws.

And there was no doubt it was me. The details were so more crisp. Nothing was hidden. I was completely naked, like all the other humans in the mural and I knew the shape of my own body, the curve of my nose, the roundness of my face, the unruly curl of my hair.

This. Was. *Me.*

My cheeks burned so hot I covered them with my hands, unable to rip my eyes from the image of my unclothed body, the expression on my face in the painting one of absolute terror. Was it the Gatehouse that created this mural? Who else could conjure my appearance so flawlessly? Who had seen me naked enough times to be able to paint with such accuracy?

Not even Bastion could say this.

I tried to make out the details of the beast chasing me but other than black skin, demon horns like Keres', and a towering, toned body, the details seemed impossible to make out. The head was turned away, leaving the face obscured by the back of its head. A head covered by long, flowing dark hair that reached nearly to the middle of its back, hanging between massive sinewy wings.

I squeezed my eyes closed, taking long, deep breaths to try and calm my racing heart. I needed to get to the dining room before I missed breakfast, but when I opened my eyes again, I couldn't stop staring at the contrast between the dark monster and myself. The fact that the face was woefully hidden, while mine was entirely exposed.

I pried myself away, rushing down the hall to the dining room. I'd have time later to sort out who and how and...*who*.

Keres looked as if he hadn't slept. He had dark circles under his eyes; his lips set in a frown that trapped my questions in my throat. He likely wouldn't answer them anyway. Something changed yesterday. Something happened between us when he'd held me in place with his magic. I wasn't sure what it was exactly, but I knew he wouldn't tell me. I resolved myself to attempt to keep my questions tucked away as best as I could, but my hands wouldn't stop trembling.

By the time I took my usual seat at the table he had already summoned his eggs and toast. My thoughts were still twisted up around the naked image of myself from the mural, and it took me several seconds to think of something edible. Once I managed to summon a bowl of strawberries with clotted cream, I ate in silence, trying my best to avoid his eyes. As soon as I'd finished my breakfast, I bolted from the dining room, determined to sulk in my suite until the next meal.

Lunch went much the same, pleasantries only, as if some code of conduct dictated that he at least asked me how my day was fairing. I responded with short answers as I continued to hold my questions back. But by dinner, they had begun to fester within me. He was waiting when I arrived, hands folded on the table in front of him, the same exhaustion written across his face. I squeezed my eyes closed and tried to push all of the confusing thoughts away. The mural, Keres, his eyes, his hands. *Keres.*

Why did I burn with the need to know why he'd missed both lunch and dinner the day before? Why did I care that he looked so tired?

Why. Did. I. Care?

"Where were you yesterday?" I asked, forcing aloofness into my voice.

He tipped his head to the side, his expression unchanged. "Was I not where you expected?"

"Don't do that?"

"Do what?"

"That!"

"I honestly don't know what I'm doing that's frustrating you, Ms. Greene," he said it with such genuine uncertainty I almost believed him.

"Answering a question with another question instead of *actually* giving an answer." I pinched the bridge of my nose in frustration. "Why did you miss lunch and dinner yesterday?"

The pause that followed drew my eyes to his, those black wells of mystery threaded with glittering silver. I hated them yet craved them at the same time.

"I wasn't hungry."

That didn't seem possible, but he couldn't lie. I reminded myself of this, over and over again as he continued to watch me before finally lifting his spoon to plunge it into the bowl of stew he'd conjured for himself. He couldn't lie. I knew he couldn't lie, so it had to be the truth.

But that didn't seem like the only reason. He took slow intentional bites, his eyes seeming to find me each time he drew the spoon from his lips. My skin tingled and the hair on my neck rose up as he chewed with intention. Every time he swallowed my eyes were drawn to the column of his throat. My fingers tightened around my spoon as I imagined my teeth dragging down the length of his chest to his navel.

He cleared his throat, his eyes seeming to attempt to focus on the stew in front of him, but his breathing was...*unsteady*.

"Are you okay?" I finally asked.

His eyes snapped to mine, wide with shock. Fuck, I forgot. I was an idiot. *He could feel my emotions.*

"I'm tired. I...I just need more sleep," he said, voice vulnerable.

Fire seared through me, heating my cheeks. I needed to smother this. I needed to reign in this attraction. As lonely as I was, I couldn't let myself like him. He was a Dark Fae. I said the first retort that came to mind.

"You need something as human as sleep?"

He smirked at this, the surprise that had only moments ago covered his face washing away.

"I need sleep, just not nearly as much."

I folded my arms forcefully. "So, you'll answer that, but you can't tell me if this is a curse? Or, you know...why my face is on the wall?"

"What are you talking about?"

I slammed my hands on the tabletop. "Don't do that!"

Without warning, he stood, forcing me to shrink back in my chair. His eyes glowed white, his dark eyebrows drawn low in anger.

"I've no time for this," he said as he turned, taking several large strides toward the door.

"No time for what? Entertaining a lowly human?" I snapped, the frustration that had been building inside me uncoiling all at once. "Answering questions you've encouraged me to ask?"

He paused, frozen in mid-step. I tried to keep the words from tumbling out but failed. It felt as if I'd been cracked open, anger and hurt that he didn't trust me poured onto the floor between us.

"What's wrong, Keres? Angry my poor, feeble mortal mind is curious? Or that I might learn something you're uncomfortable talking about? Mother forbid I have enough information to make me truly prepared for whatever horror I'm to endure on the other side of your mysterious portal."

He turned back slowly, shadows seeming to cling to his legs. The light in the dining room dimmed as he took one terrifying step toward me.

I'd pushed too hard and swallowed the last of my words.

"Tell me, Rosalin, what do you truly think of me? Of Dark Fae with our evil magic, our curses, and propensities to cruelty," he asked, sarcasm dripping from every word.

My blood was boiling and it snuffed out any good sense I might have had. If he wanted to know what I truly thought of his kind I'd tell him.

"That you think we're less than the ground you walk on. That we're lowly bugs waiting to be crushed under your shoe. That we're to do your bidding, to be sacrificed for your every whim. That our pathetic, short lives mean nothing." I took a deep, shuddering breath. "That you're arrogant and do whatever it is you please because you're beautiful, and powerful, and my life is but an insignificant speck compared to the years you'll live."

He took an impossibly graceful step closer to me, eyes smoldering with rage. "Do you know what I think of you?"

I struggled to hold his glare as my eyes flooded with angry tears.

"I think you've waited all your meaningless days for someone to pluck you from your pathetic existence." He took another step closer and I met his glare, wishing I hadn't, but unable to look away. There was hatred in his eyes. Pure fury that froze my heart in my chest. "That you humans waste your precious short lives on fortune and shallow lust, all while assuming those who are different from you must be irredeemable monsters."

He didn't give me an opportunity to respond, leaving me alone, trembling in anger and shame. For a long moment I stared at his half-eaten plate of food, then sprung from my seat to follow him. As angry as he was, I was asking for trouble. I knew I shouldn't push him anymore, but something told me if I did, if I pressed him just a little more, he'd break and tell me what I desperately needed to know.

When I reached the hall, it was dark. The braziers failed to light, and there were nothing but shadows pulsing along the walls as I tried to find my way. I turned to the right in the direction of the library, and the room I'd seen him painting in, but I didn't make it far before I slammed into a rock-hard chest and stumbled back a few steps.

Keres towered over me. One of the braziers nearby chose that moment to ignite, leaving me with the terrifying silhouette of the horns mounted on the top of his head.

"Tell me, Ms. Greene, what do you see when you look at me? A monster? A beast sent to destroy you? To drag you to a vengeful queen?"

I stared into the shadowy void of his face, my hands in fists at my sides. I was trying to decide if I was going to answer him. And if I did, whether to tell him what I actually saw or what I'd expected to see. I must have waited too long because he turned, yanking the light with him. It was so jarring I struggled to keep my feet beneath me as the world seemed to tilt and warp in on itself.

"Wait." I cried out, stumbling to one knee as I tried to follow him down the hall. "Keres, wait."

A door slammed. Based on the distance it wasn't the library, but further down—likely a room I wouldn't be able to enter. I clambered after him and found the way clearer now that his angry shadow magic had disappeared into whatever room with him. I tried the library first, but as I'd expected, it was empty. A happy brazier burning as though it was just another pleasant day in the Gatehouse. I tried the next door, but it was locked.

"Keres," I called as I knocked. But he didn't answer.

I went to the next door. Again, I knocked and called his name after finding the handle locked. Again, he didn't come.

Another door. Another lack of response.

When I got to the end of the hall I stood in front of the last door—locked like the others. I was about to knock, but some piece of me knew I should leave him alone. I'd pushed too hard. I would only make him irrevocably furious with me.

I pressed my back against the wall before sinking down to the cold floor, pulling my knees to my chest and wrapping my arms around them. I had one person in this crazy place, and I'd treated him horribly rather than assume that—maybe, just maybe—he was actually trying to help me. I'd assumed he wished me ill when it was very likely he was trying to make my stay less terrifying before I was taken to the Unseelie Court to fulfill some ancient blood debt to a Hag Queen.

He might not have had any other choice in this than I did. If this *was* a curse, he was likely just as trapped as I was. And yet, I'd treated him like he'd been the man who'd called my sister's name in the town square—or the Dark Fae who'd killed my husband.

A tear slipped down my cheek. I needed to stop treating him like a monster just because I was in this situation. I wiped the tear away and squeezed my legs one more time before climbing to my feet. I needed to apologize, or my insides might melt from the guilt boiling in my gut.

I turned to the door and reached to knock but my hand hovered. My hesitation was almost painful, but he probably had no interest in talking with me anyway. It was possible he'd been ignoring me this whole time. I turned to leave and as I did the door flew open, a rush of air and shadows flowing around me.

"You're impossible," he said, his voice a tight ribbon of frustration. The light pouring from the room behind him cast his face in shadow.

"I'm sorry," I blurted out.

"What could you possibly feel sorry for?" he spat. "Berating a vile beast such as myself?"

"You're right. I am shallow and...if this is a curse, you're likely just as trapped as I am. I shouldn't treat you like you're doing this to me on purpose, and I'm sorry."

He took a deep breath, letting the moment of silence between us stretch.

"Apology accepted. Now leave me alone, human." Keres turned back to the room he'd just stepped from and quite literally, slammed the door in my face.

Too stunned to move, I stood in place for several minutes, a mixture of fury and sadness swirling in the depths of my chest. It was how he'd called me *human* that hurt the most. I was a human, but the way the word slipped from his tongue was bitter, like wine turned to vinegar.

I took a few steps back from the door, another tear slipping down my cheek. This one burned my skin as it hung from the edge of my chin. He was right. I didn't deserve his answers. I hadn't yet learned how to see past my own hatred.

I turned and fled.

## CHAPTER 12

# Cruel Magic

## ROSALIN

I couldn't stop replaying the way he'd called me human with such disdain. I shouldn't care. I was, in fact, a human. Why did this word, spoken by him, mean so much more?

I tried to distract myself from the venom in the way he'd called me shallow by reading and practicing the etiquette prompts, forcing myself to memorize them. But I gave up, unable to focus on anything except the fact that he'd called my life meaningless. To him, I was just another maiden to be dragged through the portal to his Hag Queen. And I shouldn't care.

*But I did*, and that's what bothered me the most.

I climbed into bed, remnants of the fear when I'd first come here clinging to my bones. I yanked the drapes of the canopy tight around me. I knew they couldn't protect me, but I could pretend, just like I could pretend I hadn't noticed the hurt in his expression when he said I assumed he was a heartless monster. Because how many times had I thought that very thing?

I woke to haunting music pouring in from my sitting room. It was disorienting and I couldn't figure out why someone would be playing so loudly at such a late hour. I padded across my bedroom on bare feet and stood in the doorway, golden light bleeding onto the floor. A group of Fae and human women swayed and spoke in whispers, a few clinging to one another in provocative ways. They wore next to nothing and while I should have found this shameful, the only thing I felt was intrigued. They didn't look at me when the tug of curiosity pulled me into the room. It was as if they didn't see me at all.

But *he* did.

My breath caught fast in my throat. It was Keres, or at least it looked like Keres, his beautiful face, his strong shoulders and stature. He had no horns and coal-black hair that fell around his face in soft, approachable waves. His perfect lips curled into a smile when he saw me, igniting a flock of butterflies in my stomach. It was the way he smiled—like a spark of genuine happiness I hadn't seen on his face before. He stepped forward, my attention drawing to his apparel, or lack thereof. I should have been embarrassed by his near nakedness, but instead I couldn't look away, my eyes raking over every inch of him.

A collar of gold plates laced together with delicate chains hung over his chest in the shape of a ribcage, revealing every muscle as he moved. His stomach was bare, the lines of his abdomen shifting with each step. Low on his hips, a belt of matching gold plates was strung with hundreds of thinner chains that dangled, barely concealing him. I tried not to gawk at the way they swayed, allowing for peeks of his pale flesh.

He held my stare as he crossed the room, my blood heating with each step he took in my direction. He shouldn't be walking toward me. He shouldn't care.

"Rosalin," he said with a smooth voice, stepping so close I could feel the warmth of him seep into my skin. He kissed each of my cheeks, trailing fingers down my arm until he took my hand, threading our fingers together. "Come."

I should have had sense enough not to follow, but the heat of his palm against mine only made me crave his hands more. I allowed him to pull me through the throng of people to another room I'd never noticed before. It was small, intimate, decorated in midnight blue and black. Silks were draped from the low ceiling, trimmed with threads of gold and silver, swaying and glittering as we passed. He sat on a low futon, pulling me toward him. But my hand slipped free, and I stood frozen, gazing at the masterpiece sprawled beneath me.

He was the most gorgeous creature I'd ever seen. Every curve of muscle, every smooth plane of skin honed to perfection. He reclined with one arm tucked behind his head, a lazy smile tugging at his lips. I wanted to run from him and devour him all at once. Part of me screamed that I shouldn't be here, that I didn't belong. But another part, a louder far more insistent one, told me to stay. That this moment was made perfectly for me.

"Stay with me, my sweet Rosalin."

I should have been nervous, at the very least uneasy. Something wasn't quite right. *This* wasn't right. I shouldn't be here. I should have been terrified, I should have said no. But instead, I dropped to my knees, aching to reach for him. To touch him. To feel his hands on my skin.

"What do you desire, Rosalin? What do you want?" he asked, drawing my gaze to his dark eyes, glittering with light from the brazier. Delicate threads of silver wove through his irises, making them shimmer. His stare was unyielding. Deliciously intoxicating in its intensity.

What *did* I want?

But I already knew. The certainty had been building in me ever since I'd arrived at the Gatehouse. And now he was here, in front of me, inviting me, devouring me with his gaze.

I ached to touch him, to feel the heat of him. It was a need, almost painful in its urgency. I eased closer and his smile deepened as my fingers smoothed over his flawless skin, running my hands over the muscles of his abdomen as he drew circles up my arm. He watched with a growing hunger as my fingers traced lower.

"You have but to ask, and it shall be yours." His silky voice soaked into my blood, settling deep in my core. I traced my finger along the top of his belt, from one side of his stomach to the other, mesmerized by the way his body moved beneath my touch. I tried to ignore the way the chains draped between his legs, the way his chest tightened with each breath—the way his gaze never wavered from me.

I licked my lips, my mouth suddenly dry.

"I want..." I hesitated, breath shallow as he leaned forward.

I wasn't supposed to be here. Something wasn't right.

One of his hands entwined with mine and he pulled me down beside him. Everywhere our skin touched the heat was so intense I looked down. Instead of my dressing gown I wore nothing but a layer of sheer fabric. Every inch of my torso had been painted in black and gold with winged serpents circling my breasts and over my stomach.

I should have been embarrassed. I couldn't even remember when I'd changed, or who had painted my body. I'd only ever been naked in front of one man, but I couldn't remember why it mattered. There was only a nagging whisper that I shouldn't... Keres' slender fingers slipped under my jaw, and he turned my chin so I faced him before running those same fingers down my throat and between my breasts to my navel. Every muscle in my body tightened at the touch, a burning need uncoiling within me.

"What do you want, Rosalin?"

His hand slipped further down between my legs, pulling the gauzy material up. I tried to focus on what I'd meant to say a moment ago, but there was nothing in my mind but the feel of his fingers as they drew circles over the skin of my inner thigh, his lips gently parted, eyes never leaving mine.

"I want...this," I whispered. "I want you." I pushed his hand away and pulled myself up to straddle him.

I'd never been so forward, never in my life had I taken such control of my own pleasure. I didn't know where I'd found the bravery. I wasn't prepared for the intensity of his glare. I knew I shouldn't be doing this, not with him, but I couldn't remember why.

His hands smoothed over my thighs and up my back to pull the gauzy fabric away, exposing me entirely. Goosebumps pebbled my skin as the last physical barrier that held my desire at bay was removed.

"Is this truly what you want?" he asked as he traced his fingers over my breasts, smearing the gold paint in swirls and sending ripples of urgent desire between my legs.

I tried to focus, the word on the tip of my tongue. Was this what I wanted or was this just what my lonely body wanted?

My eyes washed over him. He looked so human. *Too human*, when I knew he wasn't. I studied his face. I'd spent enough time staring at him, the shape of his eyes, his slender nose, his decadent lips. In that moment I wanted nothing more than to feel all of him inside me—for our bodies to move as one.

But I was frozen in place.

I shouldn't want him.

This wasn't right.

I needed this to not be real.

But his skin was hot beneath me, and I could feel his hands on my breasts, on my arms, on my thighs. His eyes were drunk with wanting as they poured over me. The hard length of him pressed against my entrance.

"You have but to ask..."

I sat up in bed, my body sweaty and cold at the same time, goose-bumps prickling my arms. I couldn't take deep enough breaths. The heat beneath my skin searing between my legs, almost unbearable with need.

I ripped the drapes of the canopy back.

There was no one here. No music, no light. I stood in the middle of a dark room shivering and completely alone.

But it had been so real. I ran my hands down my body, wishing they were his. I squeezed my eyes closed and trembled with shame. I shouldn't want him. Certainly not as deeply as it seemed my unconscious-self did. This had to be magic. I shook my head in an attempt to drive the desire away. This was his Dark Fae shadows wriggling into my mind, shaping my dreams. It had to be. I glanced around the room, but other than the normal darkness of night, there was nothing.

He wasn't here. His magic wasn't either. I collapsed into a heap on my bedroom floor.

I had dreamt it all.

## CHAPTER 13
# If I Could Break Him

## ROSALIN

When I was finally able to drag myself from bed, I was a mess. Unable to stop thinking about Keres, reliving the dream over and over again. It felt so real, like a memory that had been lost in the back of my mind for years, finally released from its cage and tearing through the very fabric of my soul.

Had he put it in my head? Was that even possible? My cheeks burned with the possibility that he had controlled my dreams. I didn't know enough about Fae magic to rule it out, and I wasn't sure I was brave enough to ask. It would be a struggle to sit across from him for breakfast, attempting to forget the unforgettable way the gold chains had draped over every inch of his flawless body.

I'd been ready since dawn, both impatient and thankful Keres hadn't come to collect me for breakfast. I'm not sure I would have answered the door if he'd knocked. When I had a minute to spare, I slipped out and down the hall to the dining room.

He was waiting for me, eyes downcast. I slid into my chair before he troubled himself to look up. There was a strange expression on his face. One I hadn't seen before. It was something like confusion mixed with frustration. I glanced away from him quickly, unable to hold eye contact. Those were the same eyes from the dream, though they'd been admittedly happier to see me than they were now.

He didn't say anything, summoning his usual breakfast, he started eating without a word. But I was a ball of nerves. Every breath I took felt tight as his silence stretched for too long. I tried to recall what we'd discussed at dinner the night before. There had been angry words between us, but it had all been replaced with that fucking dream.

I cleared my throat to ask how his evening had been when I finally noticed what he was wearing. I froze, my mouth falling open as every shred of bravery washed away. His doublet, like others, had a deep neckline that exposed his chest down to his navel. But it was what hung around his neck that gave me pause. A collar made of gold plates strung together with chains in the shape of a ribcage. My whole body began to vibrate from the memory of the dream, the way his slender fingers had felt against my delicate skin, the heat of his body between my thighs as I climbed on top of him.

I couldn't stay in that room.

I couldn't be there with him.

It wasn't real. It was a dream. I *needed* it to be a dream.

I ran from the room, ignoring the confused expression on his face.

Maybe this whole thing—the Gatehouse, the curse, the sacrifice— was nothing to him. But it was *everything* to me. These were likely the last days of my life. So as I forced myself not to think about the dream, I found that I couldn't stop thinking about the curse.

I read the slip of paper that I had found tucked into the back of the Old Fae book over and over again, dwelling on each word. I'd found some sheets of stationary in the drawer of my vanity. A pen and inkwell sat on one of the shelves next to the door. With them I began making notes. My handwriting neat at first, until everything started to come together at once.

Who had written the journal entry?

It was likely Keres, but it could have been another Dark Fae. The reference to the Hag Queen lined up with what Keres had said, that I was here because of concessions made by the humans after the Fae Wars. Could there have been something else involved? Was it a treaty? Or a punishment?

Whoever had written the entry didn't want to submit the maidens to whatever fate their lover had befallen, but there was no way of knowing what their beloved's fate had been. I stared at the words hoping in my heart it wasn't Keres. I didn't need a reason to feel sorry for him right now, not when I was doubting everything I knew about Dark Fae already. In reality, I couldn't allow myself to feel anything for him at all. And a loss, so much like my own, made his angry words the evening before all the more real. That I assumed he was a monster with dark intentions when he was just enduring a punishment.

The reference to having protected forty-three maidens was enough to make my eyes well with tears. If a girl was sent to the Unseelie Court every five years, that meant whoever had written this journal entry had been enduring their punishment for at least two hundred and fifteen years. Most likely longer. The Fae Wars had taken place over five hundred years ago. And based on the age-stained paper, this wasn't a freshly written entry.

I leaned back. It was very possible Keres was over five hundred years old. Fae were immortal. They could be killed, but otherwise, he was likely to live forever. I let this settle around me, a shiver working its way up my spine.

How old was Keres? I tried to push him from my mind again, but it was getting harder.

What was meant by their faces being eternally recorded? I shuddered, my mind instantly going to the room with the portraits. There had been so many. More than forty-three with better than half appearing as nothing but dark silhouettes. What if it had been Keres who painted them all? What if he was the one who dragged every single human maiden to the Unseelie Court?

I still had too many questions, and all I wanted to do was pound on Keres' door again and ask him. I knew he wouldn't answer, and in all honesty, I probably didn't deserve his answers. He'd all but dismissed me the day before when I tried to apologize for the way I'd acted. The memory of his voice as he'd called me human washed over me.

I closed my eyes and took a deep breath, trying hard not to let the memory of the dream creep back in around all the other thoughts. I looked at the clock. It was nearly lunchtime, and I was hungry. I couldn't miss it today, but a piece of me was dreading facing Keres.

"Couldn't you conjure my lunch here?" I asked the ceiling, hoping the Gatehouse would plop a plate down on my otherwise useless table.

After a long moment of nothing happening, I gave up. I dipped the pen tip in the inkwell and circled the word portrait in my last note. I'd come back to this as soon as I could.

At lunch Keres hardly looked at me—it was better that way. I needed the distance. In fact, I pretended he wasn't there at all. I conjured a delightful lunch of onion soup and warm bread, then before he'd finished his own strange meal of what he'd called a midnight apple with a few thick slices of cheese, I left.

I rushed back to my room thinking I could pull some details out of the Old Fae book with Keres' family name on the front, but my brain was a jumbled mess. It was the gold ribcage collar that he'd still been wearing. He'd worn it in the dream, but I hadn't seen it before today. How was that possible unless he'd put the dream in my mind?

I hated not knowing if he was able to manipulate such things. I hated even more that I knew he wouldn't answer if I asked. I tried to make sense of my notes, but nothing was connecting. I'd circled the word portrait and now I wasn't sure why. After an hour of getting nowhere, I decided I'd try some different scenery. It was still a couple hours before dinner. Surely it wouldn't be suspicious if I went to the library at this time of day.

I didn't bother sneaking because I wasn't trying to hide. Instead, I walked with confidence. I was beyond thankful the halls were empty, the braziers burning cheerfully. I wasn't in the right frame of mind to deal with Keres and his shadows. I didn't creep through the door, I opened it with gusto and waltzed in, only to find him sprawled out on a chaise with a book across his knees, all long limbs and darkness. He glanced in my direction, expression never changing, then went back to reading as if me being in his library was perfectly normal.

So, he was still ignoring me. Delightful. Because I didn't have the patience for his non-answers anyway. I took a deep breath and went directly to the shelf I'd seen some other books in Old Fae and started pulling them down, flipping through until I found something that looked like a diagram of sorts. This wasn't exactly what I was looking for, but it was interesting enough that I plopped into a chair to take a closer look.

There was nothing but the sound of pages turning as I thumbed through the book. It was almost peaceful, and I'd nearly forgotten he was there with me on the other side of the library. I picked up another book, flipping until I came to strange drawings of the different High Fae. Captivated, I looked closer, noticing how detailed each illustration was. Beautiful linework twisted across the pages blending into the text with long twirling ligatures. I was mesmerized by the elegance. Tall, lean males and females with antlers and horns and pointed ears. Different colored flesh and some with very animalistic characteristics.

A shadow of a horned head crept across the open pages, and I glanced up into Keres' curious dark eyes. He seemed just as intrigued as I was, and for a moment I was lost in the kind expression on his face. I blinked a few times to make sure I wasn't dreaming again.

"Interesting read for a human," he said.

I let the snide remark roll away, trying my best not to be goaded as I went back to inspecting the pages.

"Can you even read Old Fae?"

"No, but you aren't exactly forthcoming, so I'd say these books are about as helpful as you are."

He chucked and I couldn't help but glance up at the mirthful sound of it. He met my gaze with warm amusement which I hadn't yet had the opportunity to see from him. Where was this Dark Fae when I'd been terrified or angry? I tried to snuff out the momentary flash of embarrassment at the sight of that damned gold collar and instead nodded to the book in his hand.

"What are you reading?"

He held it out to me.

"The Demise of the Blackwarden." I read aloud. I'd never heard of it but that wasn't significant. I grew up in a poor village with a small library.

"It's interesting. If a bit dry and slightly inaccurate."

Was he attempting humor? He must have noticed my confusion and took a step back glancing down at the cover as though he was reading it for the first time.

"I prefer fantastical stories if I'm honest," he continued. "This one is more of the historical variety."

"What's the Blackwarden?"

His eyes didn't leave the cover of the book as he blinked a few times in surprise.

"Another question you won't answer?"

He turned away, letting the book hang at his side in defeat. I should have stopped there. I knew better. This was how I'd made him angry before.

"Do you know much about it?" I asked.

"Them."

"Did you know them?" I corrected.

Keres turned back toward me, the muscles in his shoulders tense. He took a breath to speak, his lips parting, the words on the tip of his tongue. I'd seen this before. I knew this response. He was definitely trying to answer me. If I could break him now, perhaps I'd get an answer to the question I truly wanted to know.

"What's going on? Is this whole thing because of a curse?"

He tightened, squeezing his eyes closed in pain.

"Who are you really, Keres? Is that even your name?"

"It is." His response exploded past his lips. "My name is Keres..." he trailed off as if there was more. "Keres..." The anguish on his face was genuine and I stood as he held the book out toward me. "K..."

His eyes fluttered as he swayed, and I thought he was going to pass out. I steadied him by his arms, but there was no way I could have caught him if he fell. He looked down at me with glassy eyes.

We were so close—my hands still resting on his arms, the warmth of him seeping into my palms. He stared at me for a long moment as if trying to focus, but I was still lost in his eyes, my heart pounding so loudly in my ears I was sure he had to hear it too.

"Ask me...ask me again." His voice was strained, pressed thin as if it took all his strength to speak these few words.

"Who are you?"

"The other..."

"Is this a curse?"

He swayed again, eyes rolling before refocusing on mine. He took a breath, his lips moving in the shape of the word "yes."

A line of blood eased from his nose.

"Stop," I said, much louder than I should have. "What are you doing? You're hurting yourself."

He trembled under my hands as the blood carved a path down to his chin. The red was so bright against his pale skin. Nothing else in this entire mansion was as vivid, and I was mesmerized by it as it ran down his neck and soaked into the collar of his doublet.

"What's happening to you?" I hadn't wanted to ask him another question, but I didn't know what else to say. It was becoming crystal clear he wanted to answer me but physically couldn't. Not without consequences. The way his lips had shaped the word *yes* sent a shiver of fear writhing through me. It was as solid of confirmation as I'd likely get that there was a curse, that I wasn't crazy, and the journal page I'd found was accurate.

He swallowed, glaring at me with an unyielding agony in his expression before he turned and stumbled from the library, leaving the book he'd been reading in my hands.

This time, I didn't follow him. Instead, I read the title over and over again, letting it sink into my bones. *Blackwarden.*

Was this book about a family? Every time he tried to say his family name, he'd been unable to continue. The Gatehouse, or this curse, whatever it was, didn't want me to know. But I needed to know, and I'd figure it out if it was the last thing I did before I was dragged to the Unseelie Court.

# CHAPTER 14
# Until Her

## KERES

I'm Keres Blackwarden.

I'm the Gatekeeper, the guardian of the portal from the human world to the Unseelie Court. Condemned for my family's treasonous role in the war between the humans and Dark Fae and cursed for betraying the Hag Queen. I wanted to tell Rosalin all of this, to give her the truth. But I physically couldn't. I was already paying the price for what I had attempted to tell her.

I cleaned the blood from my face, mesmerized as it danced like red ribbons through the water in the sink basin before dissipating. I hadn't been in this terrible of shape since I'd tried to break the curse when the first maiden was brought to me. What little magic I currently possessed was decimated, along with my energy.

I stumbled out of the bathroom and over to my bed, dizzy and grasping at the post of the canopy in a desperate attempt to stop the world from spinning. It was a wonder I'd managed to make it back to my room in the first place. Sheer strength of will bid me put one foot in front of the other, until I wasn't anywhere near her convoluted emotions. I needed the distance. She'd been too close, all the conflicting feelings she'd been fighting since our argument were tearing me down. I wasn't sure how much more I could endure before I did something very stupid.

The brazier beside my bed faded to smoke.

"I know," I said aloud, even though I was well aware The Gatehouse could hear my every thought. "It was stupid."

I'd been connected to this place for so long, I could hardly remember what life was like without it eavesdropping. I didn't know where my magic ended, and the Gatehouse began. In a way, Rosalin's question as to whether I was part of the house had been an appropriate one to ask. I loathed and loved how perceptive she could be.

I flopped heavily onto the bed and rolled to my back, gazing up at the canopy draped over me as the brazier on the other side of my bed snuffed out.

It was one thing to be cursed to drag human girls to the Unseelie Court every five years—it was entirely different when you couldn't speak of it. The physical pain was torturous. I couldn't answer her questions. I couldn't lie. I was a prisoner trapped in a cage of Rosalin's curiosity.

"She's not going to stop asking."

None of the other maidens bothered to look at the walls—to look around at anything. To notice the fact that I dodged their questions with more questions. None of them ever suspected a curse was involved. They'd simply done their best to avoid me while staring at my wretchedly handsome face for the eight days they'd been in my home. They accepted that some horrible archaic agreement between a vengeful Dark Fae and long dead humans was the reason for them being dragged to the Gatehouse. Which was mostly true at least. They'd been satisfied enough with the explanation I gave them, wooed by my face and my words, just as they were supposed to be.

Until her.

She was still wooed. I could feel her desire, so strong it was disorienting. She wanted me, almost as much as she wanted to know what was going on. But it was more than lust. She wanted to anger me, to see the expression on my face change, to see me react. She wanted to *break me,* and I could feel it wicking through my skin every time she stared at me.

And her wanting was so deliciously addictive.

The problem wasn't her. It was me.

Because I wanted to answer all of her questions. I wanted to tell her everything, to give her every last precious piece of history I could about the Gatehouse, the reasons she was here, the Hag Queen, the curse, *me.* I wanted to talk with her all night and see the sun warm the sky in the morning. I wanted to show her the gallery, my paintings, the legacy of this curse. I wanted to get to know her, Rosalin Greene, the woman who wouldn't stop asking fucking questions.

I'd never been interested in spending time with the maidens. As far as I was concerned, they were all the same. Scared, shallow humans, waiting to be saved by some knight in shining armor. But not Rosalin. No, she would save herself. The determination that dripped from her flesh was intoxicating. There was no knight coming to save her, and she'd accepted as much the moment she saw me step from my shadows.

The temperature in the room plummeted, leaving my breath solid in the air. I tried to pull a blanket over myself, but I wasn't strong enough as darkness crept over my vision.

"I just need a little more time," I pleaded.

And I needed distance from her, because in truth, every time her inquisitive green eyes searched mine for answers, I loved it. And my soul would be shattered when I dragged her to the Unseelie Court where she would be destroyed by the Hag Queen's harem.

I wanted her to ask me whatever questions her heart desired, and I wanted to answer those questions even more. I wanted her to sit with me in my dining room, glaring at me with her adorable anger. I wanted her to see me, all of me. I wanted her to break me over and over again.

I wanted *her*.

"Just a little more time," I choked out, gasping in pain, my eyes rimmed with tears I hadn't shed in centuries. "Please."

The last brazier in my room went dark.

CHAPTER 15

# Keres

## ROSALIN

He didn't come to dinner and every second it took me to choke down the stew and bread I'd conjured from the stupid Gatehouse magic was agony. His empty chair mocked me. I knew his absence was my fault. I took a sip of wine and lost myself in the liquid as it sloshed against the sides, running in long threads down the inside of the glass. It reminded me of the blood that had run down Keres' pristine skin.

"Fuck."

I was trying to calm my racing heart as I made the decision not to finish my pathetic dinner. I needed to find him. I needed to make sure he was okay. I'd done this to him. I'd tried to break his silence, only to realize—too late—that whatever this curse was held him in its vicious claws. It wasn't me that was cursed. *It was him.* I was just collateral damage from some strange agreement made centuries ago to end a war.

I didn't waste any more time, walking as fast as I could without hyperventilating, the braziers springing to life as I made my way down the hall. There was a buzz of energy rippling through the Gatehouse. Something was wrong. Everything seemed lighter even though the sun had already set. It wasn't until I'd made it to the last door on the right that I realized why—*there were no shadows.*

With a shaking hand I knocked. There was no response. I bit my lower lip and waited a few seconds before knocking again and pressing my ear against the door to catch any sound on the other side.

Nothing.

"Fuck." I spun a lock of hair around my index finger, trying to take deep breaths to calm my racing heart. What if he... I shook the thought away and tried the handle. It was locked. I hadn't expected it to be otherwise.

"Keres?" I called through the door. "Are you in there?"

The silence that surrounded me was darker than any of his shadows. A tremble crept into my hands as I tried to press my fear into submission, wishing I had the cloak he'd conjured for me so I could pull it around my shoulders.

"Keres. Please talk to me. I just need to know if you're alright."

It sounded like something fell off a shelf and rumbled across the floor. I yanked at the handle wishing maybe I hadn't turned it hard enough, but it was definitely locked.

"Keres? Are you okay?"

Nothing.

I looked up to the rafters. "Can you help me?" I asked the Gatehouse. I was desperate. "Can you unlock the door?"

Heavy, uneven footsteps were both a blessing and a concern. If Keres was anything, it was graceful. I don't think I'd ever heard him walking through the Gatehouse before. He was silent, per-fectly attuned to his surroundings with his shadows doing the rest.

The door slowly swung in, and my breath caught fast in my throat. A rather haggard looking Dark Fae struggled to stand on the other side of that door. He was so much paler, which seemed impossible with how pale he usually was. His eyes were sunken and hollow. He looked half dead, and yet, he was still gorgeous. A flash of frustration ran through me at how he could look so beautiful when he was in such terrible shape.

"I'm fine, Rosalin." His voice was flat and empty. His eyes found mine and immediately slipped to my lips, a strange hunger growing in his expression as he tried to stand up straighter. "I'm sorry to have worried you."

He apologized? Keres?

I pried my eyes from his face and focused on the room behind him. It was so...*bright*. That wasn't like Keres. He surrounded himself with black and darkness. His magic was literally made of shadows. How many times had I seen him materialize from them? Surely the fact that his suite was flooded with light was a terrible sign.

"Where are your shadows?" I shouldn't have asked. I knew better but it left my mouth before I could stop it.

His eyes rolled, before he braced himself hard against the doorframe, shoulders curving forward with exhaustion. "I shouldn't have..." He seemed to stumble over his words. "I shouldn't..."

"Stop." I pressed my hand to his chest as if this would stop him from responding. "Don't. It's okay. I shouldn't have asked."

He looked down at my hand, head dipping in slow motion before he looked back up at me, agony in his eyes. I didn't know if he was mad I'd touched him, or if there was something else about my hand on his chest that caused him pain.

"I'm fine—" He stumbled against the door frame, and I reached to help keep him from falling, but I wasn't strong enough.

Instead, we both slid to the floor in a pile of tangled limbs, his head resting against mine. I couldn't move, frozen in place as my stomach bottomed out, heat building in my cheeks as I stared at his closed eyes. My arms were threaded under his and around his waist, the muscles of his back firm beneath my fingers. So close. The scent of him seemed to wrap around my throat and squeeze. After a few seconds, which felt both eternally long and not nearly long enough, he pulled his head back from mine, a withered smile turning up his lips.

"Your infernal questions, Ms. Greene."

I couldn't help it, a short laugh popped from my mouth as he lay his head on my shoulder with his lips nearly touching my neck. Mother save me, being this close to him melted any coherent thoughts from my brain.

"I'm sorry."

"It's not your fault," he said.

His soft breath on my neck was maddening. Goosebumps rippled down my arms at the deep rumble of his voice. I needed to think of something other than how close he was. I tried counting to ten, tried focusing on the light in his room. I tried to think of what I was going to have for breakfast the following day. I tried anything to pretend there wasn't a gorgeous Dark Fae essentially laying on me, clearly in need of assistance because of what I had put him through. But it was impossible to ignore that his hands were slowly moving up my back.

"It *is* my fault," I said. "I shouldn't ask so many stupid questions." I swallowed my nerves, trying to calm the trembling that was returning to my hands, to will my heart to stop racing.

"I want you to ask me all your questions." His voice was a tight whisper. "I want all of your curiosity."

Fuck, this was impossible. I tried to push the wanting that was boiling deep in my stomach away, but the way his voice curled around me sent a swarm of butterflies loose in my chest. I wanted his lips to slowly climb their way up my neck to my mouth. The need to pull him against me was overwhelming. I squeezed my eyes closed trying to focus on anything but how the quiet of the Gatehouse was so complete, it made every ragged breath he took sound twice as loud.

"I want you..." I thought perhaps he'd failed to finish his sentence, but then he said it again. "I want you...so badly, it's agony."

Then, he bit my neck. *Hard.* The sharp spark of pain ripping a gasp from my throat as one of his hands crept around the back of my head and clutched my hair in a greedy fist. I was trapped between his mouth and his hand, my entire body frozen as my blood turned molten. He pulled me tight against him with surprising strength, kissing up my neck and over my chin to my lips exactly as I'd wanted, as if he'd plucked the desire from my soul.

His kiss was hungry, devouring the last shreds of my self-restraint. I lost myself to the warmth of his hands as his tongue explored, vicious and claiming. I'd never been kissed like this, with a passion so complete my entire being ignited. Every nerve in my body was alive and begging for more of his touch, begging for his hands to be on my skin, his tongue, all of him. He moaned into my mouth before he pulled my lower lip between his sharp teeth and bit me again, the sting of his bite so delicious. I managed to free one of my arms and threaded my fingers through his hair as I kissed him again. His lips were impossibly soft, impossibly warm, the taste of him was intoxicating...*fuck.* I was losing myself.

He pulled away abruptly, eyes wide with fear, every muscle in his body tight with some nameless agony.

"Keres?"

"I'm sorry." He shook his head and pushed himself back from me. "I'm...I'm not permitted..."

"It's okay." My confidence shattered seeing him scramble to get further away from me. "You didn't do anything wrong."

"No..." He slumped on the floor, rolling to his back and covering his eyes with his hands.

I slid closer, trying to make sure he was okay, but also because I couldn't be so far away from him. Not yet. He was in pain, and I hated it. More than if it was my own pain. He shook his head from side to side, his horns smacking the floor and making a horrendous clanking noise.

"No, Rosalin, *I'm* sorry."

"What are you apologizing for?"

"I'm out of time. *We're* out of time," he gasped, his body tightening.

"Out of time for what? What's going on?"

"I have to finish it in two days."

"Finish what?"

His arms fell hard against the floor, as he stared at the ceiling, dark eyes wide. I thought he'd passed out, or maybe I'd asked another question he couldn't answer.

"I have to finish your portrait in two days."

His entire body tensed. With horror I realized he'd probably just said something he wasn't supposed to. The words, not just the shape of them on his lips. For an agonizing moment he was rigid, his face pinched in pain before he went limp, another line of blood running from his nose.

## CHAPTER 16

# Hate Me

## KERES

Cold stone pressed into my back as I woke from a dream, disoriented and unsure of where I was. I'd dreamt Rosalin had come looking for me, that she cared enough to make sure I was okay. Perhaps, in some other reality, I hadn't pissed her off as terribly as I'd thought when I'd failed to answer her questions the last time.

I needed to though.

I needed her to hate me. I *needed* to push her away, but I *wanted* to pull her into my shadows where I could keep her forever.

I dreamt I'd kissed her, hard, like my life depended on it. In a way it did, because I'd been certain about my decision before. Now I was faced with a choice. And I only had two precious days left to make it—two days left to finish her portrait, or I'd be taking her to the Unseelie Court without any protection. I swallowed my sorrow. With anyone else I wouldn't care as much. They'd all been the same, until *her*. The thought of throwing Rosalin to the Hag Queen without the shield my shadows could provide was almost more than I could bear.

Every five years I painted a portrait of the maiden delivered to me, a perfect replica within eight days before I pulled her through the gate to the Unseelie Court. Over and over again. The Hag had made the portrait part of my curse to remind me of all the humans my mistakes had destroyed. But what she didn't know was I imbued the portraits with what little scraps of magic I could to hold back a precious piece of each maiden's soul and replace it with a fragment of my shadows. The paintings grew old and died with them, their faces aging as time passed until there was nothing but a dark silhouette when their delicate mortal life ended. It shielded them from the worst of the pain they would feel when the Hag Queen siphoned their youth away, one year at a time, to strengthen her own beauty. But even more important, it gave them a layer of calm over their emotions as they faced the reality of their new life in the Hag's harem.

Sex and beauty—these were all the Hag cared about. The maidens lived with her in her winter castle; in a hedonistic paradise where the Hag Queen would expect them to entertain her and her guests at countless revels. It made me shiver just thinking about it, because soon I'd be taking Rosalin Greene there. *My Rosalin.*

Strong and stubborn Rosalin. She'd stood up to me, spat her opinions at me instead of hiding in her suite. She was bright and inquisitive—an infernal brazier washing away my shadows with her curiosity. She was the opposite of me in so many ways, with demanding emotions that ignited a spark in my cold, dark heart that hadn't been there for hundreds of years. She was a beautiful reminder that I could still feel something other than anguish, pain, and regret.

I tried to get up, but I struggled against an unfamiliar weight. I pried my eyes open and looked down to find a very real Rosalin asleep on me, her head resting on my chest and one arm slung across my stomach.

Perhaps I hadn't dreamt of her coming at all. Which meant I might not have dreamt kissing her or telling her I wanted her. Or telling her I had to finish her portrait. I squeezed my eyes closed to keep the panic building in my chest at bay. If I'd managed to say all of these things it could open up so many more questions and I hated how many I couldn't answer.

My hand hovered over her head before I gave in and dug my fingers into her hair, letting the soft threads tangle between them. How long had it been since I'd touched someone like this? Gentle and meandering, intentional, someone I wanted to touch. I savored the warmth of her pressing against my chest even as the cold stone reminded me of what I would have to do. I ran my hand over her exposed shoulder, her silken skin tempting me to tuck my fingers beneath the neckline of her dress. I knew I was only torturing myself with what I couldn't have.

The Hag Queen made sure I was kept under lock and key. I spent my time alone, here in the Gatehouse as I brought Fae back and forth through the portal. Or at her side in her palace of cruel pleasures and death. Until she needed another maiden. Every five years. And if she learned I'd touched one of her human girls before they were delivered? I never wanted to live through that punishment again.

The Hag had twisted my shadows into the curse, weaving them so tightly around her I could do almost nothing with them but bring people through the portal. She'd shackled me more than once with my own magic, reminded me over and over that I was hers, and no one else's. I shuddered at the memory of the queen's touch, her cruelty, the pain she had no qualms inflicting. Because I was hers and she could do whatever she wished with me.

Rosalin's head popped up, her sleep heavy eyes finding mine. A swell of fear washed away, replaced with such soothing relief. Her emotions were always so strong, but this close to me, they seemed amplified, burrowing themselves under my skin. And now there were countless questions already burning through her. I had to be strong, like I had when she'd first come here. When I'd still been able to ignore them. Just a little longer. I could do this if I was strong. *I had to.*

"I worried..." Her voice was raw and gritty, and she sucked in a broken breath. "I thought you died."

I swallowed hard, realizing just how much trouble I was in. There was genuine affection in her words, and I didn't think I was strong enough to push her away anymore.

I attempted a meek smirk. "I'm immortal, silly human."

She smiled weakly then nuzzled her head against my chest, a spark of heat settling in my stomach. This closeness was going to destroy me. I could feel her relief melting into a warm desire. It burned through my shirt like a brand, and I wanted so much more. I traced the line of her throat over and over again, across her collarbones and back, as if I needed reminding of the shape of her, which I didn't. I'd memorized every inch of her by the second day. I had a portrait to paint, and it had to be perfect.

For a long moment she didn't move, and I was content to spend every single second I could like this. Just a little longer. I couldn't allow myself to be this close to her again. Not when I knew there'd be grave consequences if the Hag learned that Rosalin's emotions had woven together with mine. We would both pay in pain.

"I should have guessed it sooner," Rosalin said, before she looked up at me again, her eyes glistening with tears. "It's not that you don't want to answer me, you physically *can't* answer me...I'm such an idiot."

I shook my head. I needed to protect her, but the only way I knew how was to push her away, and it was so incredibly hard.

"You're not an idiot, Rosalin." I took a deep breath trying to muster the energy to sit up but failed. "You're the furthest thing from."

One of her hands found the hem of my shirt and I flinched. Her fingertips tucked beneath, an impossible longing shot through me at the feel of her hands on my stomach. It made my head swim with the fear that I'd already fallen too far. That there was no pushing her away now because I had already lost my heart. By the Mother, if I wasn't a husk of myself...

A wave of exhaustion washed over me, tugging me down into darkness.

## CHAPTER 17

# Ninety-nine

## ROSALIN

I watched him sleep for a long time. I honestly don't know how long, but I couldn't bring myself to leave. The echo of his fingers in my hair, the way he gently traced the line of my neck over and over. The way he'd called me "silly human" with such warmth. There was something so immeasurably calming about being near him. Like he was able to take pieces of my emotions and tame them. And now I knew he'd not been intentionally secretive, that he was, in fact, not physically able to answer my questions... I wanted every moment I could get with him.

At some point I tried to help him to bed, but he was dead-weight and I wasn't strong enough to lift him. Instead, I pulled a blanket from the back of one of the chairs in his sitting room and tried to make him comfortable. The clock that hung above his door struck midnight. I glared at it, realizing I'd never bothered to ask why I wasn't supposed to be wandering around so late. Then again, maybe he wouldn't have been able to answer me. The one time I'd taken the risk; the only consequence had been him chastising me the next day.

I gazed down at his sleeping face, his lips gently parted, long thick lashes resting against his cheeks. Mother save me, he was beautiful. I was finally learning more about him, and it only made me crave more. Like each layer revealed some new secret I never thought I'd uncover. My eyes followed the curve of his horns, reminding me he was Dark Fae. How easy it was for me to overlook my distaste for his kind when he smiled at me.

Chewing my lower lip, I wondered if he'd be alright left alone. He was immortal. He'd be okay after a night of rest. But still I hesitated. What if he woke and needed me? As I neared the door, my throat tightened with every step. I squeezed my eyes shut to still my worries. I needed to let him rest. Before I lost my nerve I slipped out, closing the door behind me, hearing a lock click into place. A shiver of fear writhed through me at the ominous sound. Perhaps it was just the Gatehouse trying to keep its ward safe.

I ran down the hall toward my own suite, trying to ignore how the braziers had dimmed, and the shadows thickened. After I'd closed my door, I stood with my back against it for a long time, looking around the sitting area, trying to see if anything was different. I wasn't sure why I thought there might be, but I had an overwhelming feeling I wasn't where I was supposed to be. Even though this was *exactly* where I was supposed to be. I felt like I'd changed somehow but I couldn't pinpoint in what way.

A brazier in my bedroom flickered to life as the one in my sitting area dimmed to a low flame. A not so subtle way for the Gatehouse to tell me it was time to get to bed.

"I get it. I'm going," I said to the ceiling, as I crossed the room. "You're so pushy." The brazier flared brighter for a second before it faded again, and I couldn't help but smirk.

I changed into my dressing gown quickly and tucked myself under the cozy comforter before pulling the canopy closed for extra security. But instead of falling fast asleep, I lay there, memories of Keres' lips on mine, his hands holding me tight against his firm body replaying over and over again.

His words were branded on my skin. *"I want you...so badly, it's agony."* I ran a hand over my breast and down, craving his touch. He was right. It was agony to want so badly and know you couldn't have. Something held him back. He'd pushed me away after he'd kissed me, mumbling something about not being permitted? I tried not to think about it because I knew I couldn't ask him. But what could he have meant? He hadn't finished the statement. Was he not permitted to be with anyone or just me? The words from the journal entry flashed through my memory. *I refuse to submit a maiden to the same fate as my beloved.*

I took a long slow breath, trying to calm the fire building in my core. The way his voice resonated through me before his sharp teeth sank into my flesh. I felt along my neck where he bit me and yanked my hand away.

*My skin was like ice!*

In a frenzied panic, I pulled myself from the bed and stood before the vanity mirror. My green eyes and messy hair glared back. What could a gorgeous Fae, who could quite literally lure any woman he wanted, see in me? I pulled the collar of my dressing gown away and found a dark mark on my neck.

It wasn't exactly a bruise, and it didn't look like a bite. I stared at it in the mirror for a long time, wondering if it was some kind of magical brand I hadn't noticed since coming to the Gatehouse to identify me as one of the Hag Queen's maidens. Perhaps Keres' shadow magic had left it behind when he'd bitten me.

Again, I'd have to be satisfied with not knowing—not understanding why the feeling something had changed was overwhelming. Or why it felt as if some missing piece of me had finally found where it belonged.

The morning couldn't come fast enough. I wanted to make sure Keres was okay after I'd left him asleep on the floor of his suite. I knew that wasn't the only reason I wanted to see him, but I'd tell myself it was. I gripped the sides of my skirt to give my hands something to do as I avoided wandering down the hall to his suite instead of to the dining room. I stopped at the place where the main hall branched off, glaring at the other end. The brazier outside his suite was dark and I shook my head. This was silliness. He'd been delirious and likely hadn't been fully aware of what he was saying and doing. Still, my stomach flipped thinking about the way his gentle voice wrapped around me and squeezed. I could still feel his fingers on my collarbones.

I reluctantly turned toward the dining room. I decided if he wasn't there I'd go and find him to make sure he was okay. But I was leaving this place the following day, and I needed to get used to not thinking about him, even though right now that's all I could seem to do. I needed to accept that it was very possible he'd not entirely meant to kiss me at all, and I'd been a convenient conduit for what were a male's normal appetites. That I was present and agreeable when he'd needed a moment of intimacy in this cold lonely place.

I found him waiting in the dining room, hands folded in front of him, his usual stoic mask hiding his emotions. I should have expected this. It was possible with the shape he'd been in that he didn't remember what happened at all.

His eyes followed me as I crossed the dining room and sat in my usual place. I tried to ignore how he stared, like he usually did, and instead focused on my empty plate, summoning a breakfast of sweet bread and a bowl of strawberries. When I glanced over at his plate I almost fell out of my chair. He'd summoned a bowl of fruit similar to what I'd summoned my first morning. No eggs. No toast.

"Um...excuse me, Keres?"

He glanced up at me, a bite halfway to his mouth, lips parted in anticipation.

"Are you okay?"

"Pardon?" he asked.

"What are you eating?"

He looked at his plate like he wasn't so sure himself and set the fork down, letting the bite fall onto the table.

"I...don't know."

The look of confusion on his face made me smile, but I pressed my lips together in an effort to stop myself. He glanced up at me, brows furrowed. He stared for a long moment before a warm smile melted across his face.

"I must have been thinking about how many questions you've tortured me with, Ms. Greene." He leaned on to his elbows, folding his hands in front of his face. "Do you have any for me this morning?"

The hungry look in his eyes sent me back in my chair in an attempt to escape. It didn't work. My mind went completely blank; I couldn't conjure a single question. Instead, all I could think of was when he kissed me, his hand holding my head in place, the simmering heat of him against me.

His pupils dilated and he sat up straighter. "Actually, I need to apologize for my conduct," he said, sweeping his arms from the top of the table and tucking them into his lap, a very uncertain expression on his face. "I shouldn't have—"

"It's fine," I squeaked. "I know you didn't mean—"

"No. It's not fine." He swallowed hard, unable to hold my eye contact. "I'm..." He closed his eyes as if he needed a moment to collect himself.

"Really, it is." I stood from my seat, suddenly sweaty, my heart racing. "I need to go."

Now that I knew he was okay, the need to remove myself from his presence was intense. I very nearly slipped and fell as I fled and rounded the corner, where I came face to face with Keres as he stepped from his shadows.

"Ms. Greene," he said, a sly smile tugging at his lips. Those fucking lips that had been so soft and perfect the evening before. "You look as if you've seen a monster."

I swallowed and took a few steps back from him. His shadows unfurled from around him and crept across the floor toward me.

"Keres, I..." I blinked a few times, trying desperately to pry my eyes from him and failing.

"Can I show you something?"

The change in direction was jarring, and it took a moment for me to realize he was waiting for an answer. What could he possibly want to show me that he hadn't already? I guess there were probably plenty of things in this mansion of his that remained behind locked doors. He held his hand out to me like he had when he'd first escorted me through the front doors. I remembered how his hand had felt warm and soft—welcoming when everything else had been strange. I'd been terrified, but somehow brave enough to reach for him. I could be brave again.

He tucked my hand under his arm, squeezing it against his side before leading me down the hall. When we stepped into a pitch-black room, the creeping suspicion I'd been there before rose the hair on the back of my neck. A brazier timidly illuminated along the far wall, and I stifled a gasp. It was the room I'd been locked in on my second day. The one full of frames, some with portraits, some with nothing but foreboding, dark silhouettes.

"This was where the Gatehouse brought you on your second day. The Gallery." He refused to release my hand, instead keeping it tightly tucked against his chest. When I glanced at him his eyes were turned toward the countless frames. "There are ninety-nine of them."

Ninety-nine? If I was right and these were portraits of the maidens that had been taken to the Hag Queen, I shivered wondering if he'd been the Dark Fae to take all of them? That would mean he'd been doing this for five hundred years. He'd been cursed to rip maidens from their families for five hundred years. He'd been protecting them with his shadows for five hundred years. I couldn't craft a clever enough question. Now that I knew there were so many things he couldn't say, I was too scared to ask anything at all. Instead, I stood there dumbfounded looking at all the beautiful faces.

Ninety-nine maidens.

He glanced down at me, a strange sadness in the curve of his brow. Almost as if he was waiting for me to ask him, but I couldn't. A sickly-sweet sorrow flooded through me. I stared back at him wishing I'd never asked a single question at all, that I was blissfully ignorant of all of this. That I'd kept my mouth shut, pulled my food from thin air then taken myself back to my suite where I could hide in peace. I didn't want to know anymore. I didn't want this side of the story. The side where a very lonely Keres was cursed and forced to do something he didn't wish to do, over and over again.

I stiffened. He'd said he still needed to finish *my* portrait. Was that the canvas on his easel? I looked to the nearest painting, mesmerized by the detail. The faces looked so lifelike, as if they could step from the canvas at any moment. If it was him who painted all of these, he was a remarkable artist.

"Did *you* paint all these?"

"There's the questions." He was smiling wide enough to show his elongated incisors.

He didn't answer, he just stepped away, leaving me staring into the eyes of a woman I had a feeling I'd be meeting very soon.

## CHAPTER 18

# The Portrait

## ROSALIN

I refused to spend my last evening in the Gatehouse holed up in my suite. I'd seen everything in this place. The creepy mural, the room with all the portraits, the kitchen which served no purpose. I'd endured being surrounded by magic, the oppressive sense of being constantly watched, and having my emotions felt by someone else without my permission. There was nothing left to explore, nothing left to surprise me or scare me. So, when Keres bid me good evening, I wandered to the library and made myself comfortable on one of the settees. Part of me wished I'd see him, that I wouldn't have to spend my last night here alone. Another part knew it was probably best if I didn't.

I'd decided to read through the book he'd given me, *The Demise of the Blackwarden.* It was, as he'd confessed, horribly dry. And a good number of the pages listed nothing but conquests of what the Unseelie Court had considered one of the strongest and oldest families of the Dark Fae. They had been the guardians of the portals from the Fae realms to the human world for millennia, now they were all dead.

I felt him enter the library long before I saw him. His shadows seemed to curl around me possessively, and I didn't entirely dislike it. Keres stood in front of me with his hands on his hips, a snide smirk on his face.

"I see you found something treacherously boring to read."

I couldn't help but match his smirk. "These Blackwardens must have all been very full of themselves."

"You have no idea."

I flipped through a few more pages, seeing how much further I had left in the chapter and froze. The symbol on the chapter header was familiar. I'd seen it a few times now. It was on the Old Fae book I couldn't read, as well as Keres' pendant. I stood abruptly, the book that had been sitting beside me fell to the ground with a thump.

When I looked up at him, his stoic mask had returned. I wondered if he'd even be able to confirm if I worded my thoughts as a statement instead of a question. Keres was a Blackwarden. Was it a secret? I glanced back down at the symbol, letting this new knowledge sink in. According to this book, the Blackwardens had all been put to death for their treasonous involvement in the Fae Wars. They'd aided the humans with shadow magic, had made alliances that had cost them dearly. Maybe that meant he wasn't a Blackwarden. How could he be alive if they'd all been put to death?

"Born of shadows," I whispered. How had it not clicked when I'd read this in the introduction?

His long fingers removed the book from my hand, throwing it down on the settee before they nudged my head to the side, sweeping my hair away to expose where he'd bitten me. I squeezed my eyes shut as warmth plunged into my stomach from his touch. Vicious memories of his voice melted through me. *"I want you... so badly, it's agony."*

"This hasn't always been on your neck, has it?"

I closed my eyes, trying to push the heat away as he gently trailed his fingers over my skin. Mother save me, those fucking fingers.

"No." I swallowed hard, my voice a bit breathier than I'd intended. "I noticed it after you bit me."

He took a generous step back, hands falling to his sides in fists. When I met his gaze, I flinched. He looked...terrified.

"I marked you."

"What..." I trailed off, trying to focus on taking deep, even breaths. "What does that mean?"

He shook his head as he backed away, running his hands through his hair in such a human way.

"Keres?" I asked, trying my best not to sound as scared as he looked.

He took a deep breath before meeting my eyes again.

"It means your portrait isn't finished."

Goosebumps prickled down my arms at the tone of his voice. It was empty, broken. He turned and fled. I couldn't let him leave without giving me a proper explanation. He'd marked me? What did that mean and why was he so concerned? I refused to be in the dark any longer, whether he could answer my questions or not.

I chased after him, but his shadows seemed to pull him down into their depths, and before I'd gone more than a few steps, I was running down an empty hall. I stood alone for several seconds staring at the wall at the far end, heart racing. I looked at one of the braziers happily flickering beside me.

"Where did he go?"

Nothing happened. I'd hoped the Gatehouse and I had built a pleasant enough rapport over the last few days that it would help me.

"Please?" I whispered. "Help me help him."

I waited, wishing something might happen. Something that would guide me in whatever direction he'd gone, but I was left in the same place with nothing but the darkness. I turned to leave, intending to go back to the library to continue reading the Black-warden book, but shadows gathered around my feet, pausing my retreat. The hall became far darker than it had been just a moment ago. I spun back as the brazier at the far end of the hall flared to life.

I should have gone back to my suite. I should have spent the evening alone, ignoring all of this, pretending nothing happened, and I wasn't going to yet another strange place the following day. Instead, I was pulled down the hall toward Keres, as the shadows closed in around me, beckoning me. My steps grew more hurried, the minutes of my freedom echoing in my soul. I hadn't had a chance to knock before Keres pulled the door open, an intensity in his expression I wasn't prepared for.

He didn't say a word. Instead, he turned away, leaving the door wide for me to follow.

I'd been in this room before, but under very different circumstances. His sitting room was larger than mine, which made it seem emptier. He had a similar area for relaxing with two chairs and a side table. On the other side was the easel I'd seen before next to a small table covered with paints and various containers. I burned with curiosity as he returned to it, taking up a paintbrush and gazing at the painting. His eyes glanced past the canvas to me, studying my face then dropping to the place on my neck where he'd bitten me.

"Is that my portrait?"

He only stared at me, and I thought perhaps I'd asked yet another question he couldn't answer, but instead he nodded for me to come closer.

As I came around the easel, I didn't know what I expected. But it hadn't been a perfect replica of my face. The brown waves of my hair cascading over exposed shoulders. It was like looking into a mirror, and I took a huge step back.

"You painted this?"

He gave me a sheepish grin but didn't answer.

I might have been more interested in the painting, but I couldn't tear my eyes from his face as he stared back at me.

"Why? Why do you paint them?"

He took a breath, shoulders tightening, before he shook his head no.

I understood. There were so many things he couldn't tell me, and now I knew it was because part of this curse was his silence. I looked back at the portrait. My green eyes held more life in them than my actual eyes usually did. He'd flawlessly captured the slight crookedness of my lips, the pink of my cheeks, the way my right eyebrow hung the tiniest fraction lower than the left.

"It's beautiful," I said.

"Only as beautiful as the subject."

His compliment caught me completely by surprise, my eyes growing wide. Why was I seeing this Keres the night before I'd leave the Gatehouse forever. It surprised me more than the way he'd kissed me. He'd been delirious then, but he was most certainly of sound mind now.

"So, all those other portraits?" I hadn't meant to frame it as a question. "You painted all of them."

He nodded once, swallowing what I hoped wasn't pain before glancing at my portrait again. I'd been right. My mind was tumbling over the reality that he'd been doing this—dragging maidens to his Hag Queen—for five hundred years. I stiffened. How old was he?

"It's not perfect. I'm missing the mark on your neck." He seemed to hesitate, looking down at the palette of paint sprawled across the small table to his right. Instead, he turned toward me so fast I leaned away from him. "The mark."

He ran his fingers over it, letting them linger on my shoulder before trailing them down my arm to my hand. He wove his fingers between mine and took a step closer, rubbing his thumb over my knuckles. I shivered at such a gentle touch from someone I hadn't been certain was capable of soft kindness. He'd done such a good job of pushing me away that in that moment, believing he didn't hate me was hard.

"I know you're well aware that Dark Fae are not like humans. Like you've said before, we're more susceptible to magic and…"

I couldn't hold his eye contact and instead let my gaze rest on the center of his chest where his pendant peeked out from beneath his shirt collar.

"I didn't intend to mark you. If the Hag Queen sees this, there will be consequences." He took a step back from me and squeezed his eyes closed. "They're my consequences, but she won't hesitate to make them yours as well."

I didn't entirely understand, so I said nothing. Instead, I stared at him, mesmerized by the spectrum of emotions moving across his face before his eyes opened again.

He looked down at our joined hands. While I'd spent an embarrassing amount of time staring at him since coming to his Gatehouse, I hadn't been quite this close for so long. There was a softness to his face, it made my fingers itch to touch him. An unnaturally beautiful quality to every line, every curve, and I wondered how much of his appearance had been shaped by magic to appear so perfect. How much of him was truly this gorgeous? When his eyes met mine, my body tightened, not expecting his crestfallen expression.

"I have to take you to the Unseelie Court tomorrow."

"I know," I said, tilting my face toward his, my eyes focusing on the shape of his lips as he spoke.

"You won't recognize me there."

I blinked hard a few times, confused. "Wait. What does that mean?"

"That's all I can…" He closed his eyes in pain, and I knew that was more than I should have been told.

I reached without thinking, cradling his cheek with the palm of my hand. "I'd hope I could recognize you no matter what you look like."

He smiled sweetly, "You're not like the others."

This drew my curiosity more than I wanted to admit.

"What?"

"Your questions, your emotions. I don't know how but..." He leaned his face into my hand, his eyes slipping closed as he seemed to savor the feel of my fingers on his skin. "I feel awake for the first time in..." He trailed a hand up my arm to my shoulder as his gaze fell on my lips. "...entirely too long."

I had craved this, his slender fingers tracing the lines of my neck to my jaw. He closed the distance between us, leaning down with slow intention until his lips gently brushed over mine. It was the softest touch before he pulled back, watching me, as if asking for permission. I gave it to him, leaning closer until our lips met. Languorous and lazy, he kissed me, running his tongue along my teeth. So achingly slow, like we had all the time in the world for this moment. He kissed over my jaw, and my eyes slipped closed as he followed my neck down to the swell of my breasts.

The memory of my dream set a fire loose in my veins. Keres in nothing but gold chains and a sultry expression. But the image melted away, replacing his black hair with midnight blue and horns. It was this Keres I desired. The one whose hands were roaming over my dress and gripping my ribs with thinly veiled restraint. A vulnerable Fae who had found a way against whatever this curse was to let me in. Dark and terrifying, yet gentle and kind—a contradiction that soaked into my need and ignited it with a thousand braziers.

I snuck my hand beneath his shirt, savoring the soft skin of his stomach. He flinched as I ran my fingers higher over his chest, and I relished the way his breath hitched at my touch.

"Your hands. I'm not used to such gentle..." His voice was so soft, his eyes, two bottomless black wells of hunger, catching and holding the breath in my lungs with their intensity.

I slipped my other hand beneath the hem, just to test if he'd push me away. Instead, he wove his fingers tightly into my hair and kissed me again. I followed the lines of his muscles to his shoulders, pulling his shirt up with my arms. He grinned against my lips as he pushed my hands away.

"Is my shirt a problem for you, Ms. Greene?"

"Among other things."

He chuckled and pulled it over his head, a flare of heat plummeting through me. Before he could stop me, my lips found his chest. He gasped, a beautiful sound I hadn't expected. There was so much honesty in the way his breath caught, the muscles in his abs flexing as he took both my wrists in a firm grip.

"Ms. Greene..."

I wanted him to chastise me, to tell me I should stop. He just stared instead, his cheeks turning a delightful pink. Was he blushing? I didn't think that would be possible. I couldn't be the first person to kiss his chest.

"Yes, Keres Blackwarden?"

He stiffened when I used his full name. A name he hadn't been able to confirm. I hadn't even been certain I was right, but based on the way he looked at me now, the muscles in his neck and shoulders tight, a fear so deep in the curve of his brows, I could only assume I was correct.

He swallowed hard as I pulled a hand free, my fingers unable to resist tracing over the curve of his neck as I leaned forward. Again, I worried he'd push me away. But he tipped his head back, inviting me in as I kissed the column of his throat, tasting his skin, the oakmoss and earthy scent of him filling my lungs.

"Seems the Gatehouse has answered some of your questions," he said with a breathy voice that settled in my core.

Mother save me, I wanted him. I knew there was a very real chance everything I saw was a glamour, made perfectly to my tastes, but I didn't care. Did it matter what he looked like? I desired so much more than his beautiful face. I desired *him*. Every question he refused to answer, every wicked smirk that tugged at his impossibly soft lips, every sharp word he spoke, every breath. I wanted Keres to destroy me entirely. I wanted him to tear my desires apart and reshape them into *his* desires. I wanted him to leave me with nothing but more wanting.

His breath hitched as I tucked my thumbs into the waist of his pants, his hands hovering at his sides as though he was too scared to touch me.

"You don't know what you ask for," he said in a tight whisper.

I leaned back and glared at him with as much conviction as I could.

"I know *exactly* what I ask for."

## CHAPTER 19

# Broken Barriers

## ROSALIN

He stared with insatiable hunger, black eyes devouring me. Every nerve in my body tingled as the muscles in his neck tightened. There was something so primal in the way his lips parted before his hands captured me. One wrapped firmly around my backside, jerking me hard against him, the other twined into my hair holding me in place as our lips crashed together.

Like our first kiss, this was forceful and greedy and all consuming. The urgency ripped my breath away and left me gasping and searing with need. Keres was of sound mind this time. There was no question he knew exactly what he was doing...and he knew exactly who he was doing it with. A moan slipped from him, burning through me and sinking between my legs. Yes, he knew exactly what he was doing. Tracing his devilish tongue along my jaw and melting me into hot wax in his arms.

My mind was numb from his touch. I could do little more than trail my fingers up his arms before sinking them into his impossibly soft hair. I followed the angle of his pointed ears to his horns, my curiosity taking over as I traced over the satin ridges, down to the tips. They were warmer than I expected, and I lost myself in the surprisingly soft texture.

His hands roamed over my shoulders before he traced the bare skin at the neckline of my bodice. With deliberate slowness, he unlaced my overdress, letting it fall to my feet. He didn't give me time to be shy before trailing his lips to my chest, pushing my chemise further down with his chin as he kissed lower.

"This is dangerous," he said against my skin, goosebumps blooming over my flesh from the heat of his breath.

I couldn't speak, couldn't think. There was only his lips, his skin against mine. Even if I was able to speak, it would only have been to beg for more.

"We shouldn't," he panted between kisses. "*I*...shouldn't," he corrected, hands roaming further up my thighs and pulling my hips against him before continuing to my ribs, his fingers like brands. He climbed higher beneath my chemise, brushing agonizingly soft over my breasts and sending a hot shiver through me. "I'm not permitted to—"

I didn't let him finish what he was going to say before I pulled my chemise the rest of the way over my head, throwing it to the side. I stood half naked in front of him, worried I'd done something very wrong when he did nothing but stare, the muscles of his jaw flexing. Maybe I'd wrongly assumed he wanted more, when he had in fact been trying to push me away. I began to step away when he yanked me back into his arms, trapping me beneath his mouth. I didn't have the ability to feel his emotions like he could mine, but if his lips were any indication, he desired this intimacy as much as I did.

"What do you want, Keres?" I asked between gasps as I struggled to restrain a moan. Words were so hard to form. I don't know what possessed me to ask, other than the memory of him asking me the very same question in my dream.

He eased back from me, eyes scouring over my bareness with a delirious thirst. His eyebrows furrowed in pain as he met my gaze with sorrow.

"Tomorrow…" He squeezed his eyes closed and hung his head, hands going limp at his sides. "I shouldn't…"

I was frozen and exposed standing in front of him, and yet, he was the one that seemed vulnerable. Completely and utterly broken by this curse that imprisoned him. I didn't know why he hesitated, but I could see what he wanted, and I needed to remove whatever barriers I could. Damn the consequences.

"Not tomorrow, Keres. Right now." I reached to unfasten his pants. "Fuck tomorrow, we'll deal with it in the morning. What do you want *right now?*"

He shook his head slowly, resting his hands over mine as I fumbled. It had been entirely too long since I'd unfastened a man's trousers. I braced myself for rejection. Whatever locked him away, whatever held him back, was too strong. I felt as if he was pulling away, pulling back from me, that this was his way of telling me he couldn't go any further. That this curse was likely keeping him from saying the words.

Self-doubt slammed into me, and I closed my eyes, waiting for the sharp sting of his refusal. Instead, he brushed my hands away, my eyes flying open as he undid his trousers himself. Then he swept me into his arms and carried me through his sitting room.

I shouldn't have been surprised, but his bedroom was…*blue.* A sumptuous dark blue, the same color as his hair. I grinned as I nuzzled against his neck, relishing the warmth of his skin against mine as I traced the line of his collarbones with my fingers.

"What are you smiling about?" he asked.

"Blue instead of black? This seems a bit more cheerful than the rest of the Gatehouse."

He set me on the edge of his bed, bracing his arms on either side of me as he smirked.

"I needed a change." He cradled my chin in his hand and tipped my lips up to his, kissing me so gently, I thought I might be dreaming again. "Do you like it?"

"It reminds me of your hair."

The smile fell from his face. "My hair?"

I laughed loudly, immediately covering my mouth in embarrassment as he stood up straight, eyes wide with shock.

"Is your hair not supposed to be blue?"

"It's...that's..." He swayed on his feet as he struggled to answer.

I reached for his hands to steady him, pulling him from whatever he'd been trying to say. His eyes raked over my nakedness instead, bringing him back into the moment before he stepped closer. He took my face in his hands again and bent down to kiss me more forcefully. He pushed me back further on the bed, tucking his thumbs into the waistband of my britches. Slowly, so slowly, he slipped them down my legs, waiting for me to stop him. As if he needed to give me one more opportunity to say no. But I would never say no, not to him.

I lay back on the bed, arms over my head, entirely at his mercy. I should have been embarrassed, but there was something about the way he gazed at me—as if I was the only person who could satisfy him. His eyes traced over every line of my body, memorizing the shape of me and taking their time wandering back to my face.

Which was fine because I couldn't rip my eyes from him. The dream hadn't been accurate enough. He was all tight toned muscles flexing beneath unblemished skin. The way his open trousers hung dangerously low, teasing me with the lines of his hips was maddening. I wanted to trace those lines with my tongue. With every breath the muscles of his abdomen flexed, drawing my gaze down the length of his body. He was a study in perfection.

How was he possible? How did he exist? And how was I going to satisfy the hunger in his eyes?

"I think you can answer me, Keres. What do you want?"

He grabbed my legs at the knees and pulled me toward the edge of the bed, one side of his lips turning up in a fiendish grin.

"What if I'm not interested in what *I* want?"

My breath hitched as he kneeled, running those delicate fingers of his along my inner thighs. He gently nudged my legs further apart as his lips traced the same route. I was unable to look away from his piercing eyes, as he kissed a path between my legs. Every inch of my body was paralyzed as his kisses turned into something deeper. Held in place by my own selfish need, I gasped when he swirled his tongue over the sensitive nerves of my entrance. My head fell back as the tension in my body pulled tighter with every stroke of his wicked tongue. He stopped long enough to ask me a single question.

"What do *you want*, my Rosalin?"

Before I could form the words, he continued his delicious assault, fingers dancing over the tender skin of my thighs. I'd been rendered speechless yet again as he coaxed two of his slender fingers deep, sending tiny explosions of pleasure through me. His fingers, as I'd suspected, felt so fucking perfect.

"You." I managed to say between gasps. "I want you." I reached for his hair, letting it tangle between my fingers before I frantically grasped one of his horns and pulled. "All of you, please!"

He didn't stop, instead he moaned, the decadent sound vibrating through my core and sending me tumbling over the edge.

"Please." I clutched the bedcovers with my free hand as I cried out. My back arched in an attempt to escape his fiendish tongue as my climax rolled through me, crashing against the shores of my existence in waves.

"Please, Keres," I panted. "I want all of you. Please. *Please.*"

Finally, with a satisfied smirk, he climbed onto the bed letting his pants slip off before fitting himself between my legs. He bent low and kissed my navel before slowly creeping upward, trailing his lips along my ribs. I was frozen in place, breaths little more than broken gasps, the heat of his body steeling my words.

"To answer your question, Rosalin," he said between kisses. "I want *this*," His lips grazed my nipple, and I shivered. The waiting grew torturous. "And *this*." His mouth moved to my other nipple with slow intention before he gazed up at me from between my breasts, his expression far more serious than he had any right to be. "I want *you*."

He hovered above me, the muscles of his shoulders flexing beneath his skin as his eyes made the arduous journey over my body to my eyes. "Just you."

"Then have me," I gasped between erratic breaths. I wrapped my legs around him, driven nearly to the brink again by the hard length of him teasing against me. "Please," I begged, fearing if he waited much longer I'd die of wanting.

Keres restrained my arms above my head, and I was lost within the dark pools of his eyes as he eased himself maddeningly slowly into me, inch by inch, stretching and leaving me with an exquisite ache that melted into absolute carnal bliss. I arched my body against him as he ran his teeth down my neck. An unrestrained moan escaped him as I rolled my hips, forcing him deeper.

I struggled to free my arms, but he held them in place.

"Patience, Ms. Greene," he whispered as he nibbled my ear, his breath on my neck agony and heat and vicious torture.

I wanted to touch him, I wanted to run my hands down his flawless body, to feel his muscles flex beneath my fingertips, but he held me firmly restrained.

"Keres..."

"Yes, Rosalin?"

I wanted to protest, but every languorous movement of his body, every kiss, trapped my words fast in my throat. He released my wrists only to drag those elegant hands of his over the curves of my body, finding every sensitive place—the hollow of my hips, my breasts, the curve of my jaw.

"Keres," I begged, losing myself in the shape of his name on my tongue, in the weight of him, the taste of his lips. His breath against my face was the only thing grounding me in reality as I traced over every inch of his back, his shoulders, down his sides to that delectable line of muscle at his waist. Fuck, he was perfect. Too perfect. Inhumanly perfect.

We found the rhythm of our bodies—even and slow—as we chased ecstasy together. A steady pace that seemed to build with every beat of my heart, every breath. He looped an arm behind one of my legs to take me deeper, his hungry eyes never leaving mine as he held himself above me.

"Fuck. Rosalin." The words slipped from him in a growl as he squeezed his eyes shut and slowed to an agonizing pace. "This is so..." he moaned—a desperate sound—as he struggled for control. "You feel so good. So fucking good," he managed between broken panting.

His voice was tight, resonating and heating my blood until it boiled over, melting into the cracks of my broken soul, forging me whole again. And still, I wanted more. More of him. More of this. I wanted to be spread out and laid bare. I wanted him to break me and remake me over and over again until I was nothing but his and only his. Made for him, forged for him, just...*his*.

"Keres," I cried out, no longer able to control my voice.

He slowed again, plunging himself even deeper, and I plummeted over the edge. I felt all of him and everything at once. Every whisper of his breath across my skin, every inch of him, every touch of his exquisite fingers. My very existence ripped apart in waves. So slow, again and again, he lengthened my pleasure until I was breathless, and every scrap of my soul had been reshaped.

His own breaths changed to the most delicious whimpers as he followed me in ecstasy, every muscle in his body growing taut as his rhythm shattered. He collapsed beside me and for several minutes we faced each other in silence, slick with sweat, the heat of our bodies wicking into the air. I couldn't look away. His cheeks flushed, his lips parted as his breathing returned to normal.

He was achingly beautiful and for this moment, he was mine.

He gathered me against him, holding so tight I almost couldn't breathe, and yet I wanted him to squeeze me tighter. I knew tomorrow I'd go to the Unseelie Court. I might never see him again, and even if I did see him, I would likely never have *this* again.

I don't know how long he held me, but I was content to stay in his arms. We might have dozed, it was hard to tell. Eventually, he rolled to his back, giving me a perfect view of his flawless body stretched out beside me. I drew the line of his navel to his throat and back, over and over again, mesmerized by the way his chest rose and fell.

How had I fallen so far from where I'd started? I'd been terrified of him, a Dark Fae with magic and shadows. I'd hated him for his secrecy. Now, I struggled to imagine myself not sitting across from him at every meal, his black eyes watching me with some strange mixture of curiosity and annoyance that I couldn't get enough of.

He was quiet for a long while, staring up at the canopy over his bed, eyes wide with thought.

"What troubles you?" I finally asked. He glanced over at me, a timid smile turning up his lips.

He didn't answer right away, and I wondered if maybe I'd managed to ask yet another question he wasn't able to answer. But then, he took a deep breath, turning to curl around me, the warmth of his skin all consuming.

"I have too many wants that I can't have." He played with a lock of my hair that had fallen over my breast, drawing circles on my skin with his index finger. "I want you to stay here with me. I want to hold you like this every night. I want to keep you, Rosalin."

I pulled myself up and took his face in my hands. "Then keep me."

A sinister smile snaked across his lips before he kissed me, then trailed his tongue across my chin, down my neck, and to my breasts, his hands following. I gasped at the touch, my nerves still stretched taut with wanting. I wondered if he could feel how desperately I longed for all of him again.

The weight, the heat of him as he moved inside me, was almost more than I could bear. I was already on the edge of ecstasy as he set a decadent pace.

"The way you squirm, Ms. Greene," he whispered, restraining my wrists beneath his hands.

My only response was with ragged breaths, as I gave a half-hearted attempt to wriggle free.

## CHAPTER 20

# Waking from a Dream

## KERES

The sun rose too early. In my delirium the night before, I hadn't bothered to pull my canopy curtains and light flooded across the bed, turning the midnight blue of the covers a strange shade of green. Rosalin's hair tickled my arm. She'd stayed in my bed the entire night. I turned my head to see her better, a smile creeping onto my lips. This was true bliss. My fingers itched to trace her bare shoulder, but instead I cherished the way it rose and fell with each of her precious breaths.

My smile faded with the moment of happiness. I'd be forced to take her through the portal today. We had no more time. I'd wasted too much of it pushing her away when I should have been trying to figure out how to let her in. I'd been cursed for so long, unable to find the will to try and break it, but now that's all I wished I'd done. She was the hundredth maiden I'd take to Bevgyah, Hag Queen of the Unseelie Court, and what the Hag didn't know was I'd found a loophole in my original punishment.

After five hundred years, I could choose to have my punishment changed. I'd been given a choice when I was sentenced for treason: death or to be stripped of all my freedom and submit as

Bevgyah's consort. Now, after serving five hundred years I could make a different choice. I could choose to be put to death rather than endure another five hundred years chained to her. I swallowed my sorrow. How ironic that I'd found the will to try and break the curse after I'd finally managed to find a way to end it all.

The memory of Rosalin's face in the throes of pleasure flooded through me, settling low in my stomach. Her voice as she whimpered my name in ecstasy would echo through my soul until I ceased breathing and perhaps after. She wasn't the type of woman I was once attracted to. I'd wanted perfection and power and cared little of how it was obtained.

*Fake...*I'd been charmed by fake. I'd been attracted to lies and simple lust. But Rosalin? She was genuine and real. I couldn't look away from her. The moment I saw her standing at the doors of my Gatehouse, I was shocked that such a creature existed. I'd found all the tiny things that made her imperfectly perfect, and I cherished them. Her curiosity and confidence were something I hadn't realized I craved so desperately until she was right in front of me.

With a sudden rush of dread, I realized I hadn't imbued her portrait. I hadn't finished it at all. I swept her hair away from her neck to see the mark I'd left when I bit her. How many times had I been a complete idiot since she'd come to my Gatehouse? Opening my heart when I knew I wasn't allowed. I knew better than to leave a mark on her—something Bevgyah would notice immediately. I had hoped it would fade, but it was just as dark as it had been the day before. It wasn't a bruise or a bite which was even more concerning, reminding me of ancient stories of magical markings. It had taken on a dark purple color, like a tattoo, and if I wasn't mistaken, it looked like a serpent curled in on itself.

She looked up at me with a sheepish grin before nuzzling against me. The feel of her skin pressed to mine sent a shiver of longing down my spine. How could I satisfy this when I'd be forced to see her day in and day out in the Hag's palace without being able to so much as talk with her in private?

If Bevgyah knew what we'd done...

She'd torture and destroy Rosalin and force me to witness the consequences of my infidelity.

I took a sharp breath as her hand slowly smoothed down my chest to my navel, then lower. Fuck, her hands were so soft—such a careful caress. There was so much tenderness in her touch that I wasn't used to. I was used to forceful hands, cruelty. Pain. This was gentle curiosity and it drew a desperate moan from deep within me. She pulled herself over my stomach, the blankets falling away from her naked body as she straddled me.

There was a question in her eyes, a familiar yearning I'd felt in her emotions the night before. She was as starved for this as I was. I leaned up and kissed her, pulling her down against me, the heat of her almost more than I could take. I must have answered her question because she gently rocked her hips until she'd eased me inside of her. I couldn't stifle the whimper that escaped as my head fell back. She felt so fucking good. The whisper of her hair across my skin, her fingers on my neck, my chest, over my shoulders. I hadn't made love like this in five centuries—slow and intentional. I'd been fucked, abused, and made to perform acts I was too ashamed to admit. My body had been used in ways I wished I could forget.

But this?

This was pure, ravenous pleasure, so soft and sensual. Maybe it was because I hadn't felt this connected to another living creature in so long, but I couldn't get enough of her, of this, of the breathy noises she made. The way she watched my face, watched me, *saw all of me*. I wanted to devour every second I had with her until she was ripped from me forever.

It took all my strength to hold out as her rhythm increased. She was a hunter, and I was her very willing prey. She took me without restraint. We came together—fast and perfect, then lay on the top of the blankets for several minutes in silence as our thundering hearts slowed.

The quiet consumed any words I might have said and for a long while we were content to be swallowed up in the silence. I couldn't pry my eyes from her, mesmerized by the way her face glistened, her hair damp against her forehead. She smiled sweetly as her eyes fell closed.

"I'm not your first," I said. She was far too good at understanding her own pleasure, and mine, for that matter.

Her cheeks turned a brilliant shade of pink. Humans held such strange principles when it came to sex, and I worried I'd insulted her.

"I was married."

There was something about the words that didn't register at first, and I was about to ask more.

"He died a year ago. Killed by a Dark Fae who came to my village to meet with the Magistrate. I'm told there were words said the Fae didn't like, and he put a dagger in my husband's ribs." She turned toward me, and we lay there in silence, facing one another.

So much more of her fear and anger with me, a Dark Fae, made sense. I understood this pain. I was forced to fuck the monster who had tortured and killed my beloved in front of me, and I knew how much I despised Bevgyah for it. I took a deep soothing breath, letting my hatred for the Hag wash away. This was my time, and I'd enjoy every second I had left with Rosalin.

If I hadn't just been thinking of the queen, I might have said something more conventional, but instead, I blurted out the name of the man her emotions had been tangled around so tightly. "Bastion."

She closed her eyes for a moment then met my gaze again. "Yes."

An ache bloomed in my chest. "I'm sorry I showed you his face."

"Are you?" She smirked, but there was an edge to her voice. Her humor was a shield.

"Truly. I hadn't known." I'd dropped my voice to a whisper. "I'd only wanted to make you more comfortable in this strange place by showing you something familiar."

She narrowed her eyes as her smirk faded. "If you could change your appearance, why would you choose horns and blue hair? Why not something more human?"

I took a sharp breath across my teeth, wondering if the curse would let me answer, if I was even going to attempt.

"I don't know why, but my glamour doesn't seem to entirely work on you." I reached and tucked a piece of her hair behind her ear, trailing my finger along her jaw. "I should have black hair, round ears, no horns."

Her eyes traveled over me with confusion.

"What do you see when you look at me?"

"Fae," she said so fast I assumed she'd had the answer ready. She ran her fingers over one of my horns. "Black eyes and horns, blue hair, pointed ears and incisors."

"Even my teeth?"

"Even your teeth," she said with a soft grin, trailing that same finger over my cheek to my lips.

"And the color of my skin?"

She looked confused for a moment looking down at my bare chest then back to my face. "You're pale. Almost too pale."

So, some of the glamour worked, but not all of it. I assumed if she could see my wings she would have mentioned them, but it still made me feel so incredibly vulnerable not knowing.

"You're beautiful, you know," she whispered as she nuzzled against my neck.

I closed my eyes, adoring her skin against mine. "This face has gotten me into more trouble than I care to admit."

She giggled. "Is that so?"

I was smiling along with her, thinking I might pull her beneath me one more time before we needed to climb from this bed. I had to decide if I thought I could imbue her portrait before I took her through the portal. I worried I'd be too exhausted afterwards. If we were late Bevgyah would know why. But being exhausted was nothing compared to the pain she'd endure if I couldn't protect her. I was already trying to think of ways I could spare her from Bevgyah's harem, or how I could get her out of the Unseelie Court all together. The curse kept me from doing so many things. I would have to hope I could figure something out once we were there.

She ran her fingers over my arm to my chest, following the lines of my muscles, a look of sorrow melting onto her face.

"What do you want, Rosalin? If you could have anything." I ran my fingers through her hair. "What would chase away your frown?"

She gazed at me for a long time, her eyes wandering over my face.

"As crazy as this sounds, to never leave this place."

I pulled her tight against me. "I wish I could keep you here," I said. I wished for it more than she knew—more than I should ever wish for something I couldn't have.

"I wish you could too."

## CHAPTER 21

# Different Skin

## ROSALIN

I couldn't stop staring at Keres' tattoos as he sat on the side of the bed to pull on a pair of pants. Without sheer fabric covering his back, I was able to see every delicate detail of the serpents as they danced around his shoulder blades and twisted down his spine. They weren't quite dragons as I originally thought, they were something else entirely, long and lean, like him. The ink almost shimmered in the low light, as if made of scales, the wings spreading out to his shoulders. My curiosity got the better of me, and I reached for him.

He flinched at my touch, lifting his head for a split second before he relaxed. I traced my fingers over the soft skin of his back. So elegant. That's what they were. Like much of the Gatehouse, they were ornate without being gaudy. And while the tattoos covered his entire back, they fit perfectly. Another facet to him that I'd found behind the door he'd kept locked tight.

I knew I shouldn't ask more questions, and yet I couldn't stop myself. "What are they?"

"Ancient Blackwardens from a time before the Earth Mother created the High Fae."

A shiver ran through me at his words. So much time, a concept that was hard for me to grasp. He was speaking of thousands of years—to when the world was new. It left me with even more questions.

"Are you High Fae?"

"Yes, in a way? And no." He glanced over his shoulder at me. "Dark Fae are...complicated. There's more than High Fae in my blood."

"Are you...a serpent?"

A bright laugh escaped him as he turned toward me.

"No, but it's rumored the first of my family was created with serpent's blood and the soul of a demon."

I let his words sink in, more questions blooming in their wake.

"How old are you?"

He chuckled as he lay back on the bed beside me and pulled me tight against him, the heat of his skin against mine curling my toes. I melted into his arms, wishing I could stay there forever.

"So many questions, Ms. Greene." I blushed as he kissed my neck, gliding a hand down the length of my naked body. He hadn't made it very far in his attempt to finally get out of bed. "Old enough that I don't remember exactly how old I am," he said against my skin, before he kissed down to the hollow of my throat.

"That doesn't seem possible," I said, my voice far breathier than I'd intended, but his lips were so...

Another chuckle resonated through him and into me, heating my blood. I'd never get enough of this warm Keres—the one that smiled and laughed with ease. He'd banished the cold Keres who'd kept me at arm's length, and I hoped that one never returned.

"Does it matter how old I am?" he asked, pulling back, dark eyes wandering over my face as if he'd never seen me before.

"Not really," I managed, trying to ignore how his fingers traced over the sensitive skin at my hips then traced a line up to my breast.

"I've seen human empires rise and fall, entire kingdoms shattered into countless pieces. I've watched the human world be divided up between magistrates. I saw the Hag Queen take her frozen throne." His fingers danced over my ribs, drawing a pattern down to my hip. "I was there when the Fae Wars ignited and when the final treaty was signed in blood." He swallowed, a strange sorrow staining his words. "I don't remember my mother's voice anymore and I have long since forgotten the shape of my father's horns."

He was quiet for a long time, his eyes following his hand as it trailed over the curve of my shoulder and down my arm.

"Age is just a number, one that loses its meaning the longer it stretches." He kissed me. Softly, slowly, his tongue gliding over my lips.

I was truly undone. My mind emptied of any other questions I may have had. For a moment I forgot where I was and why I was there. It was only me, and Keres, and his delicious hands. He pulled me up with him before he slid us both to the edge of the bed, my legs wrapped around him, all without his lips leaving mine. When he did finally pull away there was a wistful look in his eyes. One I'd never seen before. It made my throat tighten.

"We need to go to breakfast before the Gatehouse gets impatient," he whispered, almost as if he didn't want the Gatehouse to hear.

"Won't it wait for you?"

He grinned before planting a sweet kiss on the tip of my nose. "Definitely not for me, but maybe for you."

I felt empty when I finally left Keres' side. Reluctant to be alone, I slowly wandered back to my suite in nothing but my chemise and the memory of his hands on my skin. It was hard to focus on anything else as I bathed and rummaged through my wardrobe for something to wear. Today, it contained midnight blue gowns for me to choose from, and it only made my growing sorrow worse.

By this evening, I would be gone. Keres would take me to the Unseelie Court and hand me over to the Hag Queen. I could see in his eyes that he didn't want to, but I also saw there was nothing he could do not to. I tried to be strong, but I knew he could feel it like all my other emotions. It didn't matter how many times I wished, or begged, or asked the Gatehouse to stop him from taking me. This was why I was here—to be taken to the Dark Fae as a sacrifice. He still couldn't tell me what that entailed, only that he would do everything in his power to make it easier for me.

But what would he make easier? That I'd be ripped from his arms? This would be agony enough, but I feared there was so much worse in store for me.

After breakfast he told me he needed to try and imbue my portrait, that I shouldn't worry about him if he didn't come to lunch. I wasn't sure what that meant, and he couldn't seem to tell me. I grew worried by late afternoon when I still hadn't seen him. I could no longer sit still. I'd read through all the books he'd left for me, practiced all the etiquette, and when I had nothing left to do, I started wandering the halls. I ran my fingers over the woodwork and admired the craftsmanship of every detail. The Gatehouse was truly beautiful in a sleek, dark way. Like Keres, shadows seemed to cling to the walls and obscure just enough to make me dreadfully curious what was beneath.

I stopped short in front of the mural, my heart rate spiking. It had changed, *again*.

The dark monster that had been chasing me now wrapped his arms around me from behind, wings curving in protectively. My face was peaceful and turned toward him, our noses touching. The contrast between his pitch-black and my pale flesh was jarring. The creature and I appeared to be opposites woven together in a lovers' embrace.

Had Keres painted this? Was the black fleshed monster supposed to be him?

The way he'd questioned me about the color of his skin came flooding back as I realized he might not be as pale as he appeared. He might look exactly like the dark creature in the mural, glamoured to look like a beautiful human man. I sucked in a sharp breath.

Did it matter what he looked like? I'd be lying if I said I wasn't wildly attracted to him, but if he'd just been an average looking man, would it change how I felt? If he looked like the monster holding me in the mural, would I care for him any differently? Would I have opened my heart if he'd looked like the creatures from my storybook?

My chest tightened. Was I so shallow to base my attractions solely on appearances? I pressed a hand to my sternum, the air around me suddenly very thick. I was *exactly* as Keres said humans were. I squeezed my eyes closed as I realized I'd assumed the creatures in the mural were monsters. The truth was, I didn't know what or *who* they were. I had no idea, and I'd judged all Dark Fae against one's actions.

But Keres had already broken the mold of my preconceptions. Why was it so hard to see that perhaps the label thrust upon him might not carry the meaning I'd given it? All my life I'd been taught that Dark Fae were monsters. Just because I'd been taught something didn't mean it was true. Yet, in my heart, monsters were ugly inside and out.

I pressed my fingers to the image of myself and the dark fleshed Fae, every muscle in my being tight. Perhaps the real monsters weren't the creatures in the mural at all. My body seemed to vibrate with terrible guilt. Perhaps I was just as much a monster as Keres, because I hadn't given a single thought to what *he* was giving, to how *he* felt. To *who* he truly was.

The atmosphere in the hall shifted. Shadows gathered along the wall, but I was still trapped staring at the mural, my breaths fast and shallow. I finally pried my eyes away and turned in time to see Keres step from his shadows, his presence instantly calming. I hadn't expected the exhaustion that clung to his frame, weighing his usually confident shoulders down.

"Are you okay?" I asked, cupping the curve of his jaw in hand.

He closed his eyes as he smiled sweetly, leaning into my palm. "I'll be fine." The momentary happiness slipped from his lips, and he stepped closer, taking my hands in his and pressing his forehead to mine. "I couldn't imbue your portrait."

"What does that mean?"

He didn't say anything, and I couldn't torture him with more questions he couldn't answer.

"It's time for dinner," he said.

I pulled away, eyes welling with tears as I glared up at him, frustrated that his voice was so calm when my heart was breaking into a million pieces. I wondered if my sorrow tasted as bitter to him as it did to me.

"Your last dinner with me." He smiled weakly.

It never touched his eyes.


I had rabbit one more time and I was certain the Gatehouse had outdone itself. I closed my eyes to savor every bite, chewing slowly, allowing the flavors of harvest to melt on my tongue. It tasted richer, more seasoned. The vegetables had been cut into little flowers and forest animals. The wine tasted brighter and more delicious than it ever had.

Keres sat across from me, hardly touching his usual meat and potatoes. There was a deep sadness that clung to his expression, making it hard for me to look at him without fear creeping in and clutching my throat.

"All of the others have been grateful to finally be leaving this place," Keres finally said, a woeful glint in his eye. "Your emotions are making this difficult."

A chill slipped down my spine, my eyes welling with tears. Words failed me. Did I need to speak? He knew how I felt. He could feel every scrap of my misery, or glee, or yearning as well as I could.

"It's time." He stood and reached a hand out to me. "Come, Ms. Greene."

I glared at his hand. The thoughts I'd originally had when I came to this place flooded back through me. What if I ran? Would the Gatehouse let me leave? Could I get out of this place and run through the forest and get away? Did I even want to get away? At least if I went to the Unseelie Court there was a chance I'd see Keres again.

His typical stoic mask covered the sorrow I knew we both felt, and I marveled at how well he could lie with his expression when his words were always true. I stood, trembling. He held my hand as he led me through the Gatehouse. It was like when he'd led me to the dining room on the day I arrived. However, his silence was so foreboding this time.

He took me to a room I'd never entered before. When his hand touched the handle, I heard a lock click open. It was pitch-black inside; no braziers came to life when we entered. The only light came from the hall, oozing over the floor and reflecting off what looked like a massive mirror.

I stopped short after entering the room, watching him walk closer to the strange mirror with confidence in every step. He'd done this before—countless times. When he glanced back at me, I was too scared to move or take a single step closer. Instead, I backed up, missing the doorway and bumping into the wall behind me.

I'd seen him move from one place to another using shadows, but it was still startling when he did it now. He stepped into my personal space, and I had to tip my face up to see him as threads of smoke dissipated into the air around us.

"I have to take you, Rosalin."

I squeezed my eyes shut, shaking my head and hoping by the grace of the Earth Mother he would spare me, and I could stay.

"Please, Keres." I didn't want to beg, but the words poured out of me, every one of them stained with the last year of loneliness and longing I'd endured without Bastion. "Let me stay with you. I promise I'll figure out how to break this curse." He shook his head, his eyes downcast. "I won't ask you any more questions until I do. I won't bother you if that's your wish. Just please let me—"

"I can't." His voice was sharp, and I flinched back, pressing flat against the wall.

The muscles in his jaw tightened as he glared with anguish in his eyes.

"Please trust me when I say, I wish I could." He leaned, bracing himself with one hand on the wall, his other cradling my cheek before slipping around my throat.

Leaning down, he pulled me forward by my neck until our lips met. There was anguish in that kiss, a tenderness in the way his fingers wove through my hair. A stolen moment when I knew we were already running late. I was lost in the scent of him, the heat of his body pressed against mine.

When he finally broke away, I was breathless. Some piece of my heart knew this was the last time I'd kiss him. He hadn't said it, but he'd implied things would be very different on the other side of the portal.

"Please, Keres."

"Rosalin..." He stepped back, a strength of will I never would have had. "I can't."

A sob escaped me as the first of my tears streamed over my cheeks. He was there again, wrapping his arms around me and pulling me away from the wall and into his warm arms. Why? Why couldn't he break these rules just this once? For me? *For himself?*

"We need to go."

I was too lost in my grief to realize he had led me over to the mirror, facing me with his usual confident posture. I swallowed past the lump that was lodged in my throat, past the fear that weighed like a block of ice in my stomach.

"This won't hurt you..." he hesitated, taking both my hands in his. "And you won't remember anything on the other side."

"Wait, what?" I said too loudly, a flash of panic spiking my heart rate. "What do you mean, I won't remember anything?"

"It's for your own good, Rosalin," he said sternly. "If you can't remember what you had, you can't miss it."

I pushed away from him, glaring with as much fire as I could muster as I balled my hands into fists. "I don't want to forget. I'll forget you, won't I?"

He looked down at his feet. This wasn't a question he *couldn't* answer. This was one he didn't *want* to answer.

"Keres. I don't want to forget you," I said, refusing to back down. "Please, don't do this."

"This isn't what I'll look like, Rosalin. I'm Dark Fae, in every sense of the term. I am made of shadows and darkness, I'm terrifying."

"Keres, I'm begging. Please."

"I'm the monster in the mural. Everything you know of evil."

"I don't care. I don't want to forget you."

He shook his head. "I *need* you to forget me."

I shook my head as I glared at him, tears making it hard to see his face clearly. Why? Why would he want me to forget? Had I done something wrong? All manner of memories flooded my mind. My sister's name. Bastion's face. The book of fairy tales. My parents. Sharing apples from my neighbor's tree. The night I'd shared with him. *Him*. Everything. It would all be gone.

Would I even know who I was?

"Please, Rosalin." A tear slipped down his cheek. "I wouldn't do this if I didn't have to." His voice cracked; anguish carved into his expression.

My heart sheared in half. *If he didn't have to*? Dragging me to the Unseelie Court where I wouldn't remember who he was or what he'd been to me? What *I* meant to *him*. He had no choice but to take me and here I was making things harder by begging for what I couldn't have.

I couldn't stop a sob from breaking free, and I buried my face in my hands. Would I remember how my heart broke before I stepped through the portal? How I'd regretted pushing him away?

How I'd spent so much time confirming there was a curse when I should have spent more time figuring out how to break it?

How could I forget?

Shadows built around us, filling the room with wispy black smoke. The mirror, which had been dark a few moments ago, glowed a faint blue as the shadows continued to swirl around our legs.

"It's time, Rosalin," Keres said, his voice shaking with emotion as he reached his hand out to me one last time. "Come."

I wiped the tears from my cheeks before glaring at his hand. It was the first time I didn't want to take it. When I glanced up at him, my heart broke all over again as his throat bobbed.

This is what I had volunteered to do. I'd volunteered to be the sacrifice to the Dark Fae in Renee's place. To be taken to the Unseelie Court. I reached for his hand. I cherished the warmth of his skin against my own. I tried to be brave. I took a deep breath and squeezed my eyes shut, waiting for whatever would happen next. He tucked my hand under his arm, tight against his side as he led me to the edge of the mirror.

When I opened my eyes, we stood before a shimmering pool of liquid silver that pulsed and rippled out from the frame's edges. Unlike other mirrors there was no reflection, just undulating colors as Keres' shadows seeped through the surface. A sudden spark of fear lanced through me as he tugged us closer.

"Keres, I..." I whispered and he pulled me through.

## CHAPTER 22

# Bevgyah's Blackwarden

## KERES

I collapsed at the guard's feet after pulling Rosalin and myself through the portal. I didn't have the energy to hold myself up any longer. A second guard collected her limp form into his arms and carried her away. I hoped he couldn't hear how my breath hitched with fear. I wouldn't have been able to stop him if I tried. I knew where he was taking her. The same place all the other maidens had been taken, and I wasn't supposed to care.

"Her majesty has been waiting, Blackwarden."

The guard slung my arm over his shoulder as he helped me up from the ground. It wasn't a gesture of kindness, so much as one of necessity. These guards despised me, but they despised a testy queen more. She tended to get rid of those who no longer served her needs.

He threw me into my suite and slammed the door. I heard the heavy lock click over as I collapsed onto the cold stone floor. If Bevgyah had requested I be locked in my quarters, I was significantly tardy. I knew I'd be punished for making her wait. I'd accepted it when I'd been desperate to imbue Rosalin's portrait and used too much of my magic, making it take longer for me to recover enough to bring her through before dinner. I lay on the cold floor, head pounding, body still vibrating from using so much of my shadows. Every breath was painful, but I needed to collect myself, change into some proper clothes, and present myself to Bevgyah before she became impatient enough to come searching for me.

Rolling to my back, I stared up at the ceiling. So much of this place felt wrong, the frigid magic rough against my own. Bevgyah's palace was nothing like my Gatehouse—a calm warm presence, always lingering at the back of my thoughts. It wasn't just being in this place again, it was that I knew somewhere Rosalin was being prepared to be introduced to the Hag Queen, and there was nothing I could do to save her.

A tear burned a path over my temple as I swallowed my guilt. I'd failed to imbue her portrait. I'd failed to figure out how to break the curse. I'd failed her entirely. My Rosalin would feel every last fragment of confusion and terror, the pain of her youth being siphoned and what she was expected to do as a maiden in Bevgyah's harem.

I tried to drag myself from the floor, needing to grasp the post of my bed to support my weight. When I stood, I had a perfect view of myself in the vanity mirror. As always, when I passed through the portal, the glamour washed away. I was the purest definition of Dark Fae. My black flesh hid the weariness that clung to my bones, but it couldn't hide the disappointment etched on my face. Entirely black eyes with silver irises stared back at me. I hadn't missed my wings. They drew more attention than I liked, and while flying was incredible, I rarely had the chance as Bevgyah's consort. My horns on the other hand, I'd missed. I'd always loved the caution they'd instilled in others. I wasn't a demon, but I definitely looked like one. It was my magic that distinguished me as a descendant of the High Fae. Shadows and ice, as cold as the world outside Bevgyah's palace. As cold as the Unseelie Court.

A sharp knock interrupted my self-assessment. I straightened as the lock clicked open and Bevgyah slipped in, her lithe form slinking through my room until she stood at my side. She gazed into the mirror with me, her hungry eyes slipping over my reflection.

Hag wasn't the best description of Bevgyah. She was a Hag in the essence of her magic—able to shapeshift and especially adept at curses. However, she was by no means haggard, as one might expect. Her pale lavender skin was flawless. She wore her teal hair to her knees in thin braids with imbued charms threaded through them to ward off all manner of Fae magic. Her perfect face was fake. I knew the truth. For centuries she'd been siphoning youthful life energy from human girls in order to maintain her beauty. The real Bevgyah was likely a withered husk of a creature.

It wasn't her true appearance that made her ugly, it was her heart. I knew this better than most. After all, I'd been enslaved as her consort for centuries and had been her lover by choice before the Fae Wars. I'd been a very different male then. Selfish, arrogant, power hungry. Willing to manipulate for what I wanted. I didn't want her crown, but I wanted the power that came with it, and I was willing to do filthy things to obtain it. I'd met my match in Bevgyah. We were two beautiful Fae locked in a game that she was far better at playing.

"My delicious Blackwarden." Her voice scraped over my skin like shards of glass. "I do hope you've brought me an interesting pet."

I tried to stand up straight but decided struggling in front of her was probably not the best idea, Instead I shifted my weight to look less like the post was holding me up.

"I haven't made myself presentable for you, my queen."

She didn't seem to care. She turned toward me, eyes wandering over my shoulders. Her cold fingers slipping beneath the collar of my shirt and trailed down my chest, her other hand snaking through my hair. My skin crawled from her touch, the muscles in my neck tightening as I tried not to flinch away. I'd endured her hands for centuries, but it never got any easier. And I knew, if I showed distaste, she would only make things far more painful.

"I want you helpless."

Fuck. She'd planned this. The guard that had helped me back to my room had likely informed her I wasn't able to walk on my own. She hauled me toward the bed by the front of my shirt, and I could do nothing but go with her. I didn't have the strength to pull away.

"You know I hate it when you've been away from me for so long," she cooed with forced pouty lips.

She'd unclasped my pants before I could push her hands away. I tried to grasp at her wrists and failed as she ripped my shirt over my head.

"On the bed, Gatekeeper."

"I'm exhausted."

"Lucky for you, I don't care."

She would have what she wanted.

She slid a hand down my pants, nails raking across my sensitive skin. I jerked away instinctively; muscles tense as I tried to slide onto the bed and further from her. The weight of exhaustion made me slow. Too slow. She caught the waistband of my pants and yanked them down my legs in one brutal motion.

I wasn't given a choice.

I was *never* given a choice.

She slammed me onto my back, my head swimming. As much as I hated her, as much as I wished I could die right then and there so I wouldn't have to endure another moment of her, my body didn't respond the same way my mind did. She expected as much. She knew how to touch me, where to kiss me, how to coax me. My only escape would be to imagine someone else's hands as hers roamed over my body. Soft, wavy brown hair brushing across my skin. Alabaster fingers following the lines of my muscles.

"You're perfection, but you know that already," she crooned.

Her hungry fingers scraped across my skin as she straddled me. I sucked in a breath, my body pulled taut with dread, but it betrayed me the moment she sank down, taking me deep. An involuntary moan ripped from my throat, raw and bitter.

I hated her. Mother save me, I hated her. But even worse, I hated myself for how powerless I'd become. How powerless she'd made me. My hands curled into fists at my sides, every muscle rigid beneath her as she moved with relentless greed.

I squeezed my eyes shut, trying to block out the sight of her head thrown back; mouth open as she grunted with each rock of her hips. I needed to disappear. I tried to retreat into the quiet of my own mind, but her voice dragged me back every time she gasped my name.

She fucked me until she was satisfied and all I could do was lie there, used up and hollowed out.

"I've missed you, Keres," she whispered in my ear, her hot breath on my neck sending goosebumps down my arms.

She didn't dare use my name around anyone else. To them, I'd be her Gatekeeper, her Blackwarden. My given name held too much power here.

She left me naked, half hard, and too exhausted to move.

"You'll be expected to escort me to the revel later. Dress appropriately," she said as her hungry eyes raked over my bare flesh. She slipped back into her gown and straightened her hair. "You'll spend the evening at my side and maybe, if you're a good little Gatekeeper, you can choose a maiden for us to enjoy together."

It was always the same. Sex, beauty, and power. I knew what I looked like. It hadn't been my choice to wear this face. Nor had it been my choice to be born into the Blackwarden family, whose shadow magic was powerful enough to activate the portals. To have a Blackwarden at your side had once been prestigious, but now there weren't any others left. I'd been the only one too weak to choose death for my family's treasonous involvement in the Fae Wars.

But I'd been mistaken.

I should have chosen death, and I'd wished I had every day since. Eternity being fucked by a monster with a beautiful face and an evil heart was truly worse than the void of the beyond.

I usually felt empty after bringing a girl through the portal for Bevgyah to siphon. But this time? I felt truly destroyed. I wanted to die. It would be better than imagining Rosalin being sucked of her life before she was sent to the bed of some Dark Fae willing to pay Bevgyah's exorbitant rates for the enjoyment of her harem.

I closed my eyes, another tear carving a path over my temple as I lay listless and broken. This was my fault. This was my punishment, and I hated that I had to share it with Rosalin. She'd done nothing but endure the hardships of a human life, to try and give her sister the life she had lost. She didn't deserve this, and I didn't deserve her. Not after failing to imbue her portrait or to figure out how to break the curse.

No, I was truly worthless.

I lost myself to sorrowful darkness.

## CHAPTER 23

# Revel

## ROSALIN

No matter how hard I tried, I couldn't remember how I'd gotten here, or where I'd come from. I couldn't remember anything, to be honest. The first thing I *could* remember was being carried from a room full of swirling shadows that seemed to weave around me and cling to my soul. There had been something so secure about them. Like they numbed the panic that started to creep into my throat. I hadn't wanted to leave. They slowly disintegrated, oozing into the floor, leaving me cold and lonely.

Someone helped a man to his feet. At least I thought he was a man, but when he stood, I could see his massive bat wings tucked against his back and two obsidian horns that swept away from his face. A face I didn't get a chance to see before I was picked up from the floor and taken to a small dark room, my head swimming with nausea.

I was laid out on a low mattress, desperately trying to focus on the face of whoever it was that had brought me there. But his face was obscured by an armored mask, and I looked away quickly, my heart racing. Thick exhaustion dragged me down until I was on the edge of consciousness. A strange girl who was half my height and the color of new fallen snow came and woke me with a gentle shake.

"Her majesty is impatient to meet you," she said.

Not a girl, a full-grown female if I were to judge her by the maturity of her voice. She led me to another room, one that was brightly lit and cheerful compared to the halls we'd just wandered through. I was pulled toward a steaming bath, nervousness prickling the hairs on the back of my neck.

"Into the tub, sweet one," she said as she pulled on the skirt of my dress. "Quickly now, we must have you ready for her majesty."

She started unlacing my overdress before I could stop her, my cheeks growing hot as she had me step out. Before I could stop her, she lifted my chemise over my head. I wrapped my arms around my nakedness, unsure why I felt so much shame. Everything was so confusing. Why was I here? I didn't think I was supposed to be, but I couldn't remember where else I was meant to be.

The tiny Fae led me to a steaming tub and after a moment of coaxing, I stepped into the bath. I was immediately rewarded with the most delicious hot water. The smell of lavender and honey permeated everything. I sank into the warmth, completely submerged with nothing but my face above the surface. The heat of the water soaked into my bones, and I was left to float for a few blissful moments, confusion swirling in my cloudy mind. I couldn't isolate any single thought, so instead, I pushed them all away and tried to focus on the heat of the water that hugged me.

"Up with you." The tiny female wasn't rude, just firm, and I was compelled to do as she said.

She scrubbed my back before using her lanky fingers to wash and comb through my hair, all while humming a strange otherworldly tune. When she was finished, she helped me step from the tub, then dried me off and dressed me in a silk slip. I didn't feel like it covered enough. The slinky fabric on my skin was buttery and distracting. Looking down my front I could see the rise of my breasts from the low neckline too well for my taste. I folded my arms over my chest, wishing I could make myself smaller.

"What's this? Are you Fate Marked?" The Fae pointed to a dark mark where my neck met my shoulder.

I leaned forward to get a better look in the mirror. Sure enough, I had what looked like a tiny serpent tattoo, spun into a twisted knot. I brushed my fingers over it, but it didn't change. A shiver writhed up my spine, blooming goosebumps over my arms.

"I don't know. I don't...remember."

She shook her head looking at the mark with concern before she turned to a shelf with various vials and jars. What was a Fate Mark and why was it a problem? I was too scared to ask, and before I could, she returned with a small bottle full of some kind of viscous gold substance. With gentle fingers she dabbed a small amount of the cream to the area and rubbed it over the mark until it vanished from sight.

"This should hide it for a few days," she said, nodding her approval before she scurried toward the door. "This way."

She pulled me down another hall, this one had a much lower ceiling giving it an intimate feel. There were several doors lining each side but we didn't seem to be going to any of these. My mouth grew dryer the further we went from the room with the comforting shadows. At the end of the hall, we ducked through a curtain of silk and twinkling gems into a massive space which was not as brightly lit. This room was draped with elegant fabrics and strands of beads in gold and silver. The braziers along the walls were decorated with crystals, which cast rainbows across the soft fabrics and smooth stone surfaces.

Low futons were scattered across the room, where several other girls lounged in outfits similar to mine—simple silk frocks, some with plunging necklines, others slit high enough to bare their thighs. The women varied in skin tone and ranged in age from around mine to much older.

"Your newest sister," the minuscule female said, leading me to the middle of the room, where she left me to stand in front of several pairs of critical eyes.

For the first time since waking on the floor, I was terrified. Why was I here? I couldn't remember anything, but I knew in my heart this wasn't where I was supposed to be. The way some of these women were looking at me didn't help.

"A bit thin, this one," a rather busty maiden commented. Her auburn hair hung in gorgeous curls around her creamy shoulders; she had deep brown eyes that pierced through any bravery I may have had left.

"She's perfect," another said as she stepped forward and took my hands. She had a friendly smile and piercing blue eyes beset with adorable freckles. Her hair was like spun gold, and I had the vague sense she was familiar. "I'm Nessa. Welcome to Queen Bevgyah's harem."

Before anyone else could say a word, a door on the other side of the room was thrown wide as a beautiful Fae female with shimmering pale lavender skin stepped through, two guards followed close behind. She was dressed in an elaborate gown, dripping with gems and pearls that jingled as she walked. A crown made of crystals that looked like shards of ice was cradled by braided teal hair, adorned with more gems and charms.

Every maiden curtsied low and held in perfect coordination. I was slow to do the same, my cheeks heating as I realized I'd missed what was likely an important cue.

"My precious Maidens." We were released from our groveling, her singsong voice gripping my insides in a way that made me want to run the other direction as fast as I could. "We shall have a revel tonight to celebrate the return of my beloved Blackwarden and your newest sister, Tesanna. Make her feel welcome and help her select something appropriate to wear. Our guests expect a luxurious display, as always."

I could only assume she was the queen. She smiled brightly at us, her gaze falling and holding onto me for longer than I liked. Then she turned and swept from the room, taking her finery with her and leaving the maidens in a buzz of low murmurs.

I let the name the queen used to introduce me roll around in my head. It didn't feel right—but then, I had no idea what my name was supposed to be. I just knew that one wasn't it.

I couldn't afford to dwell on it.

Suddenly, every eye in the harem was on me. Some women looked at me with hunger, others barely masked their judgment. It took every shred of courage I had not to bolt under the weight of their scrutiny.

"Tesanna is such a beautiful name," Nessa said with a brilliant smile. "Come, let's choose our dresses together." She ran her fingers through my damp hair without asking.

Again, I got the feeling I should feel shame or be uncomfortable with the closeness Nessa showed, but I refused to let anything destroy the smile written across her beautiful face. She seemed so happy. Besides, my current dress made me feel exposed and the thought of finding something less revealing was beyond appealing.

I was wrong. Nessa hadn't chosen something *less* revealing. In fact, none of the dresses shown to me could have been considered less revealing. They all seemed like half a dress. Some only had strips of fabric concealing private places. Others had plunging necklines and daring slits. I finally gave up after the sixth one was held up to me and asked Nessa to choose for me.

"They're all so...revealing."

"The queen loves for her guests to see what they might enjoy," Nessa said while helping me into a silky black dress that revealed my midriff but thankfully covered my breasts with a high neckline. The skirt, slit up both sides, was full and flowing, made of soft, gauzy layers that brushed the ground. I couldn't stop running my fingers over the delicate fabric.

Nessa braided my hair, leaving pieces loose around my ears and neck before she asked if I wanted to paint my face. I shook my head vehemently. I might not be able to remember my past, but the thought of painting my face seemed completely wrong. She shrugged and applied a generous color to her eyelids and lips.

"The queen always has a revel when her consort returns. He's the Gatekeeper to the human world and spends a lot of his time at his Gatehouse. The queen misses him dreadfully when he's away." She nervously folded and unfolded her hands. "He's...different."

"Different?"

"You'll see. So many of the Fae are strange looking, not like us at all. But he's...beautiful. Like *too* beautiful. He and Bevgyah make the most gorgeous pair." She beamed at me with a generous smile. "Bevgyah doesn't allow him to visit us without her," she said as she blushed, turning her cheeks a brilliant shade of pink. "He's only allowed to choose a maiden to share with her, but never to have for himself."

There was something unsettling about how Nessa spoke of having and sharing which made me shiver, but I tucked it away, along with all the other unease I was collecting to deal with later.

"What's his name?"

"She only ever calls him her Blackwarden, her Gatekeeper."

The words simmered in my throat. Something familiar about them. Perhaps I'd just heard them in passing. I wanted to repeat them but instead tried to keep my face as innocuous as possible as she led me back out to loiter with the other maidens until the revel. I would try my best to distract myself with all the new details of the queen's palace, which Nessa shared while the others in the harem flocked around me.

Nessa hadn't been entirely forthcoming. The queen's consort wasn't just beautiful, he was startlingly gorgeous and terrifying all at once. He towered over Bevgyah with onyx horns that swept back from his face. His skin the same black with a silver sheen that seemed to accentuate every line of defined muscle. A pair of massive wings lay tucked tight against his back. He wore a sleeveless shirt with a daring neckline that showed much of his chest. His clothes matched the queen's sheer gown perfectly—cream and gold with shimmering trim that caught the light every time he moved. But it was his eyes that held me. They were truly inhuman, entirely black like the rest of him with silver irises which seemed to glow.

His long dark blue hair was pulled back away from his face, allowing for a perfect view of his sharp jawline. His face was flawless. The more I looked at him, the more I couldn't help but feel that there was something almost familiar about him, like I'd seen him before, but not him. Someone who looked like him perhaps? But who could look like him? Who could be as beautiful? I was certain I'd remember. The queen's Blackwarden was unforgettable.

I felt hot all over from looking at him, and it didn't help that his gaze fell immediately on me after he and Bevgyah entered the harem. Something was so tantalizingly frightening about the way he openly stared, his eyes seeing every inch of me.

"To my loveliest maidens and my beloved Blackwarden." Bevgyah raised a glass of gold colored wine high. "The Mother has blessed me and may she continue to bless the Unseelie Court."

Everyone around me responded with a resounding "Mother bless thee." Before they collectively brought glasses of the same golden wine to their lips. All except myself and the Blackwarden. He stood perfectly still, only his chest moving with each breath, as he stared at me with an intensity that gave me shivers. Perhaps he always noticed the newest member of his queen's harem. He would have no reason to look at me otherwise. I was perhaps the least lovely of the other maidens Bevgyah had collected.

After the toast of sorts, other guests poured in behind her majesty filling the room with chaotic movement and music. I wasn't sure what to do with myself and when I glanced around to ask Nessa, she'd been pulled aside by a Fae female with green skin, four arms, and massive lower teeth that jutted out from between her lips.

It was all so strange and overwhelming that I backed away until I was pressed against the wall where I could watch the pageant of human girls and Dark Fae. They drank wine and plucked treats from trays that were carried around the room by smaller Fae creatures. Some guests had wings like the queen's Blackwarden along with antlers or horns, others had lower halves that looked like an animal's, with knees bent in the opposite direction and fur covering them rather than clothing. Some were so massive their heads or horns nearly scraped the ceiling.

Hands disappeared beneath clothing; teeth bit things other than food. I tried not to stare, but there was nowhere to look that I didn't feel as if I was interrupting some private moment. My skin was crawling as one Fae male quite literally ripped the top of one of the maiden's dresses down so he could kiss her breasts. I squeezed my eyes closed begging to be somewhere else, anywhere but here.

"I know this feeling." A familiar voice, like from a distant dream, bloomed goosebumps across my arms.

I peeled my eyes open and froze. The Blackwarden stood beside me, his wings pressed against the same wall, a glass of wine in each hand. He was watching the debauchery as he held one of the glasses in my direction.

"This makes things easier."

Perhaps if my hand hadn't been trembling when I reached for the glass, I might not have seemed like such a scared little girl in a strange place. It was everything, the music, the swaying bodies as wine was consumed from navels and...other places. It was the Blackwarden's proximity, the heat which seemed to radiate from him. The sound of his voice. Everything all at once.

I pressed the glass to my lips but hesitated. Something felt wrong. Something was so very wrong about everything around me. I was hit with the strongest feeling that I wasn't supposed to be here. I lowered the glass and closed my eyes, trying to fade into the safety of my mind where it was just me and the murky feeling that I was forgetting something very important.

I don't know how long I stood like that, a full glass of Fae wine in my hand, eyes closed, trying my best not to run in terror. It was long enough that I assumed the Blackwarden would have gone. But when I glanced up, I found his flawless face watching the crowd as if he'd seen this countless times. Seen it but chosen not to participate.

He looked down at me, the same feeling that he was familiar wriggled around in the back of my mind, causing the hair on my neck to stand on end.

"I feel like I should know you," I said softly.

What exactly possessed me to say this out loud? He didn't look away. In fact, his expression didn't change at all, and I wondered if he'd even heard me.

"I hope your memories come back to you," he said as he slipped from the wall and left me alone, my body buzzing from the sound of his voice.

I didn't bother trying to pry my eyes from him as he walked with the grace of a god toward Bevgyah. He didn't touch her. He hovered beside her as she traced lines over one of the human maiden's bodies with hungry fingers. When the queen realized her consort had returned to her side, she slipped beneath his arm, a hand climbing up the center of his chest and wrapping around his neck possessively before she yanked him toward her.

The way she kissed him was forceful, perhaps for show, to claim him as her own. I took in a sharp breath of jealousy I didn't deserve to feel as Bevgyah's hand crawled down his chest and tucked beneath the waistband of his pants. He seemed unfazed by her groping and when Bevgyah went back to fondling the human girl, his eyes once again planted themselves firmly on me.

It was how he stood, perfectly still, his hands to himself, while everyone else in the room seemed content to touch and feel and caress. I couldn't stand to watch anymore. I fled through the door

I'd been led through and down the hall, blind to my surroundings. I just needed out of there, away from whatever this was. A piece of me knew it was wrong, knew I didn't belong here. I was forgetting so many important things.

The halls of the queen's palace were just as mysterious and terrifying as she was. Night descended on my first day in this place, and I was no more comfortable than I'd been the moment I woke. Every surface seemed painted or carved with twisted monsters in compromising positions with humans and Fae and…I couldn't look anymore. I shielded my eyes with my hands on the sides of my face so I wouldn't accidentally see them and kept moving.

I'd run without direction and now I had no idea where I was. I only knew I was frantic to find a safe place I could hide for the foreseeable future. Maybe the queen would forget about me entirely, and I could figure out a way to sneak out of this place. I turned down another hall, this one wider, grander, with a vaulted ceiling that soared overhead, so high I wasn't sure how the structure could have been built in the first place. It made me feel tiny, insignificant, and lost. Braziers spaced between black wood panels seemed to burn in slow motion. Another half memory forced itself to the surface of my consciousness. I'd seen this magic before— flames taunting me with a sinister laugh.

I crept along the wall of the new hallway until I found a door left slightly ajar and slipped inside. This room was completely dark, the cool air making it feel empty. A brazier flared to life beside me as I entered and I flinched, covering my head with my arms. When nothing happened, I glanced around, finding a massive mirror on the far side. I remembered this place, I'd been here before, though the last time this room had been full of smoke and shadows. This was where I'd first woken up in this place. It hit me then—the dark figure I'd seen being lifted from the ground had likely been the Blackwarden. Those wings and horns were impossible to forget.

But now, the shadows were gone.

It was just me, the mirror, and my curiosity.

## CHAPTER 24
# Clutches of a Curse

### KERES

She disappeared from her place against the wall. I'd looked away for only a moment and she was gone. A ribbon of panic wrapped around my throat, blocking out all other emotions pressing at my mind for attention. I craned my neck to find her, but as far as I could see, she wasn't in the harem anymore.

The dress she'd been put in was hard to miss. Two slits on either side of a full skirt allowed for slices of her legs to peek through. While the neckline was modest, it showed her perfect abdomen from just under the curve of her breasts to the apex of her hips. And I couldn't stop thinking about how her skin tasted. My breath caught imagining her beneath my hands. But I wasn't the only one who had watched her with unrestrained desire. There were others in the harem who watched her, their eyes seeing everything I could see. I worried one of her other admirers may have taken her somewhere when I'd been distracted by Bevgyah.

The Hag leaned toward my ear. "Just like you to choose the one you can't have just yet."

A strange flutter of excitement mixed with dread writhed through me at the mention of *having* Rosalin. I'd hoped my concern for her hadn't been too obvious, but that was impossible. I wasn't exactly hiding the fact I'd been watching her. And I knew the rules. The magic Bevgyah used to strip away memory needed time to solidify, and she liked her maidens to get acclimated to her frozen castle before they were taken to anyone's bed. I could choose any of the maidens for Bevgyah and I to enjoy together, but not the newest addition.

She knew I wouldn't choose anyone. I had never been the one to choose. She would have to force me and she had no problem doing so.

"There's something different about her," Bevgyah said as she leaned into my space, running her fingers down the center of my chest.

I stiffened, unsure what she'd say next because there *was* something different about Rosalin. There were many things.

"She feels everything so much more intensely," she said as she pushed the waist of my pants lower with her claw-like fingernails.

I was shocked she'd allowed me to remain fully clothed. Usually at this point in the night, she would have removed my shirt at the very least.

"And I wonder how her emotions must taste to you with your...heightened sensitivities."

Rosalin's emotions were torture. Her fear was bitterness on my tongue. I'd wanted to hold her hand when I stood beside her against the wall, but I wasn't allowed to touch her. I thought if I could get her to drink some of the Fae wine she'd relax enough to get through the night, but she'd refused, and now she was somewhere in Bevgyah's palace without supervision. I didn't worry about what *she* would do, so much as what *someone* would do to her. I took a sharp breath, trying to focus on only my own emotions.

"Perhaps, I can let you break this rule just once," she purred in my ear and goosebumps rippled down my arms.

A flash of hot need sank between my legs. I hated the way my body responded, the hope that I could keep Rosalin from someone else's ravenous hands even if it meant enduring Bevgyah's depraved desires. It was hope she would shatter at her earliest convenience.

"Go, find our little pet."

I glared at her. A cruel smile turned up her lips.

"My kindness had best not go unrewarded, Blackwarden."

I didn't wait for her to change her mind. Things at the revel had begun taking a more intimate turn. Some of the guests had chosen maidens and were retiring to the small suites off the harem's hallway, where they could enjoy themselves more privately. I could feel the desire and sex as if it were my own, and though, I was usually good at pushing it away, tonight it was so much harder. But I knew, if I wasn't anywhere near Bevgyah, I wouldn't be forced to do something I didn't want.

I went straight for the main hall of the palace to get away from the cacophony of emotions and try and isolate Rosalin's. The halls were empty. A few of the guards on duty were standing outside the entrance to the harem, the others had left. No one wanted to be around the debauchery of the queen's pleasure party, unless they were taking part.

The silence was soothing. The oppressive moist heat and smell of sweat of the harem replaced with cool air that calmed the frayed edges of my mind. I stood in the center of the hall and waited, closing my eyes in the hopes it would eliminate any distractions but the feel of her fear.

"Are you following me, Blackwarden?"

I turned to find her standing in the middle of the hall, eyes wide with surprise. She wasn't afraid, she was *curious*. I'd been looking for the wrong emotion. I should have known she'd find a way back to her questions.

"Her majesty wishes for you to return to the revel."

She shuddered, wrapping her arms around her shoulders and the need to wrap mine around her was overpowering. "I'd rather not."

The slightest smile tugged at my lips. I couldn't help myself. Her honesty was so pure. The Rosalin I knew. *My Rosalin.* I held out a hand without thinking. "I promise, you're far safer there than you are wandering these halls alone."

She didn't hesitate. She took my hand. There wasn't a shred of fear where there had been before, and I shivered at the touch of her skin. I shouldn't be touching her.

I wasn't allowed.

"Is that the room where the portal to the human world is?" she asked, pointing toward a door that had been left slightly ajar.

I hesitated. Had someone told her about the portal? Or did she remember?

"It is."

"And you being the Gatekeeper, are *you* the one who takes people back and forth?"

"I am." I was grinning from ear to ear now. I wanted her questions. I wanted all of them.

"Could you take me back through?"

I swallowed, holding her gaze. She truly didn't remember the reason she was here, why she'd been brought through in the first place.

"I can't."

"You can't? Or you won't?"

Confounded questions!

"I would happily take you, but my magic is limited by the queen's desires, and she would never allow it." I could feel her frustration building as I spoke, but I craved it. I wanted more of her emotions. Ones that weren't fear, or pain, or loathing.

"I don't want to be here," she said as she pulled her hand from mine and hugged herself again. A wave of unease passed between us, and it ripped at the walls I was trying to put up around my heart.

"You're here as part of a treaty between the Unseelie Court and the leaders of your people. Unfortunately, you have no choice."

I hated saying the words. Having your choice stripped from you—your free will taken completely—was perhaps more difficult to cope with than pain. I knew it well. I'd been enduring it for five hundred years. She had yet to be compelled by Bevgyah to do things she would have nightmares about for the rest of her precious human life. I swallowed my anger knowing there was nothing I could do to save her from this. Much like her, I didn't want to be here either.

A tear slipped down her cheek. I might have crumbled at the sight of it, but I managed to slam the stoic mask I was so used to wearing over my features as her sorrow swallowed me whole. I took a long breath, trying to settle my own emotions.

"Come." I reached out my hand again.

She stared at it but didn't move. A strange almost certainty passed through her and into me.

"I know you," she said, a monotone quality to her voice. "You've guided me before, haven't you?"

I took a breath to speak, but searing pain lanced through my head. It was the same pain every time the curse kept me from answering. I took a sharp breath across my teeth that didn't go unnoticed. She watched me, her emotions dipping to concern.

"Her majesty is waiting for us." I finally managed.

She glared at me, frozen in place, her frustration wicking into my skin. I knew her feelings would be so much more intense without an imbued portrait to dampen them, but I hadn't been truly prepared. I finally took her hand and squeezed it gently before tucking it under my arm and pulling her down the hall.

CHAPTER 25

# Half Memories

## ROSALIN

The Blackwarden was true to his word, which I guess he had to be because Fae couldn't lie. I don't know how I knew this, but it was a tiny fragment of a half memory that I was one hundred percent certain was true. He pulled me through the queen's cold castle but released my hand before we approached the door to the harem. I shivered from the profound sense of loneliness I was left with as his hand slipped from mine.

The queen was waiting just inside, impatient for us to return, a scowl marring her gorgeous face.

"What took so long?" she spat at her Blackwarden.

He took the question in stride, expression never changing.

"It took me longer to find her with..." He side-eyed me. "...all the other emotions from the revel."

The queen put a hand on her hip, glaring at him in a way that made me shudder. I don't know how he managed to stay so stoic.

"Take her to a suite for now, I'm still enjoying myself," Bevgyah said as she turned, whipping her hair around and nearly smacking us both with her braids.

"As you wish, my queen."

He ushered me through a different way to the hall than I was familiar with. Several of the doors that branched off of it were closed with a handful still open and dark inside. He led me into one and the brazier ignited, flooding the space with golden light. It was a small room, an overstuffed futon in the middle and surrounded by silks draped from the walls and ceiling. I froze in place. I'd been here before. But I knew that was wrong. I hadn't stepped foot into one of these rooms so I couldn't have.

"Are you okay?" His voice curled around me, pulling me from another half memory.

When I faced him, I realized I'd been holding my breath and let it burst past my lips.

"I've been here before."

He smiled weakly. "No, not here, I can assure you."

"No, I have. Or I dreamt it?" The memory was foggy. A man was with me. He'd led me here from another room. I couldn't stop staring at his perfect body. "There was a man with me. He had pale skin. So perfect." I was lost for a moment in the fragments of the past. "I remember him."

The Blackwarden stared at me with an emotionless expression, but I didn't know what else to say. I decided it didn't matter. I might be left with these strange half memories forever, and there would be nothing I could do about it but try to recall.

"You can rest here for now," he said, after a long moment of watching me look around the room. "Bevgyah may tire herself out before she's interested in..."

The muscles tightened in his neck, his hands balling into fists.

"Are *you* okay?" I asked, resting a hand on his arm.

A strange shock of a light vibrated through me, and I squeezed my eyes shut. So much skin. Pale and beautiful. A gorgeous face in the throes of pleasure. My hands on his chest, his stomach, his...

"I need to go," his voice was breathy, and he was gone before I opened my eyes.

The queen did not grace me with her presence, and I was happy for it. The way she'd spoken with her Blackwarden had been harsh and uncaring. I knew she was the queen, and he was her consort, but she treated him like an object, rather than a person. It felt wrong. It made me want to protect him when I knew there was nothing I could do to protect myself, much less him.

I woke in complete darkness to the sound of laughter outside my little suite the Blackwarden had taken me to. I lay perfectly still trying to hear the words being spoken, but it was useless. When I sat up, a brazier burned to life, and I let out a tiny yelp as I threw a silky blanket over my head. The door cracked open, and a face peeked in before Nessa opened the door completely.

"I thought the Blackwarden brought you here," she said looking around the room and then at me with wide eyes.

"He did."

"Where did he go? He wasn't at the revel." She reached a hand down to help me up. "We've been impatiently waiting for you to sneak him out."

I shook my head, memories of the night before weren't something I wanted to revisit, but I could confidently say the queen's Blackwarden had left and had done so very quickly.

"He's never taken one of us back to a suite."

I tried to find the words to explain to her it wasn't what she thought. That he'd brought me there at the queen's behest. Instead, I just stared at her, blushing furiously as I tried to work through my jumbled thoughts.

"Come, it's time for breakfast."

Nessa pulled me down the hall back toward the harem. It was then that I realized this was my existence—the harem, revels, gossip, golden Fae wine, and half memories.

Bevgyah paid the harem a visit the next day. She wasn't accompanied by her consort; she came with two guards as she had when she'd given me my name. Every maiden, myself included, curtsied until the queen motioned for us to stand. She'd asked for the harem to be emptied except for me, and once again found myself well and truly terrified. What could she possibly want to talk with me about in private? Perhaps she tried to get to know all of her newest maidens when they first arrived?

"Tesanna, come and sit with me, my pet." She patted the futon beside her.

I did as she bade, slipping to my knees and folding my hands as respectfully as I could. I had only a vague recollection of how you were supposed to sit with a queen, and this felt entirely too casual. Shouldn't she be on some sort of throne with billowing skirts and a judgmental glare? This seemed almost friendly with the way she leaned close.

"My Blackwarden seems to have a problem, and I need your help."

I stiffened at the mention of her consort. What problem could he possibly have that I could help her with?

"Your emotions seem to be far stronger than any of my other maidens. Do you know why that is?"

How could she know the strength of my emotions? Had I been so obvious? Was it because I'd been uncomfortable at the revel?

"I'm sorry, your Majesty, I don't know," I said as calmly as I could, but I worried she could see my hands were trembling. I was hot all over, sweat soaking through my silk slip at the small of my back.

Bevgyah reached forward, long lavender fingers taking hold of my chin and turning my face to the side. Her fingernails bit into my skin as she turned my face around the other direction. I remembered the mark that the tiny Fae female had hidden with cream and magic when I first arrived. A flash of panic rippled through me as I wondered if the queen would see it. It took all of my strength not to step back and pull my hair over my shoulder to hide it.

"You seem perfectly normal, if not a bit plain." She smoothed her thumb over my chin then trailed her fingers down the column of my neck. "Perhaps he's mistaken."

I nodded, trying to suppress the shudder her touch had ripped from my insides. But as much as I feared what she would say or do next, my curiosity was building. Questions boiled in my throat, begging to be asked.

"How can someone feel my emotions?"

She smiled wide, showing sharp teeth. "My Blackwarden's shadow magic is full of surprises, isn't it? It comes in handy if he needs to manipulate someone or take advantage of a situation." Her hand slipped from my throat as she glared at me with unyielding intensity. "His evil heart is as black as his flesh, my pet. Do not let him manipulate you."

I found this hard to believe. The male who had helped me the night before had been nothing but kind, his presence calming. But perhaps it had been because he could sense the way I was feeling? I didn't have time to review every interaction with Bevgyah glaring at me.

"When he took you to a suite last night did he stay with you? Did he touch you?"

I shook my head, my cheeks feeling hot with embarrassment. Did she think I'd been intimate with her consort? "No, your Majesty. He took me to a suite and said he needed to go. I assumed to return to you."

She smirked, glancing at me from the corner of her eye. "He did not return to me. I found him in his own bed this morning." She watched me with critical eyes. "Did he speak with you about anything? Anything at all? I need to know every word he's said to you. I worry he may have ensnared you already."

I tried to recall what we'd spoken about. I'd asked him questions about the portal and how I wished I could return home, and he'd answered them. But I'd also told him I thought I remembered him.

"He told me why I was here. Something about a treaty. I asked him about the portal...I..." Too scared to confess I'd asked him to take me home; I froze in place.

"Why ever would you want to know about the portal?"

I shouldn't have said so much, but my fear had ripped the words from me. I should have lied and told her he'd said nothing. Her dark eyes burrowed into me, making me squirm under her scrutiny.

"I asked him if he could take me back through."

A flash of anger moved across her face, but she stifled it quickly.

"Tell me, Tesanna, what do you remember from the human world?"

A shiver writhed up my spine. This was a dangerous question. It was growing clearer that I wasn't supposed to remember. I tried to make my momentary shock seem more like reflection, but I wasn't sure how well I'd hidden my fear.

"Nothing. The first thing I remember is the room with the mirror and so many shadows."

She seemed to think on this for a long moment before she gracefully lifted herself to her feet.

"This has been a delightful chat, little pet. I will call for you later today so you might entertain me."

There was something so sinister in the way she used the word 'entertain' that froze my blood in my veins.

"Of course, your Majesty," I said with as much sweetness as I could muster as she swept from the harem.

I was yanked from my suite at some awful hour of the night. At first, I thought it was one of the miniscule Fae who helped us in the harem, but when I realized it was a guard, terror made it hard to breathe. Where was a guard taking me in the middle of the night? I'd tried to wriggle free from his grip, but he only tightened his hand on my wrist.

His orangish red flesh peeked from beneath black armor, and I had a momentary flash of desire to see what his face actually looked like. My curiosity was washed away almost immediately as he roughly directed me out into the hall.

"Come on, her majesty isn't exactly patient."

And he wasn't exactly patient either. I stumbled and lost my footing multiple times as he dragged me up a flight of stairs, my heart racing faster and faster, fear gripping my insides the closer I came to finding out exactly what Bevgyah meant by "entertainment." I was yanked to my feet with a frustrated grumble. Clearly, the guard wasn't interested in whether I met with the queen in one piece, only that I made it there.

I was ushered into what looked like a lavish sitting room with settees and futons spread out, framed by rugs woven in brilliant shades of blues and lavenders. The room was garishly decorated with silver trimming and gems on almost every surface. The ceiling was encrusted with thousands of massive crystals that made it appear as though it was encased entirely in ice. The walls were covered with an iridescent material that glittered in the brazier light and cast eerie rainbows over everything. A chill of warning writhed up my spine. On a settee near a massive faceted window sat Bevgyah, her Blackwarden nowhere in sight.

"Ah, Tesanna." The Hag Queen's voice was sing-songy, with a sweetness that didn't quite reach her eyes. "Tell me, what do you think of my palace?" she asked, lifting her arms to gesture to the room around her.

I was so confused. Why would she yank me from sleep to ask me this? For a moment I wanted to tell her exactly what I thought. This place was cold and creepy and nothing made sense. The last thing I wanted to do was be forced to spend my days in a room with a bunch of gossipy girls while we waited for the next party. I didn't like the way she treated her Blackwarden, and I wanted to go home, even though I had no idea if home was any better.

"It's beautiful," I lied and hoped this would be enough because I wasn't sure I could force myself to elaborate further.

"Come now. I am beautiful. *My Blackwarden is beautiful.* What do you truly think of your new home?"

She wasn't wrong. She and her Blackwarden were indeed beautiful. I took a deep breath, trying to think of something else I could say that wouldn't upset her.

"I'm still getting used to things, I guess, your Majesty." I tried to stall further, but her expression was growing impatient. "I don't like the revels."

She threw her head back, laughing with her whole chest. The crystals she wore on chains around her neck chimed like a creepy song.

"But they are so much fun," she said, a seductive lilt to her words. "I had hoped to have another when my Blackwarden returns."

"He's left?" I shouldn't have shown so much interest. I could see the flash of anger in her eyes at how quickly I'd asked about him when it had taken her so long to draw any other words from me.

"I needed him to take one of my dignitaries through the portal," she said with boredom.

She couldn't lie.

I swallowed my fear and smiled sweetly, trying to hide any concerns I might have had for him. "Will I ever be able to go back to the human world?" I finally asked, hoping that her frustration with this would overshadow that I'd asked about her Blackwarden.

Bevgyah leaned closer, the weight of her presence made the air suddenly very thin. She tucked a piece of my hair behind my ear, her finger lingering on my cheek as her eyes raked over my face to my chest.

"No, my lovely Tesanna. You are one of my precious pets. A cherished addition to my harem."

*Cherished addition.* The words rang through my head, echoing against the walls of my mind. Another half memory I frantically collected to keep until I'd recovered them all. It had been a familiar male's voice that had said these words before.

She lifted my chin with her index finger before dragging it down my throat and between my breasts to my navel. Heat radiated through me at her touch that I both craved and hated. Something so sexual in the way her eyes devoured me. I didn't dare move or react for fear she would touch me again.

"I can see the appeal."

"Appeal, your Majesty?" I asked, trying to ignore the way she looked at me, the way the air seemed to grow colder around me.

She didn't answer, instead she stood, hovering over me as she ran her fingers through my loose hair. She leaned down, putting her cheek against mine.

"My Blackwarden likes you, little Tesanna," she whispered in my ear, and instead of leaning away she licked down my neck to the hollow at the base of my throat.

I stiffened, trying not to pull away, trying to slow my heart that seemed to crash into my rib cage. Something told me that she wasn't the type of person who would accept rejection. That she might make things so much worse for me if I did. I swallowed my fear.

"He wants you and who he wants, *I want*."

CHAPTER 26

# Midnight Apple

## KERES

Why was she so different? Rosalin had vague pieces of memory. It had never happened before with any of the other maidens, but I could feel the waves of confusion. She'd asked multiple times if she'd known me or been somewhere in the few stolen moments we'd had together.

"There has to be something I've missed," I said to the Gatehouse, though it wasn't much help.

I sat on the floor of Rosalin's suite with her portrait propped beside me and a pile of books in front of me. I'd be lying if I said I didn't steal glances of her face every few moments. Bevgyah had needed one of her dignitaries brought through the portal, which gave me twenty-four hours in the Gatehouse to myself while my shadow magic recovered. And I planned on using every second to find something that could help me get Rosalin out of the Unseelie Court. After sending the male on his way I went room by room, leaving her suite for last. I wasn't able to enter when there was a maiden staying with me. The Gatehouse was very particular about this. They had to have a place where they could feel safe. But once I had my home to myself again it didn't matter.

I glanced up at the black metal statue of a horse in the corner, a strange looking apple tree sculpture beside it.

"Seems she tested you," I said with a smirk. One of the braziers flared a little brighter. "She definitely tested me." A flash of heat plummeted into my core with the memory of her lips on my neck, her hair whispering over my bare chest, her skin beneath my fingertips.

What was it about her that turned my blood to liquid fire? I shook my head before my smile fell. Her fear had never been like the other girls. It had always been layered with anger and curiosity, and it wasn't until she'd told me of her deceased husband that I'd understood why. That couldn't be what made her different though, could it? That she'd loved and lost?

"What *else* is different?"

Maybe it had to do with her being older and more mature, or because she'd chosen to come in her sister's place. That was a level of self-sacrifice that none of the others had demonstrated.

I didn't put much faith in fate, but perhaps it had been pre-ordained for her sister's name to be drawn after Rosalin had lost her husband. A sinister thought struck me. Who was the Dark Fae who'd killed her husband? I shook my head, something like that couldn't have been arranged. Not easily. Too many things would have had to fall into place for her sister's name to have been drawn, for her to have been present for the choosing and willing to go in her sister's place. These things couldn't be planned, could they?

I pushed the thoughts away, trying to accept that—for whatever reason—Rosalin had been brought to me. And when she looked at me, she'd seen past her fear and anger, straight to the person buried beneath this face.

I couldn't help but wonder if the fact that she wasn't protected by my shadows actually helped her recover some of her memories in the Unseelie Court. What if those memories had something to do with breaking the curse? I shook my head. I hoped that wasn't the case, because if it was, I'd been making it harder to break the curse for five hundred years in my attempts to protect the maidens the only way I could. I already felt like a total idiot. I didn't want to add another reason. But the more I thought about it, the more I focused on Bevgyah's attention to the memories. They were important enough for her to strip away. She insisted on precautions to ensure the magic had time to solidify and the maidens' memories were truly gone forever.

I shivered. Even if it was the memories, there had to be more. A catalyst so to speak.

I laughed loudly, the sound echoing through the halls of my empty home.

Emotions.

Bevgyah expected me to be able to feel their emotions, and proximity made them stronger. I wasn't allowed to touch them because touch was even more intense I was the last connection they had to their world thus my appearance was changed, my given name never uttered.

Perhaps it was my stolen moments with Rosalin that had sparked fragments of memories. If that was true, I needed to ignite them. I needed to find something she'd remember that wasn't tied to me. Something she could hold in her hand and keep with her. But other than her old brown dress she hadn't brought anything with her. It was one of the stipulations of the choosing. They could only bring what they wore.

I rummaged through the books in the room. Maybe I could find something she'd spent more time with. Perhaps one of the etiquette books, or a piece of jewelry I hadn't noticed her wearing. I pulled another stack of books from her side table, desperate to find something I'd seen her reading. Instead, I found a book I'd never seen before. A book of fairy tales—a children's story book. I flipped it over, admiring the swirls of gilding that wrapped around the cover. A lovely depiction of a wood sprite graced the front. I knew it hadn't been in my library. I would have remembered it.

"Did she ask you for this?" I was desperate for the Gatehouse to actually answer me. Why hadn't it been given a voice? I glared at the rafters high above before looking back down at the book.

Rosalin's name was scrawled on the inside in a child's handwriting. I flipped through, admiring the illustrations. They were beautifully detailed if a bit naive—depictions of Fair Folk with various skin tones and elegant willowy statures. I lost myself in the descriptions of magic and mischief, smiling at the pictures of sprites and dwarves and elves. It was when I turned to the section on Dark Fae that I paused.

They were ugly and foreboding—the details skewed in a way that made each illustration seem evil. Descriptions of curses and wicked magic that could destroy a human or lead them astray. I flipped through the pages trying to ignore the grotesque faces of the creatures that looked more like monsters and demons than people. Pages of warped darkness that would give any human child who didn't know any better nightmares of the worst kind.

I stopped cold.

*It was me.* Not me exactly, but a black fleshed, winged male with horns, and dark shadows that billowed around his feet. A note had been written in the margin beside the description of what this book simply called a Shadow Guardian.

"An apple is just an apple, whether green or midnight."

I traced my fingers over her handwriting. It was different from the childish writing of her name. This writing was new. It wasn't an answer, but it was something. A way of seeing things, of seeing people as people, whether human or Fae even though she'd come here with a very unfavorable opinion of me and my kind. I stood and tucked the book under my arm, glancing around the room one more time for anything I might have missed before I left. I had one more place to visit.

I'd been painting the mural long before I'd been trapped as Devgyah's consort. I never knew when the Gatehouse would clear it away in the middle of the night, and I would need to start anew.

It seemed to know when things changed enough that it needed to be refreshed. This was the reason I'd forbidden the maidens to wander at midnight. I didn't need their curiosity. Rosalin had been the only maiden to even notice it.

Over the years I'd perfected the dragons and serpents and dark creatures that honestly looked a fair amount like the illustrations in Rosalin's book. It was after I'd painted her the first time that I'd truly been curious where the images came to me from, because I'd painted her long before she came to the Gatehouse. I hadn't thought anything of it. A brown-haired girl in a brown dress was nothing unusual. Thinking back now, it had been months before she'd come.

I stared at my last rendering of Rosalin and myself, my mouth going dry. I held her protectively, wrapping her in my arms and wings. I knew what my subconscious was telling me. I needed to protect her, but I didn't think I could truly keep her safe, not until I'd found a way to bring her back through the portal. And if the key to breaking the curse was memories, it was possible I'd already run out of time. I was left with my pathetic plan of being put to death now that I'd fulfilled five hundred years of my original punishment. Rosalin would eventually grow accustomed to the harem like all the other maidens.

Perhaps it was better that way.

I shook my head, feeling like a dreadful idiot. Because that's what I was. Curses always had something that broke them. As ironclad as mine seemed, there had to be *something* that broke it. Except, I had run out of time to find it. Combined with my punishment for treason, this was my existence. Death was the only way out. I touched Rosalin's face on the mural before it faded away like a dream. A flash of panic gripped my chest. The wall was blank as if Rosalin had never been.

I blinked a few times. It wasn't midnight, yet the Gatehouse had cleared it.

"Really?" I asked with weariness clinging to my voice. "Now?"

I was reluctant at first, but after staring at the empty wall for several minutes I trudged to my suite, grabbed a paintbrush, and squeezed a few colors out onto my palette. I stepped into the hall, my eyes snagging on the brazier outside my suite. The flames shifted in slow motion—haunting as it danced to silent music.

"I have nothing to paint." I shook my head. "I have no hope left."

The brazier flared brighter before dimming again. I looked over at the children's book I'd left lying on the floor in front of the door to the portal.

*An apple is just an apple, whether green or midnight.*

I took a deep breath and began.

It didn't take me long. I only had a small place to paint. I left the rest of the wall completely empty, dropping the paintbrush and palette to the floor before I stood straight and stared at my work. It was rough, not much more than silhouettes. That's all it needed to be. There would be no imbuing, no magic, no hope. It would just be a reminder of what had been and what would never be again.

I glanced up at the brazier and swallowed my sorrow.

"Thank you, old friend. It's been a pleasure."

I retrieved the book and turned to the portal. The last thing I wanted to do was make Bevgyah wait.

## CHAPTER 27

# The Queen's Precious Pet

## ROSALIN

I promised myself I'd be okay—that this was all just a nightmare, that I only needed to breathe and think of anything but Bevgyah's hands.

She had touched me.

I squeezed my eyes shut, willing the tears not to come. Her touch made me feel dirty, burning with shame. Fear kept me frozen—fear she might kill me, or worse—as her fingers lingered on my breasts, the silk of my dress offering no protection at all. And now I was standing against the wall again, Bevgyah's guests flooding into the harem for a second time.

She stood alone—her Blackwarden hadn't returned from his Gatehouse yet. It was better that way. I had a feeling when he did return the queen would ask more of me than I could handle. I hugged myself, feeling entirely exposed even though I'd managed to convince Nessa to let me stay in the silk slip that covered more of my body than the other frilly gowns.

A dark hand held a glass of wine in my direction, and I flinched before glancing over. How long had he been standing beside me while I was lost in my thoughts? I wondered if the Blackwarden could feel my terror. If he had any idea the conflicting emotions raging through me at that moment. I was both elated he was here and terrified he'd returned so soon. And beyond curious if he wanted to be here anymore than I did. I took the glass, my fingers brushing over his unintentionally, sending butterflies loose in my chest.

"I left something in your room. I thought it might make you feel more...comfortable." When I looked over at the Blackwarden, he was looking down at his feet. I wondered if he'd said anything at all, or if I'd imagined it.

He didn't say another word, instead he looked over the harem with a stolid expression, taking tiny sips of wine. His movements were so graceful. He had to know how beautiful he was, and how hard it was to see past that beauty to the kind male that stood in silence beside me—no expectations, no questions, no small talk. Just a warm presence at my side when I needed it most. Knowing he was here now calmed my nerves enough that I thought maybe I could get through the revel without breaking down into tears.

The people in attendance were drifting toward one area of the harem, and I leaned forward to see what was going on. It was Nessa, in a beautiful blue sheer gown made of strips of fabric accentuating every gorgeous curve of her figure. She moved with the music, her hands running down the length of her body as she danced, removing a strip of gauze every few seconds as she twisted and turned. I didn't realize at first what she was doing, but once I did, I couldn't stop my mouth from falling open, embarrassment on her behalf igniting my cheeks.

All eyes were on her as she continued the erotic dance, stripping piece after piece of cloth, until she was left with nothing but a thin thong covering her nether region. I gripped my wine glass so tightly my knuckles turned white but was unable to look away as a blue-fleshed male with tall, twisted horns rose to dance with her. He ran an unnaturally long tongue between her breasts before pressing his face where his tongue had just traveled.

I squeezed my eyes shut. Is this what would be expected of me? I felt disgusted just watching. I took a long sip of the wine, letting the gold liquid slip down my throat and coat the inside of my stomach with a warmth that radiated into the depths of my being. The Blackwarden had said it would help make things easier, but now I wondered what *things* he was referring to.

I glanced in his direction. He wasn't watching Nessa, he was looking at me, his silver eyes following my movements as I took another generous gulp of wine.

Bevgyah's words echoed in my mind. *He wants you and who he wants, I want.* I realized I was staring at his lips, stained gold from the wine. His striking black skin only made those lips look that much more delicious. He finally looked out over the harem likely searching for Bevgyah. He took another sip, the muscles in his neck drawing my attention as he swallowed. I needed to stop staring at him, but if I wasn't staring at him, I was staring at the debauchery around me.

I hugged myself, hoping Bevgyah would wander off with one of her other "pets." When I glanced toward the Blackwarden again he had slipped away, moving toward a cluster of women who were huddled tightly around someone I couldn't quite see. I took the opportunity to sneak back down the hall to my room, closing the door behind me, and wished I had some way to lock it. I leaned against it for several minutes, trying to calm my racing heart. Maybe I'd be left alone. Maybe I could escape another revel without having to put myself on display. Maybe I was a fool who needed to learn how to accept that this was my life now.

I found a book beneath my blankets. Perhaps this is what the Blackwarden had left for me? My head swam too much to look at it. Instead, I tucked it under the futon before I cocooned myself in the covers and tried to ignore the music filtering down the hall, a brassy laugh, drunken cheering, a muffled yelp. I just wanted to sleep. I wanted to leave this place, or at the very least, be left alone. Even though I couldn't remember it, I wanted to go home.

I must have fallen asleep because I was awakened by the sound of my door being thrown open and a very drunk, very disheveled queen stumbling in. Still half asleep, I didn't know what to do or how to act. I scrambled to extract myself from the blankets, fumbling in my rush.

"Tesanna." Her voice was too loud, as though she didn't realize how crass she was being.

When I managed to push myself up, I realized she was unaccompanied. She'd left her Blackwarden behind. The straps of her dress had been pulled off her shoulders, the only thing keeping it from falling down was how it clung around her breasts.

"Come with me, my precious pet," she slurred as she grabbed my wrist and yanked me toward the hall.

The music had stopped, and as she dragged me back to the harem, I noticed most of the doors to the smaller rooms were closed. We stumbled through the gem curtain at the end together and I flinched, realizing it was only her Blackwarden who remained. He was sprawled out on one of the futons in nothing but a pair of loose-fitting pants that were pulled low on his hips showing every inch of his incredible torso. As Bevgyah led me closer I could tell he was drunk, his eyes two slits of near unconsciousness, his arms thrown over his head. He was beautiful, every muscle in his chest and abdomen flexing as he breathed.

"My Blackwarden and I require your entertainment."

I took a sharp breath preparing to disappear into myself, my silk dress clinging to the sweat on the small of my back. I knew what she meant by entertainment.

"Oh, come now, my sweet Tesanna." She dragged her finger up my arm to the strap of my dress before slipping it off my shoulder.

The queen held my arms pressed against my sides as she kissed over the swell of my breasts. I squeezed my eyes shut. I wanted to run. I wanted to hide in my little room. Bevgyah trailed her hands up the length of my body before she slipped the other strap off my shoulder. I felt exposed, even though I was still fully clothed, as her hands meandered across my stomach and down to where the dress was slit at my thigh. Her fingers disappeared beneath the fabric, and I took a sharp breath at her touch.

"Perhaps you should have some wine to help you relax." She turned away, grabbing up a half-consumed glass of Fae wine. "Drink this."

Something told me the last thing I wanted to do was drink the wine from that particular glass. That it wasn't wine at all. My eyes found the Blackwarden's. He was watching me with a terrifying need swirling in the depths of his silver eyes, his lips gently parted. I couldn't pry my eyes from him. If I wasn't mistaken, he shook his head, the movement almost indiscernible.

"I don't like wine, your Majesty."

She came closer, anger in the curve of her eyebrows as she grabbed my chin and turned me to face her. "I didn't *ask* if you liked it. I *told* you to drink it."

Before I could step away, she grabbed the hair at the nape of my neck and pressed the glass to my lips.

"Drink."

I did as I was told, swallowing large gulps, as she pulled my head back and poured the contents of the glass down my throat. It overflowed past the corners of my mouth and rolled down my neck and her tongue followed, lapping the wine from my skin.

"Delicious," she said against my neck as she traced a hand down my spine to my backside.

The drink made me lightheaded, and the room seemed to warp and tilt. I no longer felt I had the strength to push Bevgyah away. I no longer knew why I would want to. She ran her hands over my silk dress, and I suddenly needed those hands on my skin. I leaned into her, wanting nothing more than to kiss her plump lavender lips. Her hands were in my hair, holding my head in place as she explored my mouth with her tongue, sending sparks of fiery need through me.

Strong arms wrapped around my middle, the warmth of the Blackwarden's hands on my backside seeped through the fabric of my dress. He'd pushed his queen away and held around my waist tightly, pressing his cheek to my stomach. So much decadent heat from his chest burned through the silk and I wanted more. I needed more.

"Not this one, my Queen. Please," he said between breaths.

He looked up at me, and I was frozen in place, those devilish silver eyes devouring me entirely. I squeezed my own eyes shut, trying to clear my mind, my fingers weaving into his hair. It was so soft, so delectable as I dragged my hands down the length of it to the bare skin of his shoulders. So good. He felt so good beneath my fingers. Like the most amazing dream. Firm and soft and warm. When I looked at him again, he'd closed his eyes, a pained expression on his face.

"Another of your maidens, but not this one," he begged, his voice trembling.

Bevgyah yanked him off me, throwing him back down to the futon. "You can pretend to push her away, Blackwarden, but I can see your desire hard between your legs."

His chest heaved with each breath, the muscles in his stomach taut as he tried to sit up and couldn't. The room was still spinning, and I took a step closer, unsure what to say or do. My vision was failing me because it looked like shadows oozed up from the ground and wrapped around the Blackwarden's arms and throat.

"Tesanna." Bevgyah's voice was a song. I was drawn closer to her as she coaxed me to my knees. "What do you most desire?" she asked as she leaned closer, bringing her lips to the shell of my ear.

The question hung in my head, another half memory. I'd been asked a question like this before. I blinked a few times but couldn't clear away the fog. The room wouldn't stop spinning, and my entire body was on fire with terrible desire. I didn't push her hands away when they pulled my silk slip up slowly, the fabric sliding over my skin felt like butterfly wings and I needed more. Her fingers found their way between my legs, groping for the edge of my undergarments. I pressed myself against her hand, and I wanted more. I needed more. She kissed my neck, her tongue tracing the line of my jaw until her lips were on mine again.

I felt like I couldn't catch my breath. Like I needed the heat of her body on my own.

And yet.

I didn't want this. I never wanted this.

I was floating outside my own body, helpless to stop her, as she eased my undergarments down around my knees.

"No," I whispered against her lips. She pulled back, her expression one of bitter judgement.

"You would deny your queen?"

I glanced down at her Blackwarden as he struggled against what looked like black shackles around his wrists and throat. Had she restrained him with shadows?

"Bevgyah, she doesn't—"

"She will speak for herself," she spat at her Blackwarden, her tone severe.

"I don't...I don't want this." My words were more confident this time, as if his voice had helped me find my own.

"But don't you want *him*?" she asked, as she sank to the ground beside him, her pale violet hands contrasted against the dark skin of his stomach. A flash of jealousy squeezed my throat as her fingers meandered over the ridges of his muscles.

I couldn't answer her, because the truth was, I did. I very much did. And I knew I shouldn't. Her fingers danced at the waist of his pants, pulling them down far enough to expose him entirely, opening a chasm of shame inside me as I struggled and failed to rip my gaze from his nakedness.

His eyes were clear for the first time as they held mine. All the drunkenness of a moment ago was gone, replaced with a terrible fear in his expression that burrowed deep into my chest, banishing the blazing fire that had ignited between my legs. He squeezed his eyes shut, his head falling back as she stroked him, leaning her face down to take him into her mouth.

He moaned as he struggled against the shadowy bindings. It wasn't a sound of pleasure. It was the sound of agony. The muscles in his neck and shoulders grew taut as he fought to free himself. I didn't know how to help him. It felt like everything I did or said had to pass through layers of sticky honey. I was still on my knees, half dressed, half coherent. An anguished scream was building in my chest, ready to burst free, but I couldn't find a way to let it out. And I never got a chance. Bevgyah lunged at me, her hands slipping over my hips to my stomach and up to cup the lower curve of my breasts, her thumbs rubbing over my nipples.

"Don't you want to be touched, Tesanna? To touch *him*?"

I pushed against her shoulders, squeezing my eyes shut, begging to be somewhere else, anywhere but here. The room continued to tilt in on itself until I lost my balance and sprawled out on my backside. She towered over me, a wicked smile turning up the corners of her lips as terror completely replaced the desire running through my veins, leaving me cold.

"Leave us then, unless you'd rather watch," she said with a dangerous seduction in her voice. "He's so much more delicious when he's restrained like the monster he is."

I scrambled to my feet, yanking my undergarments up as she crawled toward him like a predator in heat.

I was useless—nothing more than a lowly maiden in the queen's harem. I couldn't help him like he'd helped me so many times. He fought hard against the bindings, his muscles shaking from the effort, head lolling back as he struggled. I was frozen in place as she kissed him, down his throat to his chest as she straddled him.

Something dark stirred inside me as her hips moved against him. The reality of what she was doing ignited a molten fury so intense it burned away the haze—I was instantly sober. But still frozen. The shape of the word *"Go"* on his lips shattered whatever spell held me.

I turned and fled, leaving the queen alone to have her way with her Blackwarden.

## CHAPTER 28

# Punishments and Pleasures

## KERES

I stood staring at the portal. The events at the last revel had been agony, and every waking moment since, my mind tumbled over any possible solution to get her back through.

It was obvious I wasn't going to be able to keep Bevgyah from destroying Rosalin.

*My Rosalin.*

I closed my eyes, forced to relive the moments over and over again. Bevgyah's hands as they roamed over Rosalin's body. The shift in Rosalin's emotions—from terror to anger.

"What an unusual place to hide."

I straightened as the Hag's voice shaved over my skin. I was hoping she wouldn't bother looking for me quite yet. It usually took her a day before she grew interested in me again. The bruises from the shadows she'd shackled me with hadn't healed yet.

"I'm curious to know why you seem so adamant I not enjoy my newest maiden."

I closed my eyes, taking deep breaths, trying to keep my expression as innocuous as possible.

"Have you touched her without my permission?" she asked as she circled me.

I tried to force the fury that was burning in my chest deeper down where it could simmer until I had a moment to myself. Getting angry in her presence never served me well.

"I've only embraced Tesanna in your presence, my queen." I couldn't lie. But she wasn't Tesanna until she'd come to this place.

"Have you met with her alone? Have you talked with her?"

I tightened. Bevgyah knew there was something different about Rosalin, and I knew I couldn't hide it forever. She'd eventually ask the right questions.

"Is she intrigued by you?"

"Yes."

"Is she attracted to you?"

I rolled my eyes. "They're all attracted to me. *You* are attracted to me. *Everyone* is fucking attracted to me."

She laughed, the sound grating against my growing anger.

"You poor, pathetic, beautiful monster."

Her hands dragged down the length of my silk shirt, her fingers tucking into the low neckline so she could touch my skin. Always my skin, because she owned me and could do whatever she wished with me. She never failed to remind me, like she had the night before. I wasn't sure if I was angrier about the fact she'd fucked me in the harem, or that she'd drugged me and restrained me to do it.

"Tell me, Gatekeeper, did you fuck her in the human world?"

I couldn't lie. No Fae could lie. I wasn't supposed to touch these women, not in the human world, not in the Unseelie Court. She would punish me and while I'd accepted that in the moment, I knew I'd regret my decision when the time came for me to actually receive my punishment. I swallowed, hoping she'd ask another question before I had a chance to answer.

"I can taste your attraction to her. It's thick and sweet." She groped lower. "How many rules have you broken, my tantalizing Blackwarden?" she crooned in my ear. "How am I to punish you this time?"

She stepped around to face me with a sinister grin. I had long since learned the beautiful face she wore was the greatest lie anyone could ever tell. Uttering lies was impossible, but there were other ways to change the truth without using words. For instance, her powers of glamour and shapeshifting, which were magnified by the lifeforce she siphoned from the human girls.

"Perhaps I should punish her—"

"Leave her—"

"Then tell me what is different!" she spat, her voice loud enough it echoed down the hall.

I squeezed my eyes shut. If I told her about imbuing the portraits I risked all of the maidens. When I opened my eyes, Bevgyah was waiting, her face a beautiful emotionless mask.

It didn't matter. I'd be accepting death over another five hundred years as her consort. And there was nothing she could do to remove my shadows from the portraits tucked away at the Gatehouse. At least not until she found someone else to open the portal.

"I imbue the portraits of the maidens before I bring them here. It helps dampen their emotions and shields them from the worst of the pain when you siphon their life away." I almost choked after I said it out loud. "I..." I took a deep breath. "I didn't finish her portrait. I can't imbue an unfinished portrait." I took a deep breath, letting it out with a shudder. "She's unprotected from your cruelty, and her emotions are entirely her own."

Bevgyah glared at me with an unyielding fury simmering in her eyes. "So, you've shielded all of them?"

"Yes."

"Since the very beginning?"

"After...Sara." I swallowed the sound of the name on my tongue.

When the Blackwarden family had been caught helping the humans in the Fae Wars, the Hag Queen had given me a choice. I could be put to death with my brethren for treason against the Unseelie Court, or I could submit as her consort until such time as she no longer desired me. But I was a fool. I had a lover in the human world.

When she found out, the punishment was far crueler than I could have ever imagined. She cursed me with my own magic, binding my shadows so I couldn't use them against her. She forced me to drag her human sacrifices through the portal every five years. And as one last gleeful addition to her curse, she locked away my ability to speak about any of it.

Then, as though trapping me in an endless cycle of dragging innocent girls to be slaves to her deviant desires wasn't bad enough, Bevgyah tortured my beloved Sara before siphoning her life all at once, killing her. All while I was shackled, naked to a wall, bound by my own shadows to bear witness to what my mistakes could truly cause.

I'd vowed to myself never to let anyone into my heart again. And I'd succeeded for nearly five hundred years.

"And what kept you from finishing this girl's portrait?"

I knew she'd come back to this. She knew the answer, but she would force me to say it. I shut my eyes a moment, letting the memory of Rosalin's lips on mine, the whisper of her breath over my skin, clear my head.

"Because..." I swallowed hard, trying to maintain my composure as my magic gathered behind me where it would remain useless against her. Rage built in my chest and sat in my stomach like hot coals. "Because she spent the night in my bed."

Bevgyah glared at me, and I glared back. If I was going to be punished for my *indiscretion*, I would make sure she felt every word of my confession like a spear through her chest.

"We made love. Slowly. Ravenously. Worshiping each other's bodies."

She tipped her chin up, struggling to mask the anger oozing from her and muddling with my own. She knew she couldn't hide her emotions from me. I felt all of her jealousy, rage, and disgusting joy at knowing she could justify torturing me.

"I didn't *fuck* her; I made sure every inch of her body was well and truly satisfied and then we made love again...*and again*. She slept curled in my arms until the sun woke us, and then we made love again."

Bevgyah's anger pulsed from her in rivulets that seeped into my mind, spurring my words, ripping them from me until I'd said everything I'd ever wanted to say.

"*Love,* Bevgyah. Something I will *never* give you. Not while I breathe. Not while I stand in the shadows. No matter how many times you try to take it from me, destroy me, tear me down, and lock me away. You will never have all of me."

I'd dug my own grave before handing her the blade to cut out my heart.

A wicked smile cracked her flawless face. "I may not be able to take your love from you, but I can take away that which you *do* love, Gatekeeper."

I'd known this would happen. In a way I begged for it. A merciful death that would end Rosalin's pain rather than prolong it until she died broken and used up.

Bevgyah took a step toward me, wrapping her hand around my throat and squeezing. Perhaps she'd kill me now instead. But she yanked me against her, bile rising in my throat at the touch of her skin. I clenched my jaw so tightly my teeth ached as her lips crashed into mine. I made a point not to reciprocate, my lips as immovable as the ice her crown was crafted from. My shadows spread out around me and pooled at her feet—useless and pathetic.

"We aren't done with this matter," she said as she turned and left me standing alone at the portal, shaking with fury, and the most profound sadness I'd felt in centuries.

## CHAPTER 29

# Without Permission

## ROSALIN

A sour unsettled feeling had taken up residence in my gut after the last revel. I knew it was only a matter of time before Bevgyah came for me again. She didn't seem like the type of person to let my rejection go unaddressed and unpunished.

But it wasn't just the queen. It was everything. It was how she'd treated her Blackwarden, the harem, the way I was expected to submit myself to her every whim. I sipped on floral tea at breakfast and decided eating was probably not a good idea. I tried to sit off to the side in the harem, but Nessa found me. She always found me. She was far more kind to me than I deserved.

"Are you okay?"

"I'll be fine."

She gave me an adorable frown. "I worried when you left so early from the revel."

"I don't care for them," I said, trying to keep my voice from wavering as tears prickled my eyes.

She rested a kind hand on my arm, her gaze holding mine. "I didn't like them when I first came as well, but you get used to them." There was so much honesty and well-meaning in her words. She was trying to be helpful, and I truly liked her for that. Even though I couldn't get the image of her dancing nearly naked out of my head.

After a long moment she smiled and left me to sit alone and think over everything that had happened. There'd been something in the wine the queen had forced me to drink. I couldn't remember all the details. It was like I only had pieces of what had happened. She'd touched me, kissed me, and I hadn't entirely disliked it. At some point she'd tried to do more, but her Blackwarden had stopped her. After that all I could remember was his eyes as they'd watched me. The image of him sprawled out on the futon half naked and beautiful. He'd protected me...again.

I wandered back to my room, hoping I could avoid the gossip of the other maidens. Their eyes made my skin crawl and reminded me how much I wanted to go home, even though I couldn't recall anything about it. Standing in my tiny room I remembered the book the Blackwarden had left for me. It was still tucked safely beneath the edge of my futon. The illustrations were beautiful, even the ones of the Dark Fae. As I flipped through, I realized there were notes in the margins. There was something so incredibly familiar about it. I continued to thumb through until I came to a page with an illustration that looked a shocking amount like *him*.

"*An apple is just an apple, whether green or midnight.*" I read aloud, the hair on the back of my neck standing on end.

I closed the book and slipped it back under my futon before I sat in the silence of my room for a long moment trying to decide what I was going to do, and why I felt I needed to do anything at all. When I couldn't figure it out, I flopped back on the futon and glared up at the silks hanging above, letting my mind wander over all the half memories, the way so many of them seemed to overlap with *him*.

As the day slipped into evening, I was so certain something terrible had happened that I snuck from the harem, determined to make sure the Blackwarden was okay. I'd already wandered these halls alone. If I needed to, I'd use the excuse that I'd gotten lost. I had, after all, only been in Bevgyah's palace a short time.

Lucky for me, I didn't need the excuse. The palace seemed empty. Braziers lit my way as I wandered from hall to hall, then ascended the elegant flight of stairs to the upper floor. I'd been here once before, but I'd been rushed along by one of the queen's guards. I hadn't noticed there were fewer braziers, and the walls like the hall below, were decorated with murals of monsters and Fae chasing naked humans. I made the mistake of looking closer and quickly turned away, that feeling of having seen something similar before coming to this place creeping through me.

The further down the hall I went the more certain I was that I'd come to the right place. I don't know why, but up ahead, a single door at the end called to me. I could feel it, like a beacon burning through the palace. I was about to knock but decided to do something brash and likely very stupid. I turned the knob. The door was unlocked, and I slipped in, careful to pull it closed behind me quickly, for fear someone might have seen me enter. A brazier flared to life as I turned to face the room.

I gasped, unable to believe what I saw. He was chained up like a prisoner, hanging from a bracket on the ceiling. His head lolled between his arms as his long blue hair draped down his chest. The chains were only long enough for him to stand, and he sagged with the effort. His wings hung wide behind him, as though he didn't have the strength to hold them tucked against his back.

"Blackwarden!"

He lifted his head, his face weary with exhaustion and confusion. I realized he was naked, shadows seeming to wrap around him and partially obscuring his lower half. I swallowed the tickle of embarrassment that I'd barged in on something I shouldn't have, realizing the brazier had been dark.

He'd been left alone like this.

Rage flashed through me so hot it threatened to rip from my chest in a growl. I rushed to him but stopped short at the way he glared, those silver eyes of his like frozen daggers.

"You can't touch me," he said, his voice gravelly from disuse.

"Why has she done this to you?" My hands hovered in front of him, wanting to sweep the hair from his face, to try and pull him down from where he was chained, to do something to help him when I was likely the reason he was in this position.

"It doesn't matter. I'll be fine." He gave me a weak smile, beautiful and sad. "She'll have her way and then let me go. She has to, or no one can pass through the gate."

He was right. As the Gatekeeper he was necessary. It was his magic that brought people back and forth from the Unseelie Court to the human world. Without his shadows she would have to find someone else who could accomplish the task.

"I can't leave you like this."

"You can, and you must," he said with so much anguish in his voice. "Please. I've accepted this to stop her from..." He hung his head in defeat. "I won't be able to help you, if she finds you here."

He'd told me not to touch him, but I reached for his chin cradling his face in my hand. He didn't pull away, instead he relaxed into my palm, the warmth of his face drawing me in.

"Why does she do this to you?"

He swallowed, squeezing his eyes closed. "Because I was a different person once. I did things I shouldn't have done to get what I wanted. I was cruel to her and this is my punishment."

I don't know what possessed me. Some half-hidden piece of my heart insisted it knew him from a life before this one. It was a craving so deeply rooted in my soul, burrowing into my chest. I couldn't stop myself. I stepped closer.

He took a sharp breath, as if my proximity was too much, too intense. It wasn't fear, it was...longing. I leaned closer, brushing my lips over his, the heat of him soaking into my blood. When I shut my eyes, he was there, with gold-stained lips from the last revel. Sprawled out on a futon at my feet. There was another male, almost superimposed. Gold chains, his skin beneath my fingertips.

I closed the distance, kissing him gently at first, feeling his tongue glide along my lips before I opened my mouth to him. Fire writhed through my veins—hot and delirious and terrifying. I needed more. I wrapped my fingers around his neck, feeling his pulse flutter against my palm.

I lost myself in the delicious scent of his skin, my fingers tracing the muscles of his arms to his neck and over his collarbones. A memory of a man sitting across a table—his hair was short, but the same color blue. He had black horns but was so pale. He smirked at me with daring eyes.

I knew him.

The Blackwarden strained against the shackles, pressing his body against mine and deepening the kiss. A soft moan vibrated through him into me, igniting my entire body as my hands trailed down the sides of his torso. Firm muscles flexed beneath my touch. So soft. His skin was so soft. I'd felt this skin before. Pale skin, a beautiful face.

I knew him.

When I finally...reluctantly stepped back, his silver eyes glowed a dangerous white, his lips still parted as he stared at me with more wanting than I was prepared for. The need in the way his shoulders rose and fell with each ragged breath he took broke me in half, yanking a piece of my soul to leave at his feet.

"You need to go," he growled, as shadows built behind him, swallowing his wings and reaching around him like twisted fingers. "Please."

I blinked a few times, not fully registering what he said. Slowly his words settled over me like new snow, cooling the heat that writhed through me like a boiling river. I turned and ran, not looking back, not bothering to close the door behind me. I ran through the empty hall of Bevgyah's palace with tears obscuring the lower half of my vision and a fading memory of a man who looked like the Blackwarden.

I didn't make it far.

As I rounded a corner I ran square into a guard and stumbled on to my backside. Shaking away my momentary double vision, I found myself looking up into the armored mask of one of Bevgyah's guards. It was the one with orange skin hiding beneath his visor, the one who had dragged me to the queen before. He lunged for me, but I scrambled away, slamming my back against a wall and pressing the breath from my lungs. Choking, I tried to sidestep, but he was faster and a hot hand clamped down hard on my wrist.

"Her Majesty has been looking for you."

Something about the way he nearly yanked me off my feet was different and dangerous. There was conviction as he dragged me back down the hall I'd just come. My feet scraped over the stone as I writhed in his solid grip. I wasn't strong enough, and after a moment of struggling against him, I changed tactics.

"What does she want with me?"

He didn't answer, instead he jerked me along harder, sending threads of pain down my arm. I'd managed to escape Bevgyah's hungry hands, but how many times had it been her Blackwarden stopping her? And if he wasn't there to help me because he was shackled in his room...?

I'd seen what she did to him, it wasn't hard to believe she would do the same or worse to me. With renewed fear simmering in my stomach, I tried to pull away from the guard again, but his hand squeezed tighter, bruising my arm. I had no choice. I was going to the queen whether I liked it or not.

He knocked before entering then thrust me to the ground, my knees slamming into the unforgiving stone. I yelped in pain as I collapsed in front of Bevgyah where she sat on a plush sofa, twirling a braid of hair around her index finger. She was alone, a glass of golden wine in her other hand.

"Ah, my favorite pet. We have much to discuss." She waved away the guard, and he pulled the door closed behind him. "Tell me, have you touched my Blackwarden without my permission?"

I was frozen in terror. I had. I'd kissed him when I found him chained up in his room. I'd run my hands over his gorgeous body. I'd longed for more. How had she found out, I'd only just fled from his room? Was there some way of knowing? Some Fae magic that could reveal the shadows of my fingers on the Blackwarden's beautiful skin?

"He was chained up in his room," I slammed my hands over my mouth. I hadn't meant to speak. The words had tumbled from me before I could stop them.

Her eyes narrowed. "And what were you doing in his room?"

She stood, walking with slow deliberate steps in my direction, every sway of her hips mesmerizing as I tried to think of the answer to her question that wasn't absolutely ridiculous. I'd been there because I'd had a bad feeling. But how could I explain this to her when she was the reason for the bad feeling? She traced her fingers over my bare shoulders as she walked around me then stopped abruptly, smoothing over the spot on my neck that the miniscule Fae had pointed out when I'd first woken in this place.

"I haven't noticed this before." She pushed my hair away, running her fingers through to the ends. "Where did this mark come from?"

My breath hitched. How was I going to explain this? I didn't remember where I'd gotten it. Only that the little Fae female had been concerned enough that she'd concealed it.

"I don't know, your Majesty." I swallowed hard. "I had it when I arrived."

She sucked in a sharp breath across her teeth. "I see."

She circled me again as I started trembling beneath her merciless stare. "Sweet Tesanna. I have only a few rules for my maidens." She stood in front of me, anger glittering in her eyes as shadows seemed to swirl up her legs to her torso. It was the same magic she'd used to restrain her Blackwarden at the last revel, and it only made my trembling intensify. "The most important being that you cannot *touch* my Blackwarden without my permission."

I couldn't move as the shadows curled around my legs, freezing the blood in my muscles firmly in place. I just stared into her frigid eyes, my heart racing, body rigid. She would kill me, or worse, she would punish me as she'd punished him.

And I deserved it.

## CHAPTER 30
# Broken Rules

### KERES

I honestly assumed Bevgyah would leave me chained up in my room until the next revel. I'd broken all her rules and intended to break a few more as soon as I was physically able. After she'd pulled me down and had her way with me, she'd left me sprawled out on the floor with my wrists still shackled. I was too exhausted to move when a guard came and finally released me. At some point I'd managed to drag myself to my bed, but a sick feeling had settled in my stomach and made it impossible for me to rest.

I thought I could endure, but I couldn't. My heart had woven so tightly around Rosalin, I couldn't bear to see her suffer. Her hands on my body when she'd kissed me branded my soul with certainty. I had to find a way to get her out of here, and I was more than willing to die to do it.

Rolling out of bed, I held on to the canopy post for balance as I stood straight, tucking my wings against my back. Every inch of my body ached from standing in chains for twenty-four hours. The bruises around my wrists were beginning to fade, but the pain penetrated deep into my bones.

This curse kept me from taking Rosalin back through the portal, but there had to be another way to get her out of the Unseelie Court. I needed to continue distracting Bevgyah until I figured it out. And I needed to do it fast because I was running out of time to request my sentence be changed. Once Rosalin was safe, I could remind the Hag Queen of the loophole, and once I was dead, my hope was Bevgyah would lose interest in Rosalin. This was all I could do for her now. If only I had full use of my shadows, but I'd failed to figure out how to break the curse, and I was truly worthless as the queen's Blackwarden.

I trudged down the hall toward the Hag's suite in nothing but pants. I didn't bother getting completely dressed. She'd want me naked anyway. If I was lucky, she'd be readying herself to wander down to her harem. She'd barred me from entering there until further notice, and after the years of enduring her punishments, I knew I had little hope of forcing my way.

I didn't knock. I barged in, half expecting to find her in the middle of some nefarious entertainment. Instead, my heart plummeted into my stomach. A pale human girl had been shackled up in Bevgyah's room. One with very familiar brown hair. I had a perfect view of her bare back, ligature bruising around her thighs and ankles. I sucked in a breath, trying to control the shadows building around me as my fury ignited.

A sob escaped Rosalin as she wriggled in an attempt to look behind her and see who'd just entered. "Please, Majesty," she whimpered as she shifted her weight. "No more. I beg you."

"Don't move," I said, rage dripping from my voice. This was my fault. I was the idiot who had confessed to loving Rosalin knowing Bevgyah would retaliate. I was responsible for every scrap of Rosalin's punishment. Every bruise, every pain she felt. Something raw and terrible cracked open inside me as I took each step closer.

I reached up and fumbled with the shackles at her wrists. I'd need a key. A sob escaped her as I started throwing open drawers in a mad attempt to find some way to get her down. There was nothing. I turned back to her, anger and fear vibrating through me in a strange mix as she hung there, naked and broken. I'd have to try and use my magic, what pathetic slivers of it I could manipulate.

She watched me with weary eyes as I stepped closer. Without thinking, I reached for her face. She flinched at my touch, and I cursed myself. Bevgyah had likely done more than siphon her. I'd been abused by the Hag for hundreds of years. I would have flinched too if I didn't know what was going on.

"I'm sorry," she said, another tear gliding down her cheek.

"You have nothing to apologize for." I closed my eyes, begging my shadows for help. If the Mother abandoned me entirely after, I'd accept my fate.

Here in the Unseelie Court, so close to Bevgyah, what little magic I had was unpredictable and hard to control. She'd done such a good job of twisting my shadows around her own magic, they were nearly worthless to me, other than for opening the portal.

But I had to try.

I focused on the locks at Rosalin's wrists. I was familiar with these shackles. They'd been around my own wrists earlier in the day. Taking a deep breath, I reached with my mind, hoping my shadows would follow, willing them to turn the tumblers in the locks. I hadn't attempted anything like this in ages, but I was desperate. It had to work because I had to get Rosalin down.

There was no other option. I had to save her.

Seconds slipped by as I focused. It was taking too long, and I worried Bevgyah would come barging in at any moment. I was too busy focusing on the locks to pay attention to any emotions other than Rosalin's hope that radiated out from her like a beacon. She had far more faith in me than I had in myself.

She was silent, her soft breaths calm as they caressed my shoulder. I wanted to open my eyes, to hold her, to close the distance between my lips and hers, but I needed to *focus*. Another moment, and I heard the unmistakable click of a lock then reached up to pull one of her wrists free. She clung to me as I switched my focus to the other shackle.

When the second lock clicked open, I pulled her against me, holding her weight entirely. I was scared I'd hurt her if I touched her in the wrong places, but she didn't shy away, wrapping her arms over my shoulders and clinging to me as she trembled in fear. When she finally stood on both feet, she swayed from the effort. Worried she wasn't strong enough to stand on her own, I swept her into my arms.

"I've got you," I said as I set her on the bed and took her face in my hands.

She avoided my gaze as I looked her over for injuries. Her eyes were hollow and lined with dark circles, lips deathly pale. Her usually rosy cheeks had been reduced to a sickly pallor. They were all signs of being heavily siphoned.

"Are you hurt?"

She squeezed her eyes shut, shaking her head. I could feel her despair, her shame. She was trying to disappear from what Bevgyah had done to her. Horrible embarrassing things. But I just needed to know that she would be okay.

"Please, Rosalin. Talk to me."

She looked at me with wide eyes. My own growing round. I blinked hard a few times as if clearing my mind from a dream.

How had I been able to speak her name? The curse had kept me from saying it out loud since coming to the Unseelie Court.

"What did you call me?"

## CHAPTER 31

# Hag's Heart

## ROSALIN

The name he used wrapped around me and squeezed, like the most glorious embrace I'd ever been blessed with. *This* was my name.

But how had he known it?

He took a step back, the muscles in his neck tightening. There was something so familiar about the way he looked at me, a desperate ache in his expression. *I knew him.* I had to have known him before coming here, but pulling the memories forward was... painful. Searing white light lanced behind my eyes as I tried desperately to remember, but I couldn't push through the agony.

He glanced over his shoulder at the door before grabbing a silk robe off the back of a chair and holding it open for me.

"I need to get you out of here."

I slipped my arms into the sleeves and wrapped the fabric tight around my nakedness. Before I was able to do anything else, he lifted me back into his arms and carried me from the room. I pressed my face against his neck, trying to hide from the world, from this place, from everything. I wasn't sure I'd survive the memories of Bevgyah's hands, the ropes she'd tied me into position with. The way her mouth felt on my body. Instead, I focused on the way he kissed the top of my head, how warm his skin was against mine, his familiar scent. I knew as soon as Bevgyah found out he'd taken me down from the shackles, we'd both be in trouble. I shouldn't have touched him. I shouldn't have looked at him. I definitely shouldn't have kissed him. And I shouldn't have been in his arms at that very moment.

He ducked into his own suite and set me down on the edge of his bed, glancing around the space with wild eyes.

"I don't know where to take you." He ran his fingers through his hair, leaving it wild around his horns and over his shoulders.

I tried to sit up straight, but my whole body ached, and I slumped over, losing my fight against the pain. He was there in an instant, warm hands helping me lay down at the foot of his bed where I curled in on myself. A moment later he was covering me with a blanket.

"I have to get you out of the Unseelie Court."

I don't know when I started, but I was crying again, squeezing my knees to my chest. I just wanted to die. It seemed so much easier than this life I was living, that I didn't seem to have any other escape from.

The bed moved, and then the blanket before he tucked himself against me. I was too tired and broken to push him away, and even if I could, I wasn't sure I wanted to. If there was one person in this place that I wanted near me, it was him, but I still couldn't understand why. What was it about him that was so comforting? So familiar?

"I failed to protect you." His voice was soft beside my ear, smoothing over the rough shards of my nerves. "I'm sorry." His voice caught with anguish.

I turned toward him, not realizing how close my face would be to his. I swallowed hard as I gazed into his silver eyes, desperate to ignore the need boiling inside me to close the distance between our lips.

"Why are you helping me? She'll punish you again. Why would you do it knowing that?" I took a shuddering breath, squeezing my eyes shut to focus my thoughts. "She'll hurt you. Why does she hurt you?"

His fingers slipped through my hair. I craved his touch, pressing my face against the palm of his hand. I felt like I wasn't close enough to him as I turned and wrapped my arms around his chest and nuzzled into his neck.

"I need you to remember," he whispered into my hair. "Because I can't..."

He tightened around me, and I glanced up at him. His face was pinched with pain, his breath shallow. I pushed back; fearful I'd hurt him. After an agonizing moment, he pulled himself up, leaving me cold where he'd just been lying beside me.

"I won't be able to go with you," he said as he started looking for something in his wardrobe. "It's the only way. I'll have someone else take you away from here."

As much as I wanted to stay wrapped in a blanket at the foot of his bed, I struggled to my feet and stumbled toward him. I didn't make it far before he turned to catch me from falling over my own clumsy feet. He drew me against him, tucking my head under his chin, strong arms wrapping around me.

"I'm sorry I don't remember," I said with a quiver in my voice.

"It's not your fault. None of this is your fault. Please. It's my—" He stiffened and stepped back from me. "Fuck." His eyes went wide. "She's here."

The hair rose on the back of my neck as he pushed me toward the door that led into his bathroom. Once inside, he clutched both my shoulders, glaring at me with glowing silver eyes.

"I need you to stay in here. Please. No matter what I say or what she does." He was turning away before I could protest.

I was about to push out of his bathroom after him when Bevgyah barged in, and I had a dreadful view of her fury from the bathroom door left ajar. It made me burn with anger the way she treated him. Really, the way she treated all of her "precious pets" as objects with which she could do whatever she wished. I clutched the doorknob with more force than I'd intended as she struck him across the face, throwing his head to the side.

"Where is she?" she shrieked. "Where have you taken her?"

Bevgyah's eyes were wild as she looked around his room, holding on the blanket at the foot of his bed a little longer than I liked.

"Who are you looking—"

She struck him again.

"You know who, Blackwarden."

"What makes you think I'd hide her from you?" His voice was so calm. Far calmer than it had any right to be. I don't know how he managed to keep his tone so even with the way Bevgyah stepped closer to him, digging her sharp fingernails into his hair and yanking his face toward hers.

"You can try to weave around my questions, but I know your ways." She kissed him before she slapped him again. "Try to protect her all you want. You will fail. And when I find her, I will destroy every scrap of her soul."

Why did she treat him this way? What had he done to deserve this?

"You knew what you did when you marked her. You happily condemned her."

A shiver writhed down my spine as my fingers reached for the mark at the base of my neck, the memory of Bevgyah's rising anger when she'd noticed it.

"You knew what you were doing," Bevgyah sneered as she stepped closer. "Beg me for her life on your knees, Blackwarden."

I struggled to watch. It was the revel all over again. And again, there was nothing I could do but watch her hurt him. I was helpless. I covered my mouth to hold my anguish inside, searching half memories and foggy thoughts to find something that could save him.

He'd told me to remember. Remember what? There was nothing in my mind but fragments of another life and terror of this one.

He kneeled before Bevgyah, defeated, his arms limp at his sides as she yanked his face toward her by his horns. Why didn't he do anything to stop her? He should have been strong enough to fight back, but he didn't.

His wings sagged behind him revealing tight toned muscles and...from this angle I could see what looked like silver markings that snaked around where his wings met his shoulder blades. *I knew those tattoos.* I'd seen them before. I *knew* I'd seen them before. Delicate serpentine dragons that danced down his spine. A piercing headache flashed behind my eyes, and I squeezed them shut. So many things that were only half there, but I needed to remember.

"Have you lost your will to live?"

"I haven't had it for quite some time, I assure you."

Bevgyah leaned down closer to his ear. "I plan to make her suffer, bleed, and die before you for this," she said with a breathy voice. "I'll make her beg for death before I'm finished with her."

He didn't move, a beautiful black statue that came with a flash of a memory. Serpents on either side of stone steps. I racked my brain. There had to be something there. Something important that I could remember. The foggy edges of a place, black walls and golden light. A delicious green apple.

"Has life been so horrible at my side, Blackwarden?"

He didn't answer, and I suspected it was because whatever he'd say would have been unfavorable. True, but definitely not what the queen wanted to hear.

"I've tried so hard to tame your arrogant heart. Perhaps this hasn't been an appropriate punishment?"

Arrogant heart... There was a smirking face, beautiful, with dark eyes and pale skin and black horns. A hand reaching to take mine.

"Why is it you never do as I ask?" she spat.

"I've done your bidding for five hundred years, Bevgyah. Perhaps you've forgotten."

Five hundred years? He'd been her prisoner, her consort for *five hundred years*? This was how he managed to stay so calm. As horrifying as it was to think, he was used to her torture.

"I forget *nothing*. That's why you're here!" she said.

"There's one thing you've forgotten, Bevgyah." His voice held a silky tone; it curled around me and pulled my hand to the doorknob again.

I knew that voice. There were faces. So many faces in golden frames. A man sitting across from me at a table. Two delicate black glass egg cups in front of him.

"You gave me a choice, death or to submit as your consort, but after five hundred years, I can choose differently."

Bevgyah didn't move.

The air seemed to freeze in the room. What was he saying?

"You would choose death now? When you're so close to having your pathetic human lover?"

"I would choose death over spending another day chained to *you*."

Thick silence clung to everything as his words settled into my bones.

The sound of a blade being pulled from a sheath scraped across my consciousness as Bevgyah's lips curled into a snarl.

She would kill him.

And I would watch him die.

He took a sharp breath as she pressed a dagger to his throat.

"I *should* kill you. All the hardship you've caused me. Your traitorous heart, your unfaithfulness. You thought you could outwit me, could fool me into stealing my crown." She shook her head slowly. "I should have killed you long ago, you wretched beautiful beast."

"Then do us both the favor," he said, his voice even and fearless.

I channeled his bravery. If he could be fearless in the face of death, then I could too.

I stepped from the bathroom.

Bevgyah's eyes snapped to mine, a fury so thick burning in them my knees felt weak. A wicked smile crept across her flawless face.

"I knew you'd found your little plaything," Bevgyah said as she looked back down at him, pressing the blade harder against his throat, a dark trail of blood running over his Adam's apple.

"Please, don't hurt him," I begged, but words weren't going to save him.

"I can do whatever I want with him," she said as she took a fist full of his hair with her other hand and jerked his head, the dagger slicing into his skin a little deeper. "He's mine, and he will always be mine."

"I've asked for death, Bevgyah," he said with a deep contempt staining his words, leaning into the blade at his throat. "Kill me."

"Keres, no!" The words slipped from my lips as I took another step closer.

His name seeped through me, hot and perfect, and with it my memories came flooding back all at once with blinding, painful ferocity. The Gatehouse with its dark hallways. Volunteering in place of my sister. Renee. Keres, the stubborn, gorgeous Dark Fae. The frustrating brazier outside my suite. The ever-changing mural. His soft, decadent lips. His boring breakfast of two eggs and toast. The book of children's fairy tales. The delicious weight of his body. His laugh. A green apple. His silky soft skin beneath my fingers. The surprise in his eyes when I'd asked a question he knew he couldn't answer. The single tear that had slipped down his cheek before he'd brought me through the portal.

Keres.

My head felt as though it would split in half, my knees trembling beneath me. I'd spent eight days with him. Eight maddening days. They had been both the most terrifying and the most amazing days of my life. I spent those eight days breaking down his walls to find a very different Keres than the one I'd first met.

Perhaps it had all happened too fast, but standing here, watching Bevgyah hold a knife to his throat...

I remembered everything.

"I love you, Keres," I whispered through the pain in my skull.

The room went dreadfully still.

Like melting ice, Bevgyah slowly shifted back from him, taking the dagger with her. She shook against whatever force it was that held her.

"What are you doing?" she said with a shrill voice. "You can't use your shadows on me! I own them! They're mine! *You* are mine!"

Keres rose from his knees, wings spreading wide like a magnificent, midnight dragon. His hands were fists at his sides. I risked stepping closer as Bevgyah fought against whatever invisible force held her in place. But it wasn't invisible. Shadows crept around her legs and snaked over her skin to wrap around her wrists and neck. They pooled between her and Keres, thick like muddy water—the same shadows she'd used to restrain him at the last revel.

Keres took a smooth step forward and ripped the dagger from her hand as if she'd been turned into stone.

"May this thaw your fucking cold, dead heart, Hag."

And he plunged it into her chest.

## CHAPTER 32

# Out of Time

### KERES

Gripping Rosalin's hand, I pulled her into the hallway behind me. We needed to get to the portal. We had precious seconds, and I wasn't even sure if I'd be able to get us both through.

The curse was broken!

She'd remembered my name. It wasn't just my name. *She'd said she loved me.* Somewhere hidden in her words had been the key to releasing me from five hundred years of misery, and I refused to fail to get her safely back home.

I'd just used my magic against Bevgyah for the first time in centuries. It had felt so deviously good. But I knew it was likely only because she hadn't expected it. Bevgyah was far more powerful than I had ever been.

"Wait, wait." Rosalin yanked her hand from mine, pulling the silk robe closed around her. "Where are we going?"

As much as I loved them, we didn't have time for her questions. I had to get her out of the Unseelie Court before Bevgyah killed one or both of us. We didn't have time for anything else, otherwise I might have grabbed my Blackwarden pendant, or her book of fairy tales. None of that mattered. They were things. Our lives couldn't be replaced, and I had a very renewed interest in living.

"I don't understand. How did I...How did you...?" She was shaking so violently, her voice trembled.

I took her face between my hands, hoping to reassure her. "You'll remember everything once I get us through the portal, but we have to go now." I took her hand, pulling her toward the stairs down to the main hall, thankful she didn't resist me. "A dagger to the heart won't stop a Hag for very long."

A blood curdling shriek echoed through the halls of the palace, and Rosalin flinched before entwining her fingers with mine. Her terror was so potent as it washed over me it made my knees weak.

I yanked her into my arms and jumped from the top step. I hadn't flown in ages, but it wasn't something one forgot how to do, especially not when an angry Hag was barreling through her palace after you. The halls were much narrower than the open stairs, and I was forced to drop to my feet as I rounded into the main hall.

"Stop him! Stop that fucking traitor!" Bevgyah shrieked, her voice shredding through the palace, burrowing into my courage like a maggot. I'd been cowed by this female for so long, it took all my strength to disobey her now.

Six guards ran toward us from the throne room and skidded to a halt when they saw us. I set Rosalin on her feet as gently as I could. I needed my hands for this. I would have transported us directly to the portal, but it had been so long since I'd attempted it with two people that I wasn't willing to take the risk. Not yet anyway.

I yanked at the shadows, feeling the full strength of them for the first time in entirely too long. They pooled at my feet waiting patiently to be commanded. The guards swayed with anticipation, polearms and swords at the ready. A soft hand on my bicep drew my attention. Rosalin's green eyes glittered in the light of the bra-ziers. She held my gaze, fear swimming between us until I felt her emotions shift into powerful conviction.

Without a word, I nodded then turned back to the guards, sending my shadows across the space between. They were sys-tematically yanked down into the darkness, one by one, as they screamed in agony. They'd live. My shadows couldn't kill; they could only terrify. They would face their greatest fears before being dropped into a heap somewhere on one of the lower levels of the palace. It was easy magic, not like transportation exactly. I didn't get to choose where they landed, and frankly, I didn't care.

By the sixth guard, I swayed on my feet. I'd used too much. It had been so long since I'd been able to do this, I'd forgotten my limits and as my vision blurred, I worried I'd used everything up. Rosalin took my arm, tucking hers against my chest to steady me. Blessed creature. I still wasn't sure I deserved her after all my failings.

"I'll fucking destroy you, Blackwarden!" Bevgyah's wicked voice sliced through the air, so much closer than I liked.

I shook off my moment of weakness. We needed to keep moving. I pulled Rosalin behind me as I stumbled into the portal room, not wasting any time as we approached the massive mirror. I summoned every last shred of my shadows. I didn't need to be alive on the other side; I just needed to get Rosalin through. We had seconds left, and I wasn't sure I could summon my magic fast enough.

Shadows oozed across the ground like heavy smoke, wicking into the mirror and turning it a brilliant shade of blue. The silver surface shimmered and twisted as I pressed the last remnants of my shadows into it, my vision doubling before straightening back out. I turned in time to see Bevgyah round the corner.

I might not have recognized her if I hadn't been expecting the Hag that stood before me. Her face was little more than a skull, with withered, sagging flesh clinging to the bone like melting wax. All the beauty she'd cultivated was gone, leaving nothing but her true face. It was startling after I'd known her mask for centuries. She'd needed to use every scrap of her own magic to heal herself after I'd put a dagger in her heart.

"You..." She pointed a long bony finger in my direction. "You vile monster! I should have known exactly what you were when I met you."

Four more guards flooded into the room behind her, but they were immediately confused. The withered old Hag between us wasn't the queen they'd come to know.

"Get him," she yelled.

But the guards didn't move. They hesitated, looking from her to me. My face was recognizable, but she was a stranger.

"I said, get the Blackwarden," she shrieked.

One of the guards took a step closer to Rosalin, drawing his sword. I refused to take any chances. Not with Rosalin. I wrapped a protective arm around her waist, pulling her to my side and lifting my wings behind me.

"The curse is broken, Hag. I'm not your pet any longer." I took a few steps back toward the portal as the guards edged closer. "Let me go. Let me take her home, and I'll continue to be your Gatekeeper," I said, keeping my voice as calm as I could manage.

In truth, I was terrified I hadn't pressed enough of my magic into the portal. Terrified that at any second, the guards would lunge, and I wouldn't be fast enough to push Rosalin and myself through. Terrified that after everything—after she'd endured Bevgyah's hands, suffered the agony of being siphoned, remembered my name, and broken the curse—I would still fail to protect her. One final time.

After all she'd been through because of me, I couldn't fail her. I swallowed my fear, letting her words wash over me. *"I love you, Keres."* How could I tell her I loved her more than life itself, that her love had given me a second chance I didn't deserve, if I failed her now? How could I *show her* if I let her die?

"You're a fucking disgusting beast," the Hag spat. "You deserve worse than death, and I shall give it to you." She sprang past her guards, fingers curled into claws.

I wrapped Rosalin in my wings and stepped back through the portal.

# CHAPTER 33
# My Blackwarden

## ROSALIN

I woke on the cold floor, disoriented, the world spinning as I tried to push myself up. The warmth of a body touched my arm, and I turned toward it.

Blue hair, dark skin, black horns. *Keres.*

I touched the tip of his pointed ear but he didn't stir.

"Keres?" I rolled toward him, cupping his face in my hands, my stomach bottoming out. "Keres," I whispered. My eyes flooding with tears as his eyes remained woefully closed.

He'd used too much of his magic. He was immortal, but that didn't mean he couldn't be killed. I gathered him into my arms and pressed my face against his neck, smothering my tears in his hair. I'd lost him—my Blackwarden, my second chance. He'd protected me so many times and I'd lost him.

"Please, Keres."

His arms wrapped around me. A sob broke free in my relief. It was real and hot, washing through me as he gathered me against him, tucking my head under his chin and ceaselessly hugging me. I melted into him, ignoring the silk robe slipping from my shoulders, savoring the heat of his bare skin, the scent of him. I was lost in his arms, and I never wanted to be found.

"You remembered," he said into my hair before kissing my head.

He pushed us up, pulling me onto his lap, my legs immediately enveloping his waist. I snuggled against him, wrapping my own arms over his and digging my fingers into his long hair. I refused to let him go. Not yet.

Maybe never.

My time in the Unseelie Court was blurry, but based on what I could remember I didn't want to remember it clearly. I pulled back to look at him, cradling his face in my hands as his eyes washed over my face. I was seeing the real Keres for the first time with all my faculties, and my heart intact. I'd always found him beautiful, but he was...painfully gorgeous. The way the light glazed his black skin with a silver sheen that accentuated every muscle, the curve of his lips, the line of his jaw. I struggled to look away. He was Dark Fae, as he'd said, in every sense of the term. So inhumanly beautiful.

A line of blood trailed down his throat.

"You're bleeding." An insatiable urge to check him over for other injuries flashed through me as my hands roamed over his shoulders.

"It's nothing."

"I...I'm so sorry," I said through another sob. "I couldn't help you."

He leaned forward, pressing his forehead to mine. "Never apologize again, Ms. Greene."

I pulled back enough to glare at him as a smile crept across his face. I must have looked completely confused.

"Glorious creature, you broke the curse." He held my chin firmly in place.

I wasn't prepared for the ache his gaze left in me. The smile slipped from his face as his eyes fell to my lips. I didn't wait for him to kiss me. I crashed into him, hungry for the taste of him. He moaned into my mouth, the sound sending sparks of heat through me as my fingers followed the lines of his neck to his bare chest. I eased back from him breathless, remembering the moments before he pulled me through the portal.

I remembered his name. That wasn't what broke the curse. I'd told him I loved him. I'd confessed in front of the Hag Queen. *I loved him.* It didn't matter what face he wore; I loved *him.* Somehow, a Dark Fae wormed himself into my angry heart, and I didn't know how or when, but I wouldn't change it for the world. He was my midnight apple, and I loved him.

"Rosalin?" The sound of my name from his lips was the sweetest thing I'd ever heard.

I smiled as I kissed him again.

I'd struggled to help Keres to his suite. After using so much of his magic to escape Bevgyah and then to open the gate back to the human world, he was beyond exhausted. I'd forced him into bed to rest. Even though he'd begged me to stay with him, I feared my presence would only be distracting. I knew I, for one, would struggle to keep my hands to myself.

Instead, I told him I was going to see if I could find anything in the library on warding the portal, or his Gatehouse against anyone coming through, and he reluctantly let me slip away. I don't know what I thought I was going to find, but when I entered the library the braziers flared to life, a stack of books waiting for me on a side table next to a comfortable chair.

"I missed you, too," I said to the ceiling, the nearest brazier flickering in response.

Diving into the books I skimmed quickly, finding most of them were in Old Fae. I'd have to give these to Keres when he was well enough to read through them himself. I set them aside and focused on the ones I could read instead, trying to find something on wards or hexes that might keep certain people away. I worried that if we didn't do something, once

Bevgyah managed to find someone to open the portal she'd come for him.

I couldn't lose him. Not again. I had almost lost him forever, in the cruelest way possible. I shivered realizing he had been forced to see me every day, unable to call me by my real name, unable to speak with me without risking the Hag Queen's punishments. And now that I knew what those punishments were, I shuddered to think of how often he might have had to endure them.

I squeezed tears back with a deep breath and set the book aside, an overwhelming need to make sure he was alright washing over me. I slipped out into the hall but stopped short.

The mural was gone.

I was frozen in place, staring at a blank wall. I ran my fingers along where I was certain it had been, but there was nothing. Just the textured black walls. No dragons, monsters, or naked humans. No trees or landscapes. I traced the length of it all the way to Keres' suite where there *was* something.

It was small. Two silhouettes with their backs to the outside world. One of them had horns, the other leaned against him, her brown hair obscuring much of her details. It was rushed. Each brush stroke was intentional but rough.

When had this been painted? I looked up at the brazier, my mind reeling.

"Did you paint this?" The brazier dimmed. But I knew in my heart who painted the mural. It made sense. He painted the portraits with such pristine detail, why wouldn't he be capable of painting this mural as well. I had vague memories of the same type of mural on the walls of Bevgyah's palace, the only other place he spent significant time.

I touched the silhouettes, certainty blooming in my chest. Something about them helped ease my fears that I wasn't just another human passing through Keres' long life. Maybe he cared for me as much as I had come to care for him.

"Can I stay here?"

I don't know why I asked out loud. The brazier outside Keres' door flared brighter in response. I smiled at the ceiling before I turned and slipped into his room.

## CHAPTER 34

# For the First Time

## KERES

I woke to Rosalin reading in a chair beside my bed. My throat tightened. I had almost lost her forever, and I still wasn't sure I deserved her at all. The fact that my actions over five hundred years ago had been the catalyst of all her pain was overwhelming.

Her soft pink cheeks glowed with more life than they had in the Unseelie Court. Her green eyes shining much more intensely. Perhaps I saw her through a different lens, but she was achingly beautiful—human and imperfectly perfect. I smirked at how her lips moved as she read. Those fucking lips. Heat simmered deep in my core at the thought of them on my skin. Why had I waited so long to kiss them? Why had I pushed her away?

But I knew why. I'd been forbidden. My heart had been locked in Bevgyah's clutches for centuries. I'd lost hope that I could give it to anyone ever again, knowing what the Hag would do when she inevitably found out. This wasn't the only reason, though. I worried no one could see past my face to the person beneath. And even if they did, I was terrified of what they'd find.

I'd been a true monster once. The purest, most dangerous beast, hidden beneath a beautiful face. I'd betrayed people—manipulated them. I'd done vile things to get what I wanted. My arrogance had gotten me to this place and in all honesty, I deserved every moment I spent chained to Bevgyah's side. I deserved her torture, her sadism, her hatred. She'd been a young queen, easily wooed by a handsome Dark Fae, and I'd taken advantage of my status as her lover. I'd found all the ways to lie without words. I'd made her what she was with every manipulation, every traitorous act.

I knew one thing for sure. My punishment had changed me, and I never wanted to go back to being the Keres Blackwarden I'd been all those centuries ago. I shivered at the thought of the things I'd done; the people I'd destroyed to get what I wanted. Even now, I wasn't sure I deserved the second chance I'd been given. Especially since that second chance included the rare creature beside me. A human who'd been able to see past her own hatred of my kind, past the monster I tried to be, to see the me that hid in the shadows. I swallowed hard, unsure if I deserved the happiness she brought me just by staying by my side while I recovered from using too much of my magic.

I don't know how long I lay there watching Rosalin read. I would have watched her longer, but she glanced up, her eyes brightening when she met my gaze, a smile melting onto her lips.

"Hello, dark stranger," she said, reaching a hand over and resting it on my arm. "How are you feeling?"

"Like I brought twenty people through the portal."

She smirked. "Well, you only brought two people through, but one of them had these massive wings."

I rolled my eyes and reached for her. She giggled as she snuggled in next to me, fingers tracing over my bare shoulder and sending goosebumps over my flesh.

She pulled back suddenly, eyes going wide.

"Something the matter, Ms. Greene?"

"The mark..." She pulled her hair away from her shoulder so I could see

I wasn't sure what I was looking at, at first. A tiny serpent with wings twisted around itself into the shape of a very familiar symbol.

"It hasn't always looked like that has it?" I asked as I ran my fingertips over her skin.

She shook her head. "It changed. I think when we came back through the portal."

There were ancient stories about marks left by magic. Stories of things like Fate Marks and brands that showed up when two Fae claimed one another as mates. But Rosalin wasn't Fae. Still, I couldn't deny what the symbol looked like. It was the Blackwarden family name in Old Fae. I touched my chest. I'd left my pendant behind in our mad rush to get through the portal. Not that it mattered. I knew what it looked like.

I swallowed hard. The guilt that welled in my chest as I realized I might have claimed her without her consent was painful. It burned deep, like a thousand fire demons trying to rip their way from my ribcage. I squeezed back tears that I refused to shed. I couldn't feel sorry for myself, I needed to do better, to *be* better. I never wanted to ensnare someone after I'd been chained to a heartless bitch for five hundred years. I hadn't exactly asked Rosalin what she wanted when I bit her neck in a moment of vulnerability, and I refused to take someone's choice away from them. *Never again.* I would let her choose, even if it meant she'd likely return to her family and leave me alone with my Gatehouse.

I would always let her choose.

"I don't entirely know what it means." My words were misleading, but true. I didn't *entirely* know. "Is that all that's troubling you?"

She watched me carefully, her glittering eyes burning into me. I was certain she could see the tears I'd refused to shed, the pain that was searing a hole through my lungs. She knew I wasn't telling her everything. After a long moment a smile tugged at her lips.

"You know, right now, I can honestly say there's nothing."

It took all my strength not to let out a massive sigh of relief, a sudden need to have her closer, to have her skin against mine gripped my insides.

"There is one thing wrong," I said as I lifted a corner of my blanket. "You're entirely too far away from me right now."

She snuck beneath the covers and straddled me, her lips immediately falling on my neck, hands smoothing over my chest. Her lips found mine, a slow and lingering kiss heated my blood as her tongue explored. This hadn't been my intention, but the last thing I was going to do was push her away. I'd been forced to do things I didn't want to do, with people I definitely didn't want to do them with, for so long that being kissed by her was like being kissed for the first time. And I refused to be embarrassed by how she made my body respond.

I gasped at her touch, so soft and gentle, as though she knew that it wasn't just my overuse of magic I was recovering from. She sat up, her hands whispering across my chest, eyes wide as if asking permission. I struggled to pull myself up to her lips, but she stopped me, pushing me back down onto my pillow with a slow head shake.

"You're recovering, Keres." A mischievous glint overshadowed the look of seriousness she tried to wear as she kissed down my chest, slipping beside me and pulling the blankets back as she continued to my stomach.

"Rosalin..."

"Yes, Keres?" she asked as she circled my navel with her tongue then kissed lower, her fingers feather soft as they pulled my pants further down.

"You don't have..." The rest of the words slipped away as she wrapped a hand and her lips around me.

Every muscle in my body tightened as her other hand splayed across my abdomen. Fuck, her mouth was...

"That's..." I couldn't hold back a whimper as she licked up the length of me. "...so good. So..."

"Something the matter, Keres?" she asked before she took me back into her mouth.

I tried to speak, but all I could manage were breathy moans.

When the curse broke, other things changed. I didn't entirely understand how, but I felt different. Perhaps it was because I was in the human world, wearing my own skin and not a glamour created to make me seem less Fae. Every lie I'd been forced to wear had been stripped away. I had the overwhelming sense that while I'd been given a rarely bestowed second chance, it could so easily be taken away.

I stood in front of the portal, hands clenched tight at my sides. I couldn't risk Bevgyah coming through. Maybe she wouldn't. Maybe she'd send an assassin to do her dirty work, but I couldn't take that chance.

There were more portals. Ones that lead to the other courts. There were ways Bevgyah could get here even without using this particular portal, which made me all the more certain of what I needed to do.

"Here you are." I flinched as Rosalin slipped her hand into mine and leaned her head against my shoulder. "I know what you're thinking, but I worry if you destroy this portal, you'll…" She choked on her words.

I already knew what she was going to say. I would no longer be immortal. I'd lose my connection to the Unseelie Court. As a Fae, I needed a tether to the Earth Mother's magic and the way I did that was through this portal. *My portal.* Which meant, I wouldn't have my shadows either. I swallowed, wondering if the Gatehouse would suffer as well. It wasn't entirely made of Dark Fae magic, but something much older.

"But that means…" Rosalin gazed up at me, fear in her eyes. "You'll grow old and die."

"Grow old and die, *with you*," I said as I leaned my forehead against hers. "Maybe I don't mind that so much."

She stepped away from me, that adorable frustration wrinkling her forehead. "Keres, I can't ask you to—"

I pressed a finger to her lips. "Ms. Greene."

She just stared at me with wide eyes, and I couldn't help the smile that spread across my lips.

"You didn't ask. The last time I opened my heart to someone, I didn't have an opportunity to give myself to her entirely before she was taken from me."

Heavy words pooled in my throat. Ones I should have said to her before I took her to the Unseelie Court. Ones I had given up on ever being able to tell her.

"I didn't think anyone could love me, the real me beneath this face."

I tried to keep myself firm as she stared at the center of my chest. I could feel her emotions, but love meant different things to different people. Humans lived such short lives that I wasn't sure if they were capable of love in the same capacity.

"The moment you stepped into my Gatehouse, I felt something different about you, but I didn't understand what it was."

She looked up, green eyes rimmed in tears.

"You could see me, *all of me*, and you didn't run and hide." I took a deep breath. "No, you asked your infuriating questions until I craved them."

She smiled at this, a tear slipping down her cheek. Her emotions had melted into something so dreadfully soft and caring; it caught my breath fast in my throat. Perhaps it was Fae who struggled to love, because she was clearly very capable of it.

I turned to the portal. There would be a way to fix it if needed. It had been created once; it could be created again. I clutched the highest point I was able to reach and pulled.

It tipped precariously, and at first, I thought it might wobble back into place. After it seemed to float, suspended on one corner, it swayed forward, falling in slow motion until it shattered into millions of tiny pieces that spilled across the floor like brilliant crystals. The sound had been so loud, echoing through the Gatehouse and snuffing out the braziers in the room.

After what seemed like an eternity in thick silence, a single brazier on the far side timidly illuminated. I turned to find Rosalin, eyes wide with fear.

I couldn't go back now. I'd made my choice. The weight of that decision pressed the breath from my lungs, and I swayed in place. The magic that had been a part of me—my very essence—was stripped away in an instant, leaving me raw and exposed. The last fragments of my shadows melted into the air, and I was left with the unfiltered reality that I could never reclaim them. The fragile remnants of my being had been cracked open and spread out at Rosalin's feet.

With deliberate slowness I walked to her, the stone beneath me far more solid than it had ever been before. For the first time, I couldn't feel her emotions swirling around in my mind, tugging at my own. That constant connection that had tethered me to her was gone, and in its place was a terrifying silence. It left an empty space that was immediately filled with fear, and excitement, and anxiety that I'd never felt before. I cradled her face in my hands, trembling as the reality of what I'd given up settled over me. Wishing I could put all my own emotions into words, but so many of them felt too fresh and precious. I had given up immortality for this life.

For her. My Rosalin.

I stood straight, my hands falling to my sides as I stepped toward her. "Can I grow old with you, Rosalin Greene?"

She closed her eyes, another tear slipping over her cheek as she smiled. She leaned up to kiss me.

Every kiss we'd shared I'd had both our emotions clawing their way into my heart. This time it was only my own, a heat so strong I needed to pull her closer. She gasped as I deepened the kiss, wrapping my arms around her, fully intent on keeping her with me forever if she so chose.

When she finally stepped back my cheeks were wet with tears I'd held back but couldn't any longer.

"Are you crying, Keres Blackwarden?"

"Are you answering my question with a question, Ms. Greene?"

"Yes," she said with a smirk. She wrapped her arms around my neck to lean closer, her breath tickling my ear as she whispered, "And yes."

# My Love

## ROSALIN

I found him in the hall, his long hair a mess around his horns where he'd pulled it back from his face, his wings tight against his back, a paintbrush in one hand and a palette in the other. When I woke to find him gone, I'd panicked, worried something had happened. He'd never risen earlier than I had. He usually watched me sleep until I woke before he'd take me into his arms.

He was a gentle lover, and I suspected it was from the years of abuse at the hands of the Hag Queen. It was hard for me to imagine everything she'd put him through and how he could ever want to be touched again. It made me cherish every caress, every kiss, every moment together even more. The way my pale hand looked as it smoothed over his gorgeous dark, silver skin.

It had been a few months since he'd destroyed the portal, and I'd noticed small changes in him, things I wondered if I might have imagined. The color of his hair had darkened. His tarnished silver complexion had taken on a purple tint on his cheeks. The biggest change had been around his eyes from always smiling. Maybe it was just happiness? His existence as Bevgyah's consort for hundreds of years had destroyed his hope. I needed him to never lose it again because his laugh was quickly becoming one of my most favorite sounds in the world.

"Here you are." I came to stand beside him. "Did you sleep?"

He hadn't anticipated the amount of rest he'd need as a mortal, and I felt like I was constantly reminding him.

He'd covered a large section of the wall with sprawling hills of grass that flowed into fields of wheat, interrupted by the occasional tiny farmhouse. It reminded me of Fennigsville, and I couldn't help but wonder how my family was doing, a sudden ache to see them writhing through me.

He stood back to admire his work before he glanced over at me. "I've seen this place in my dreams."

"It's my home," I blurted out, wondering if there was some strange Fae magic still at work. Maybe it was the Gatehouse, which had thankfully retained its sentient charm.

He said he hadn't been able to feel my emotions since he'd destroyed the portal, but I wondered if he still had a tiny connection to the Earth Mother. If he ever managed to return to his home through one of the other Fae portals, could he regain his magic and his immortality?

"I'd like to go there," he said as he took a step toward me, paintbrush and palette still in hand.

A sudden rush of jealousy gripped my heart. I didn't know if I was ready to share him with anyone. Keres was gorgeous—*arrestingly* gorgeous. He would draw attention anywhere he went. Even more so for his distinctly Fae traits. It was hard to hide horns and wings when you didn't have the magic to glamour yourself.

He leaned down to kiss me and my thoughts were instantly banished. This was a promise, a claim. No one else mattered but us at that moment.

Would I ever tire of this? Of him? *Of us?* The paintbrush and palette hit the tile and clattered away as he pressed me against the wall. I knew the answer to my own question.

No, I would never be tired of this. I would never be tired of him, or the way he made me feel alive, precious—completely his.

"Ms. Greene," he said, voice low and breathy, pulling me deeper into him.

"Yes, Keres?" I breathed, my pulse racing.

"What do you want, my love?"

I couldn't take in breath fast enough as he kissed down my neck, his lips leaving a trail of goosebumps in their wake. A grin spread across my lips. I knew what I wanted.

"My midnight apple."

He smirked, a wicked gleam in his eyes, as he swept me into his arms.

# Acknowledgements

This little book started as an escape from everything going on in our world. I needed a place to "go," and dove into writing a version of my all-time favorite story, Beauty and the Beast. As things tend to happen with me, the story diverged very quickly.

I'm not sorry about it.

This was my first attempt at writing Fantasy Romance and because of this I leaned **HEAVILY** on some of my Alpha and Beta readers to ensure I was hitting the right story beats (iykyk). I didn't want it to be TOO ridiculous, even though, I will admit, I set out to make it as unapologetically romantic as possible, pulling in some popular Romantasy tropes and either flipping them or leaning into them as heavily as I could allow myself.

To my Alpha readers: Zaid, Essie, Allison, and Sara, you guys kept me from spiraling and hitting the delete button. When I was doubting I could make this book into something worth publishing, you were yelling at me to pick myself up. When I needed people to read and tell me I wasn't totally crazy, and this story is actually "acceptable," you were there telling me it was amazing (debatable). When I was obsessing over Keres before I'd even shared a single word on IG, you were swooning with me. Thank you, because without you, this would still be in my drafts.

To my Beta readers: Kim, Bekah, Chelle, Taylor, Tiara, April, Chantelle, and Ana...and to Zaid, Essie, Allison, and Sara AGAIN... thank you for helping me hone this story into a respectable book.

You helped me see some things that needed more work, some things I didn't need, and some things I definitely needed to add (like MORE Keres.)

To Amber at Bibliobean Editing, thank you for giving me my first developmental evaluation (hides under a desk) and a great line edit. With your help I've made my first attempt at first person POV pack more of an emotional punch. Because this story wasn't emotional enough already, amiright? But seriously, thank you for cleaning up my drivel and making it worth reading by the general public. I appreciate you!

To Sara for doing the final clean up on this book baby (as well as your help with Alpha and Beta reading). You'll never know how lucky I feel to call you my friend, you glitter queen, you! I'm always happy to share Keres with you...or you know, my next dark stranger.

AND FINALLY, thank you to my readers. Am I terrified that you hate this book? Yes, I'm terrified you'll hate every book I write. Am I grateful you've bothered to read it though? You have no idea how grateful I am. Do I hope you're secretly obsessed with Keres and Rosalin's story as I have been since the moment I sat down at my laptop on November 6th of 2024? Oh definitely.

Sorry, not sorry. *insert snarky emoji of your choice*

# About the Author

Ciara (Keara) Hartford is a Romantic Fantasy and Romantasy writer of character driven love stories full of magic, heartache, bloody action, flawed characters, and brutal cliffhangers. When she's not writing she's working on illustration and graphic design freelance, as well as reading every fantasy book she can get her hands on. She lives near Cleveland, Ohio with her mad scientist husband and amazingly talented daughter.

For more, visit www.ciarahartford.com or connect on social media @ciarahartford.author

## READ MORE OF CIARA'S WORK

### The Sundering of Rhend Series
*The House of Starling* (2024)
*The House of Amfithere* (2025)
*The House of Rhend* (2026)

Printed in Dunstable, United Kingdom